The Murder of
Edgar Allan Poe

The Murder of Edgar Allan Poe

A NOVEL BY

George Egon Hatvary

CARROLL & GRAF PUBLISHERS, INC.
NEW YORK

First Carroll & Graf edition 1997

Carroll & Graf Publishers, Inc.
260 Fifth Avenue
New York, NY 10001

Library of Congress Cataloging-in-Publication Data

Hatvary, George Egon.
The murder of Edgar Allan Poe : a novel / by George Egon Hatvary.
—1st Carroll & Graf ed.
p.   cm.
ISBN 0-7867-0358-X
1. Poe, Edgar Allan, 1809–1849—Death and burial—Fiction.
2. Authors, American—19th century—Fiction.   I. Title.
PS3558.A754M87   1997
813'.54—dc21   96-36793
                                                                                        CIP

Manufactured in the United States of America

Author's Note

This is a work of fiction, but I stay close in many respects to Poe's life, which can be culled from standard biographies. The best recent one is by Kenneth Silverman. Dupin is of course Poe's own detective hero, here resuscitated. What I quote by Poe can be found in many editions; the most authoritative one is the Mabbott/Pollin edition of the *Collected Works*. Poe did plagiarize— or borrow, to put it more politely. I did some work in that area myself several years ago.

For Laurel and Maura

The Murder of
Edgar Allan Poe

1

THE NEWS of my dear friend Edgar Poe's death came in the letter the concierge had slipped under my door, which was the way she sometimes delivered my evening mail. Wrapped in my old silk dressing gown, I had been sunk in a deep chair, so absorbed in Chateaubriand's *Mémoires* that I barely heard the swooshing sound coming from the dark hall. Finally I roused myself from my stupor and shuffled out in my carpet slippers. As I brought the letter into the candle-lit room I saw that it was from America. The sender was Edgar's aunt, Mrs. Clemm.

A fear took hold of me as I tore it open. I glanced at it and cried out, *"Mon Dieu!"*

Fordham, N.Y. 13th Oct. 1849

M. Auguste C. Dupin
33, Rue Dunôt, Faubourg St.-Germain
Paris

Dear Monsieur Dupin:

It is with heavy heart that I inform you that my beloved Eddie passed away a week since. He was returning from a trip to Richmond, and while in Baltimore he fell grievously ill, was taken to a hospital, and there expired. He was buried on the 9th in the Presbyterian cemetery of the same city. I hasten to write to you, knowing of your close friendship and working companionship with my Eddie while he resided in Paris—something the world knows as well from Eddie's various writings.

With much personal esteem, I remain yours,

Mrs. Maria Poe Clemm

"Edgar dead!" I gasped, devastated, my voice swallowed by the silent, lofty room with its heavy, faded curtains and two thousand dusty volumes, where we had spent so many hours together. Part of my brain refused to register his loss. It seemed but yesterday that we sat there on that sagging plush sofa, or one of us at the cluttered writing table, reading, writing, philosophizing; at times solving some enigmatic crime of the day. We saw no one, save foolish M. Gaston, police superintendent of the 6th Arrondissement, when absolutely necessary. We both loved the night, and early in the morning we closed the shutters, lighted candles, and "busied our souls with dreams," as Edgar put it so well. Then at the advent of true darkness we would sally forth arm in arm and roam far and wide amidst the wild lights and shadows of Paris.

I felt an overwhelming need to go out and seek human contact, as if fleeing from my own death. For the past several years, since Edgar's departure from Paris, I had become more and more of a hermit. I saw almost no one. Worse, my creative—or to use Edgar's word, resolvent—faculties had lain fallow. I could scarcely remember the last time I had been asked by the police to solve a crime. Or the last time I had written a poem—not that my poems had ever been very good. All I could do was read and read and read until I thought I'd go mad. I would put the book down, then reach for it again, with nothing else to reach for. Sometimes I had the distinct feeling that Edgar—our past life, his letters, some exciting new work he'd sent me—had kept me alive.

Now Edgar was gone.

I shaved off two days' growth of beard and dressed, finally pulling my old black cape about me and donning my tall silk hat. I roamed down dark, narrow, unevenly cobbled, desolate streets, then sought the noisy crowds along the garishly gaslit Boulevard St.-Germain. Yet I was only partially aware of the carriages drawing up before restaurants, discharging fashionable men and women, of the music seeping out of cafés, of the clusters of painted *filles de joie* lingering at every crossing. At one point, distracted, I let one approach me with a smile and a "Monsieur?" For a split second I didn't know what she wanted. Then I recovered myself, said, *"Non merci, mademoiselle,"* and walked on.

I stopped at a small, quiet café, ordered a grog, and pulled out Edgar's aunt's letter and read it again. I wished she had written more about Edgar's death. Who was there in Baltimore with him?

Who took him to the hospital? Who witnessed his final moments? I intended to write to her—and to anyone I could think of as a friend of Edgar—as soon as I returned home. But a letter by transatlantic steamer took two to three weeks, so I had to be patient.

I wondered about the nature of Edgar's illness, which, for lack of better evidence, I associated with his nervous, often melancholy, sometimes agitated temperament—in some ways like my own. We were the same age; in our physical aspects, too, we were strikingly similar—something we recognized the first time we fell into conversation at a little library on Rue de Montparnasse.

Our meeting was occasioned by a book we both reached for at the same time. The convergence of our hands on this volume evoked a startled merriment from both of us, then immediate courtesy:

"*Allez-y, monsieur*—go ahead, sir."

"*Mais non, allez-y*—no, go ahead, please."

The book was a recent study of mesmerism, or the magnetism of souls, and we solved our little dilemma by retiring to a quiet corner of the library and reading aloud from it to each other. Edgar read French very well, though with an accent that I immediately recognized as American. We agreed that mesmerism was perhaps the most remarkable discovery of the age.

"I believe it provides the proof we have been seeking for the immortality of the soul," Edgar declared. "I'd be willing to wager that if we mesmerized a dying person we could continue contact with his soul after death."

"If you could do such a thing—*mon Dieu!* Think of the philosophical consequences!"

After the library closed, I invited my new friend to my rooms. I brought out a bottle of Armagnac and two glasses, but Edgar said he had no tolerance for alcohol and I put away the bottle and brewed tea instead.

We continued our discussion—partly in French, partly in English—about mesmerism and a great many other subjects.

"Is it not remarkable," Edgar said, "to consider our mental affinities—and physical ones as well—in light of our wholly different family histories?" He blew a smoke ring toward the phantasmagoric shadows on the lofty ceiling.

"True," I said, made conscious of his wavy raven hair and large, dark-gray, luminous eyes. His other features, too—his broad brow, narrow, longish nose with a relatively short space between it, and the sensitive mouth, not to speak of his very pale complexion even by candlelight—were strikingly similar to my own. He said earlier that he was twenty-nine, which was my own age; and we were both medium tall, more slight than robust in stature, although I was perhaps more athletic. "I confess," I went on, "that when we reached for that volume at the identical moment, I thought I was confronted by my mirror image."

Edgar laughed. "So did I. I think we both have a Celtic strain. More importantly, given our mental affinity, how can it not find expression in our physiognomies?"

"You spoke just now about our different family histories. I fear you allow my title of *chevalier* to mislead you."

"Ah, my friend. My family history is so troubled: I was orphaned early, taken in but never adopted, struggled with poverty all my life. Yours must be infinitely superior."

"To be sure," I said, "I come from an illustrious house, but I inherited a fortune too early in life, I wasted it, lived dissolutely, and now I am poor like you."

We drank another cup of tea to our poverty—and the mental riches it encouraged.

When two souls are in such close communion as we became that evening, it is not always possible to ascribe the origin of some idea or even mode of behavior to one or the other. The *bizarrerie*, for example, the "wild whims" in which Edgar wrote that he had joined me were frequently his own; as were the brilliant analyses when our friend, Gaston, whom he had promoted in his fancy to prefect, called on us for aid in some baffling crime. Edgar was too modest in his accounts. Much of the credit in our getting to the bottom of some of these bloody or diabolic deeds was due to his genius.

*   *   *

I FINISHED MY GROG and roamed on, sometimes on the verge of believing that Edgar was walking next to me. At St.-Germain-des-Prés, the square dominated by the old church on one side and a noisy café on the other, I turned toward the Seine. A short walk past somber buildings and high, shut portals brought me to the *quai*, where in warmer weather men would go down the steps to the very edge of the water and fish. Edgar used to like to stand here leaning on the stone parapet and gaze down into the river. This was a blessedly peaceful part of Paris compared to other parts where our President, Louis Napoleon, had begun to demolish ancient buildings and cut across historic streets to build more grand boulevards in imitation of his illustrious uncle. I stood looking at the gaslit façade of Notre Dame in the distance, trying to take comfort from the lines I remembered from one of my friend's most beautiful poems:

> Thank Heaven! the crisis—
>   The danger is past,
> And the lingering illness
>   Is over at last—
> And the fever called "Living"
>   Is conquered at last.

2

I HEARD FROM AMERICA sooner than I had dared to hope, three items arriving within the next few days. The first was a letter from Dr. Snodgrass, a magazine editor and physician.

Baltimore, 15th Oct. 1849

M. Auguste C. Dupin
33, Rue Dunôt, Faubourg St.-Germain
Paris

Dear Monsieur Dupin:

Mrs. Maria Clemm wrote to me to say how much she regretted not to have been able to give you more details of her nephew's recent death and asked me to do so, since I was with him in his final days.

On September the 3rd I received an urgent message from Gunner's Hall, a tavern serving as a polling place for the election held that day, that Poe was "the rather worse for wear" and "in general distress." It was a terrible day, a hard wind driving cold rain into one's face, and I found poor Poe in thin and shabby clothing which didn't seem to be his own, semiconscious from drink and feverish, with a look of vacancy about him. I called a carriage, but Poe, who had been seated, was unable to stand up; he had to be carried. I directed the driver to Washington Hospital, where Poe was put under the care of the young physician on duty, Dr. Moran. Poe remained largely unconscious for the next two and a half days, often sweating and tremulous, sometimes talking out of his head, addressing imaginary people and objects. During moments of lucidity he begged that his brains be blown out with a pistol. At one point he called out a name that sounded like "Reynolds." His final words before death were more distinct: "Lord help my poor Soul."

I wish to add only a few more details. There has been some speculation that Poe may have been drugged and taken from one polling place to another to make him a "repeater," then abandoned. His poor clothing may have been the result of robbery, or perhaps, since he had lost the trunk with which he traveled, he may have sold his clothes in his desperate and dire need. I regret that I cannot provide a satisfactory diagnosis of Poe's final illness. It may have been an aggravated case of delirium tremens, since unfortunately he drank, or cerebral congestion, or brain fever.

Yours very truly,
Dr. J. E. Snodgrass

The final paragraph startled me with its sinister suggestions. Edgar drugged? Edgar robbed? Criminal offenses against him that perhaps shortened his life—even caused his death? I felt myself in the grip of a gnawing anxiety.

The second item, also a letter, distracted me at first from such speculations. The sender's name, Mrs. Elmira Royster Shelton, looked familiar. Edgar had written to me shortly before his death saying that now that two years had passed since his beloved Virginia's death, he was thinking of marrying again, mentioning two ladies. One, as I remembered, was this Mrs. Shelton of Richmond, a childhood sweetheart recently widowed.

My dear M. Dupin:

What grief, what pain! My dear Eddie was with me but ten days before the Lord took him. May I write to you as a friend? He was the dearest object on earth to me, and I know you loved him; he spoke of you with the deepest affection. How could anyone know him and not love him? Yet there were those who did not. May God have mercy on their hard hearts! We were to be married. Eddie left here feverish and agitated, but then he was frequently in that state; his decline and death occurring in less than a fortnight was frightening and unexpected. O my dear friend! I have to pause frequently as I'm writing lest my tears soak my stationery . . .

This lady's words had a strange effect on me. I have never seen any painting or daguerreotype of her, but Edgar had spoken about her in such vivid detail that I now saw her before me—comely, statuesque, infinitely sad. I wanted to take her hand and draw her to me in an attempt to comfort her. Her words were so heartfelt and moving that I found myself full of reciprocal affection, fascination, curiosity. It was as if, since I felt so close to Edgar, I had taken his place in her heart, as if her place once in his heart were now in mine.

Yet in this letter, too, there was something to cause me anguish. There were those who did not love Edgar. Did Mrs. Shelton hint more? Was she reluctant to use the word "hate"? Edgar had enemies, he had told me. Her next sentence, "May God have mercy on their hard hearts!" suggested more than mere absence of love. And then: his death was "frightening and unexpected." Add that to the possibility of Edgar drugged, Edgar robbed . . .

The third item, a lengthy obituary that had appeared in the New York *Tribune* on October 9, was sent to me anonymously.

> Edgar Allan Poe is dead. He died in Baltimore the day before yesterday. This announcement will startle many, but few will be grieved by it.

What? I leaped up from my chair and began to pace angrily, stirring up a cloud of dust through the room. Few will be grieved by it? What villain wrote this? I turned to the end. The article was signed "Ludwig." Who was this detestable Ludwig? Had he personally sent this thing to me to taunt and torment me?

> The poet was known, personally or by reputation, in all this country; he had readers in England, and in several of the states of Continental Europe, but he had few or no friends and the regrets for his death will be suggested principally by the consideration that in him literary art has lost one of its most brilliant but erratic stars.

The newsprint flowed together before my eyes and I sat shaken by my pounding heart. Few or no friends? An erratic star? Erratic?

> He was in many respects like Francis Vivian in Bulwer's novel, *The Caxtons*. Passion in him comprehended many of the worst emotions which militate against human happiness. You could

not contradict him, but you raised quick choler; you could not speak of wealth, but his cheek paled with gnawing envy.

"Lies! Odious lies!" I cried out, hurling the paper from me and upsetting a burning candle that nearly caused a fire. But I wanted to get to the end of this hellhound's spouting.

> Irascible, envious . . . cold, repellent cynicism . . . sneers . . . no moral susceptibility . . . little or nothing of the true point of honor . . . morbid excess . . . hard wish to succeed that he might have the right to despise a world which galled his self-conceit.

I was on my feet again, raging against the enemy—our enemy— refusing to accept that he was unknown and removed by three thousand miles. In my state of fury I wrenched open a cabinet, threw back the cover of a leather case, pulled out one of my pistols and fired into a distant dark corner of the room as if the monster were standing there.

The loud report and the smoking weapon in my hand brought me back to my senses. Reason was once again uppermost in my mind. If Edgar could be hated so much as this Ludwig hated him . . . Also, considering the unexpected, frightening, sinister cir-cumstances of his death, was it not a possibility, even likelihood, that his death was the result not of natural causes but of foul play?

"Oh, my dear friend!" I of course owed it to his memory to cross the Atlantic and investigate.

*   *   *

I BOOKED PASSAGE on the *America* which was to sail from Le Havre in a fortnight. I had just enough time to arrange my affairs, pri-marily to secure a loan on a tiny bit of land I still owned in the Champagne region. Meanwhile, if there was one person to whom I owed a report of Edgar's death, it was his great admirer, the young poet Charles Baudelaire. We had been close at one time when we both lived lavishly and ran up enormous debts. After his inherited fortune was placed under *conseil de famille* and mine dwindled to near zero, he took refuge in Bohemia and I in solitude. Making inquiries at the café I remembered as his favorite, I learned that he was living on Rue de Babylone and was ill. I found the old, seedy building, trudged up to the fourth floor, and rang.

The door was opened by Jeanne Duval, Baudelaire's mulatto mistress, in a haze of perfume. Her beautiful tan face was drawn in a puzzled frown, which aged it slightly, but then she recognized me with a brilliant smile.

"Monsieur—er—Master Detective!"

"Dupin," I helped her, noting that in her low bodice and wide skirt her figure was as lovely and slender as ever. "I apologize, madame, for this intrusion."

"Not at all. Charles will be delighted to see you."

"How is he?"

"Not terribly bad, monsieur. He's taking arsphenamine, which helps."

I did not have to ask about the nature of Charles's malady. He had told me about his syphilis years ago. One false step in youth. But how can we avoid such false steps? It's all a matter of luck.

Entering the bedroom, I was struck by its emptiness. There was a wide brass bed, a wardrobe, a couple of straight chairs, one serving for a nightstand.

Charles was in bed, propped up by pillows, with books and papers spread out around him. He was twenty-eight but looked older. He was balding and his face was gaunt. His eyes seemed feverish, the pinpoint pupils showing the effect of laudanum, and his lips were compressed with apparent pain. But he gave a smile and extended a well-kept, flaccid hand.

"Ah, Auguste, my old friend! Forgive me for receiving you like this. Pull over that chair and sit down. I'm sorry I can't offer you a more comfortable seat. I found this place in September, and I started to furnish it but couldn't get any more credit."

"I fear I have bad news."

"About poor Poe? I heard. It was like hearing about my own end. I'm sure it reactivated this cursed pox. Or perhaps it was that despicable obituary, which an American acquaintance had sent me. Don't they have a law in America that keeps curs out of cemeteries? How did he die?"

I took out the three letters, just as Madame Duval came in bearing a silver tray with two glasses of vermouth. There was no place to put it down and I went to get another chair. "Won't you join us, madame?"

"No, monsieur. You have literature to discuss. I know nothing about literature."

Charles read the letters with absorption, sometimes emitting a deep sigh. "I felt it coming," he said, looking up. I dreamt of it night after night. I've always felt this uncanny identification with Poe from the first moment I read him. Would you believe that I found poems and stories and even sentences that I'd thought of, but in a vague, confused, disorderly way and that Poe had been able to bring together to perfection? Translating him is the only thing I'm able to do when I'm ill. I can't work on my own poems or articles—I don't feel held together, I relapse into lethargy. To think I'll never be able to meet him! You knew him, you were his close friend. I envy you for that, Auguste—"

Suddenly there came a crash and a scream. "You damn evil beast!" The door was flung open. "I'll kill her!" She meant the black cat who ran in and jumped up on Charles's bed. The door slammed shut, and we could hear shards of pottery being swept up.

Charles stroked the cat, who started purring. "She threatens to kill her or give her away every day, because she knows I love the creature. Jeanne can be kind but also malicious. Do you know anything about this Ludwig?"

"I have the feeling it's a pseudonym. But the article reveals a number of facts. The author is a writing man, he has a facility with the pen, but he lacks the self-confidence of true genius. He could've strung together some fancy phrases in disparagement of Poe, but he preferred to quote Bulwer, a second-rate writer himself. Ludwig concedes that Poe was a brilliant writer—that's a well-established fact, which he doesn't have the courage to deny. Phrases such as 'few will be grieved' and 'he had few or no friends' suggest that he knew Poe well, that he in fact pretended to be his friend in order to cut a figure before the world, meanwhile being gnawed by envy and hate."

"He sounds like a vampire!" Charles exclaimed. "You analyze him brilliantly. I keep thinking of the doctor's letter. Why did Edgar let those terrible things happen to him? One might almost say he drank to that purpose. One might almost say he committed gradual suicide. Any wonder? He, a rare genius, an aristocrat, subjected to a society ruled by the *canaille*."

"Or perhaps he was murdered. If so, Ludwig is my prime suspect."

"Murdered? *Mon Dieu!* What do you base that supposition on?"
A rash appeared on Charles's face at the idea.

"The hatred, the envy, of the likes of Ludwig. There must be
more scribblers like him. Poe had enemies. Note Mrs. Shelton's
letter averring as much, however delicately. Note how readily the
doctor suggests criminal offenses against Poe."

"And your next step?"

"To investigate. I sail in less than a fortnight."

"You astonish me. Yet you don't. That's just what Auguste
Dupin would do. I confess I'd be reluctant to visit that land where
someone like Poe could be treated so badly."

We finished our vermouth and I rose to go. "You'll soon be
better, Charles. The medicine will help."

"I need to live a while longer. I want to translate everything by
Poe. And write more poems. I've barely written any. Listen—

> Be what you will, black night, red dawn,
> There's no fiber in my trembling body
> That doesn't cry: Beelzebub, I love you."

He smiled. "Beauty wedded to corruption." His bony, elegant
hands clasped each other. *"Les Fleurs du Mal—The Flowers of Evil.*
How's that for a title?"

"It's a great title."

We shook hands. "Feel better, Charles."

"Bon voyage, mon ami. I'll be waiting eagerly to hear from you."

*   *   *

I WENT TO SEE Superintendent Gaston at the Commissariat on Rue
Bonaparte in the hope of obtaining from him some letters of introduction to the American police. I waited for him for some time in
a bleak anteroom contemplating the physiognomies of wanted
criminals on the wall, while a policeman came in and out, assuring
me that the superintendent would see me presently.

Finally I was ushered into his august presence behind an ornate
Empire desk, under a portrait of President Louis Napoleon. In a
niche there was a bust of Julius Caesar.

"Ah, Monsieur Poe—I mean Dupin. Momentarily I'm never
sure which one of you I'm talking to. It's been a long time and you
look rather alike." He offered more his little finger than his hand.

"To what do I owe this pleasure?" he asked with a touch of sarcasm, as if implying that there was no way in which he might require my services. He was a short, fat man with tiny curious eyes, a weak chin, and small, gesturing hands. "Please sit down."

"I have come to you with a request," I said bluntly. "But first a sad piece of news. Edgar Poe is dead."

"A pity. He was a brilliant fellow—though he wasted too much time with poetry and such stuff."

"Poets have imagination, monsieur, which is useful in investigating crimes." It was one of Edgar's favorite theories, which he had expressed to Gaston more than once within my own hearing.

But Gaston had a short memory. "An odd notion," he said, laughing heartily.

"I thought you might have come across it before."

"I don't recall."

The superintendent was one of the most irritating persons in my acquaintance, but it was just as easy to smile. As Edgar had put it so aptly, there was nearly half as much of the entertaining as the contemptible about the man.

"What can I do for you, Dupin?" he asked.

"I need some letters of introduction to the American police."

"What on earth for?"

"I suspect Poe may have been murdered."

"And you intend to go there to find out?"

"Yes, of course."

"What an odd idea."

I recalled Edgar making the point that Gaston had a habit of calling anything odd that was beyond his comprehension and thus lived amidst an absolute legion of oddities.

"How many letters do you have in mind? America is a vast country with many police departments."

"Poe died and was buried in Baltimore; I expect my investigation will probably cover Richmond, Philadelphia, and New York as well."

"I want to see these places on the map." He shook a small bell and a policeman came in and saluted. "Bring me a map of the United States of America."

"Yes, Monsieur Superintendent."

"They're all on the East Coast," I said, trying to understand why he needed to know the exact locations where his letters would be presented before favoring me with them.

To feed his self-importance, I realized as I watched him bend over the map the policeman had spread out on his Empire desk, his fat forefinger jabbing at each of the four cities, as if he were about to send a conquering army to the new world.

Then he straightened up and began to strut up and down, his pudgy right hand inserted under the lapel of his coat, à la Napoléon.

"Send in a scrivener," he commanded.

"Yes, Monsieur Superintendent."

The uniformed scrivener entered, sat down at a small desk with pen in hand, and Gaston dictated:

> This is to introduce M. Auguste Dupin, who wishes to investigate the mysterious death of the American poet, Edgar Poe. M. Dupin is an able detective who has been of considerable help to me in numerous criminal cases. Any courtesies accorded to him will be greatly appreciated.

What more could I expect? Something like, "M. Dupin solved crimes in Paris, such as the famous murders in the Rue Morgue, or the case of the letter purloined from the Queen's boudoir, that totally baffled me"?

When the four letters were presented to Gaston, he signed them, pressed his official stamp on them and gave them to me. He extended his little finger for a handshake and wished me luck on my odd quest.

3

IT WAS A COLD, stormy November crossing, and the old ship with its huge side paddles was not taking the waves and the wind too well. For the first three days I was wretchedly seasick. The moment I tried to stand up I had to clamp my hand on my mouth and run to the lavatory. A degree of peace came to my viscera only when I lay prone in my berth, and the temptation to remain here for the rest of the voyage and refuse all food and drink was strong. The American businessman sharing my stateroom, a man of robust build and red, laughing face, who chewed tobacco and wore a detachable shirtfront, urged me to go on deck.

"It'll help, I assure you."

I just wanted to be left alone. I took fifty grains of laudanum, which first relieved my nausea and gave me blue and gold visions— I seemed to be hovering in a balloon high above the ship—but after a while the nausea came back with a vengeance, and the relentless motion and the groaning of the ship's joints produced in me the terror of Edgar's cataleptic hero in one of his tales who, sleeping in the narrow, coffinlike berth of a sloop, dreamt that he had been buried alive. With a shock I saw Edgar himself in the grave. Had he really been condemned to it by an evil deed? Various modes of violence ran through my mind—gunshot, knife, cudgel, rope—all leaving their terrible, unmistakable signatures on the victim. In Edgar's case, since he was believed to have died from natural causes, poison was the only possibility.

I was proficient in the study of poisons, having mastered Mathieu Orfila's great work, *Toxicologie,* as well as others—probably more proficient than Edgar's attending physicians. Dr. Snodgrass's letter raised the possibility that Edgar had been drugged by corrupt and violent political workers, but no one seemed to have pursued this further: drugged to what extent? by whom exactly?

17

Nothing less than an exhumation of the body would allow me to investigate—but here I immediately ran into difficulty: the only poisons that can be clearly and decisively detected by chemical means are those of the mineral kingdom, such as arsenic or corrosive sublimate. Others of the vegetable kingdom, such as opium or strychnine, will in all probability, especially after several weeks, leave no trace.

But exhume I must, whatever the family or legal resistance!

Interestingly, this resolution crystallizing on the third day, when my body was considerably weakened by lack of nourishment and water, I felt a corresponding resolve to try what my cabin mate had been urging me to do. I gritted my teeth, clamped down on my stomach to suppress its urges, and fought my way up through the maze of corridors, saloons, gangways. A great surprise waited for me: the wonderful air, the sky, the sea. I stood at the railing, rising and falling with the ship like a good sailor, crying, "Ha, ha!" My next test was to go to the dining saloon and eat. I tried this, a little timorously at first, but I was able to keep down a light meal. Through the remaining two weeks I had a good voyage.

*　　　*　　　*

WHAT A STRANGE WORLD, this America! I was given but a glimpse of its great natural beauty as we sailed up Chesapeake Bay, which extended in my mind to its vast mountains and plains, its primeval forests and broad rivers stretching westward to another ocean. But this grand vision was put to flight by glimpses of Baltimore that I caught between the jolts of my hackney coach—rows of red-brick houses relieved only occasionally by a pretentious Greek façade or monument or church. How recent and raw and primitive the town seemed after Paris. Some of the streets were not even paved; at one point the coachman cursed and whipped his poor nag to get us out of a mud hole. The crowds of people I saw troubled me. I am not speaking of the miserable ones in rags loitering about the harbor amidst the low gin shops and hovels—all cities have them—but the prosperous ones along better streets: jaunty, noisy, the men chewing tobacco amidst jets of expectoration, the women in all colors of the rainbow, with frills, ribbons, ruffles blowing in the wind, their hair molded into fantastic curlicues. Newsboys ran everywhere crying the latest *Sun* hot off the press, sometimes shoving each other for a sale. Before me was the most dramatic result of our own great

Revolution before my birth—Blessed Democracy. I thought of Tocqueville's profound study of democracy in "the most enlightened and free nation of earth," as he called America. Something about the crowds before me, however vulgar, reminded me of the point Tocqueville made about the importance of civic societies in this country, how they furthered a multitude of aims like public safety, commerce, industry, even morality and religion. But the crowds also made me think of Tocqueville's warning about *individualism,* that product of democracy, which first seems such an improvement over the mere *égoïsm* of our fathers, but which, by tempting a person to isolate himself from his fellows, ultimately degenerates into downright *égoïsm.*

The thought led me to Baudelaire's condemnation of "the *canaille* that ruled here and destroyed Poe," and before I could take hold of myself I was falling into melancholy, a loss of purpose, a deepening doubt. I saw little hope of discovering anything about Edgar's death; my long voyage seemed a waste of effort. Why had I undertaken it?

I am subject to these oppressions of the spirit, as most creative persons are. I call myself creative, even if as a poet my claims are modest. As an investigator I am more successful and better known. True, no investigator with the keenest analytic powers can hope to be crowned by the muses. Investigators might serve law and order, but poets, as Shelley wrote, are the legislators of the world—if unacknowledged. To be best in a lesser field and only second best in a greater inevitably results in discontent in a sensitive soul. I, too, had been chronically discontented on this account until the day I met Edgar. Henceforth, I can truthfully say, my own doggerel ceased to matter. I began to live through Edgar as a poet, as he began to live through me as an investigator—or, to broaden the term, a logician or analyst. For ultimately, as he put it so well, the two are one: analysis is a matter of imagination, the fountainhead of the poetic power. Elsewhere he spoke of us having a bi-part soul: the creative and the resolvent. Strangely, our absence from each other, instead of diminishing, had only enhanced our oneness.

But now Edgar was gone, and on this day of arrival, as my mood became darker and darker, I saw only one distant saving hand to cling to, the angelic hand of one who had loved Edgar and had written of that love to me. I leaned out the window and called to the driver on the box to stop.

"Go back to the wharf." There was nothing for me in Baltimore. I would take the next steamer to Richmond to see her.

But as the man swung his horse around and cracked his whip I was brought face-to-face with my own folly. How did I know there was nothing for me to discover until I made the attempt at discovery? Was I going to leave Baltimore without even visiting Edgar's grave? If this madness was the work of love kindled in my lonely soul by a lady's despondent letter, then love must wait.

I leaned out the window and called to the driver once again to stop and turn around and take me after all to the modest but respectable hotel he had recommended.

It was about three-quarters of a mile northwest from the harbor, a dull three-story brick building by the name of Miller's. But it seemed satisfactory—now that I was once again governed by reason, and I sent for my trunk. My room with its dimity curtains and bedspread and oleographs of mountain scenes seemed commodious; a fire was blazing in the Franklin stove, and the bed felt soft.

After washing, shaving, and changing my linen I went down to inquire the way to the Presbyterian Cemetery.

"Why, sir, it's just a couple of blocks from here, on Fayette and Greene," the hotelkeeper told me.

A strange coincidence. Or perhaps fate.

The cemetery had no fence or gate, only a small building at the entrance housing the keeper. Across the street there was a flower market and I bought a wreath, then had the keeper lead me among the tombstones to Edgar's grave. It was a mere mound as yet, the earth had to settle before a stone could be laid; but with a willow tree bending over it, and wreaths and evergreen branches and holly nestling amidst patches of recent snow upon it, I felt the full sadness of Edgar's passing, that same poetic sadness which he had evoked in so many of his own writings.

> Ah, broken is the golden bowl!
> The spirit flown forever!
> Let the bell toll—A saintly soul
> Glides down the Stygian river!

As I laid my wreath I made a silent vow to him that if his death was the work of a villain I would find him and bring him to justice. A moment later I realized how abstractly I had made this vow, how far apart it stood in my mind from my earlier resolve, to exhume the body lying underneath this mound and cut it apart. It was as terrible as it was necessary. Did I have the mental strength, the courage to undertake it?

*   *   *

I WAS ANXIOUS to meet Dr. Snodgrass. The city directory listed his magazine as the *Saturday Visitor,* located at 114 Baltimore Street. It was getting dark, the streetlights were by no means frequent, and I waited for the approach of a wobbly lantern marking a cab. A couple had fares, but the next one delivered me to my destination. The four-story building housed several offices, with light burning in some of the windows. Upstairs, in the outer office of the *Visitor,* two young men, one wearing an eyeshade, sat behind desks piled high with papers. The astonishment in their faces when they saw me suggested that they had known Edgar. I asked to see Dr. Snodgrass.

"He is at a conference, sir," the one with the eyeshade said. "He may or may not be back before we close for the day."

"Very well, I'll try to see him tomorrow." I took out my card, wrote "Miller's" under my Paris address and gave it to him.

Seeing my name, he said, "Ah, Monsieur Dupin!"

Outside, full darkness had descended and I noted that the city was poorly lighted—which would be to my advantage when it came to opening Edgar's grave. I caught an omnibus back to my hotel, where I put one of my pistols in my pocket as a general precaution before going out to dinner.

"Are there any good restaurants nearby?" I asked the clerk, a bright, alert boy about eighteen.

"Yes, sir. The General Wayne Inn is only a block away."

"Who was General Wayne?"

"A hero of our revolution against the British, sir."

"I see. Have you ever heard of Edgar Allan Poe, my lad?"

"No, sir."

"All right, show me the way to go."

Interestingly, the inn brought me even closer to the cemetery. I could see a weatherbeaten sign squeaking in the wind, no doubt showing General Wayne's picture, but I could not make it out by the feeble light seeping out of the place. I went in, sat down by a much-carved table and ordered veal roast and a bottle of my native country's Rhône wine.

Poor Edgar, I thought as I was drinking it. One glass would set him off and he would become wild and irresponsible. It was the chemistry of his blood. And that one glass was sometimes impossible for him to refuse. He made the most determined vows not to touch liquor, but he would get into pleasant company, and friends—false ones I'd call them—would press a glass of wine on him and that would undo him. Then a period of deep remorse, guilt, and another vow to be broken.

While we lived together in Paris I refrained from drinking just so he wouldn't be tempted. We smoked hashish occasionally, but that brought about no such torment in him.

The roast was good, but the place was noisy. "The greatest American in Congress," I heard from the next table, "is Daniel Webster of Massachusetts. And he worked for the Whig cause. Any sensible President would have made him Secretary of State. Not General Taylor, that bungler."

"I don't predict a long future for the Whigs in any event," his companion said. But then their meal came and they seemed to enter a contest to see who would finish first, both bending into their plates and bringing up food rapidly and noisily—largely with their knives.

While I ate, a plan was crystallizing in my mind. I needed help in carrying a load of about two hundred pounds—including the coffin. I needed a cart. I needed a laboratory equipped for chemical experiments. I needed above all the quiet of the night. Who would be a better person to turn to than a young doctor who had access to a laboratory, who could also assist me and corroborate my findings, and, most importantly, someone who besides his literary work was also a physician, one who, judging from his letter, had been fond of Edgar? But the role I was assigning to Dr. Snodgrass without even having met him in person was perhaps presumptuous.

On leaving the inn I stood for a minute on the sidewalk, feeling that I was being observed. I saw no one but I wanted to draw the person out. My hotel was to the left, so I started to walk to the right, toward the cemetery. Halfway down the block I made myself stumble and looked back as if at the uneven paving. I saw a dark figure press himself between two houses.

As I continued my steady, casual gait—but with my pistol

cocked in my pocket, my finger on the trigger—several possibilities ran through my mind. The fellow might be a thug who wanted to rob me, or he was Edgar's murderer, or one hired by him. My arrival in Baltimore was no secret; passenger lists were available at shipping companies. Edgar's killer might well have anticipated that I would respond to his crime by coming to America to investigate. My need to know my antagonist's identity overpowered all fear.

By the time I came to the cemetery I knew I must enter it, for my pursuer was not likely to make a move on the street. I was now at the southeast corner. I remembered that the entrance with the caretaker's cottage was a block north, at Fayette and Greene, and that from there a curving path in a generally western direction led to Edgar's grave. However, the cemetery could be entered at other points, too. A break in the low hedge provided one. I passed through and felt gravel under my feet. I intended to take a position behind a tombstone.

But the last gas lamp I had passed was no longer of any use: before me lay undifferentiated darkness. I placed my hopes of seeing in the faint glimmering from the sky, which seemed turbulent with clouds of various thickness passing over the moon. The moment there emerged the faintest outline of a tombstone I leaped behind it, crouched, and waited.

Again I considered possibilities. If we exchanged fire and he killed me and the police caught him, they might also have Edgar's killer. If I killed him, learning his identity might lead to the same result. But there were many ifs in my reasoning. My best hope was to overpower him, disarm him, learn his identity, make him confess.

Then again, he might be a mere robber.

I saw him for an instant, and now fear gripped me and a chill passed through me. But I took hold of myself and strained every nerve to observe. He was engulfed in darkness again, then I could see him, still outside the hedge but closer to it than previously.

Before he faded again, a shot rang out and a branch broke overhead and fell near me. I fired in response—into the air, just to show him that I was armed.

But he had apparently seen me at one point; I had to change position. The darkness was total now and I advanced slowly with my hands out before me. I seemed to be on a gravel path that was curving confusingly; suddenly I felt soft earth under my feet. The next moment I hit what felt like a horizontal slab of stone and I groped on until I felt a vertical one to crouch behind. I waited.

It took a long time for the moon to send the faintest light down and I began to shiver from the cold.

Finally a glimmer, but I did not see him. He had melted into the night like a phantom.

But then another shot rang out. I couldn't tell where it came from or if it hit anything, but it had obviously been meant for me, personally. No random robber would be so persistent. If he'd only show himself. I was ready to return fire. I wanted to kill him in self-defense, in revenge for Edgar's murder.

Yet again the gnawing question: how could I tell with absolute certainty who he was, what he was?

As for overpowering him and disarming him—what folly. Unless he suddenly materialized near me with his back to me. A vain dream.

I groped in the darkness for a stone about a quarter or third of a pound in weight and when I found it I hurled it as far as I could, toward the western part of the cemetery. I heard it hit a tombstone.

But my enemy wasn't responding.

I heard something else. Hoofbeats. Not from just one horse but several. They approached among flickering lanternlight glancing off brass buttons and buckles. The police.

My first impulse was to run deeper into the cemetery: this was not the way I had planned to meet the Baltimore police. I didn't care to be questioned, searched, accused.

Trying to turn the encounter to my advantage, I gave out a shout: "Police! Police!" and made my way back toward the hedge— cautiously, not knowing whether my antagonist was still lurking near, ready to shoot me from close. But now the mounted detachment saw me and I seemed to be safe. I ran toward them.

"Thank God, you came. Some ruffian was shooting down the street. I ran into the cemetery and fell—" I had to account for my disheveled appearance, my muddy hands.

"Which way did he go?" the sergeant in charge asked.

"I don't know. I'd just come out of the General Wayne Inn when I heard a shot and saw a sinister-looking figure in the shadows— and I ran—"

"We may need you for a witness, sir. May I have your name?"

I had to give it; they might ask for my papers. "Auguste Dupin." But I doubted any of them had heard of me. "I just arrived from France for a visit to your beautiful city. I'm staying nearby at Miller's."

"I regret you were given such a poor reception, sir."

"I appreciate your concern, Constable. And I hope you catch that ruffian."

And perhaps he was only that. Entering my hotel frozen, exhausted, I recognized my adventure as a last-ditch effort to prove that Edgar was a victim of a crime without having to disturb his grave. But now I had no choice. The hotel boasted indoor plumbing and I ordered a bath—also some brandy to be sent up.

4

IN THE MORNING a letter was brought up with my breakfast tray.

Dear M. Dupin:

It has come to my knowledge that you are in Baltimore. As it happens I am here also from Richmond, visiting my sister, Mrs. Craig, and it would give me great pleasure if you would call on me at 175 Exeter Street.

Yours truly,
Elmira Royster Shelton

I couldn't suppress a cry. What singular good fortune! It lifted me from my lingering unease about last night's adventure. The lady was here in Baltimore—as an answer to my wanting to go to Richmond. Good God! Yesterday when I was about to take the steamer, then decided not to, did I have a preternatural knowledge that she was about to step off the steamer herself, or had already done so? Such questions could drive one wild. As I studied her well-formed, determined script—one I knew from her previous letter—I was newly seized by the fascination I had experienced in Paris; I was newly convinced that I was fated to be Edgar's successor in this romance—something she perhaps sensed as well. I gave myself to the fantasy that she had decided to visit her sister because she knew that I would be in town.

Ah, but how? Whether she knew it beforehand or learned of it today, what was her source? And how did she know I was staying at Miller's? Presumably she knew Dr. Snodgrass, who told her.

Or perhaps her source was someone completely unknown to me. This possibility troubled me. It was one thing I hadn't given sufficient thought to thus far, that in America I was perhaps as well known as in France. For Poe was well known here. The surprised looks my card and face had gotten from Snodgrass's two assistants should have served as a reminder.

I studied my face in the soft light of the mirror above the dressing table. I was clean-shaven, as Edgar had been the last time I saw him; during recent years he wore a moustache. Still, there was that almost uncanny resemblance between us; even the two sides of our faces were similarly asymmetrical, and of course we both had the same build. My trunk contained items of the disguise I sometimes used in my work: unkempt beard, greasy wig, tinted glasses, a coarse, tattered coat. In case I needed not to look like Edgar, I was prepared.

I went to see Mrs. Shelton in the early afternoon, in Colonel Craig's modest but well-appointed Georgian house. A Negro admitted me, then ushered me into the drawing room with its graceful sweep of curtains, Aubusson carpets, and airy Sheraton furniture. As the lady came forward to receive me, her obvious astonishment over my resemblance to Edgar gave her face a stern, narrow-lipped expression; momentarily I couldn't reconcile it with the passionate sorrow, the love in her letter. But as she offered her hand, a warm smile lit up her handsome features.

"My dear monsieur, it's a pleasure to meet you."

"The pleasure and the honor are mine, madame." I felt quite lost in her large, deep-set, ice-blue eyes. In her high-necked brocaded gown and with her straight chestnut-brown hair smoothed back from her high forehead she was statuesque.

"I take it you received my note."

"Both your note and your earlier letter. My visit to your country is in some ways a response to it."

She looked puzzled—and again stern. She was so unapproachably American—such a challenge to a man, even a Frenchman. Had Edgar the boldness to woo her? And been actually accepted by her? Oh but there was a vivacity, a passion underneath—her letter provided ample proof. She was thirty-eight; she had to be if at the time of their first romance Edgar had been seventeen and she fifteen. But there were only the subtlest shadows of age under her eyes.

"Let's just say that in grieving for Edgar we have been brought close."

"Mr. Dupin, you didn't sail across the Atlantic just to grieve with me. Your name alone suggests far more. But let's sit down."

She indicated a pink sofa near the fireplace in which a log was sputtering and rang for tea. I stood at one end of the sofa, waiting for her to take the other, but she chose a chair.

Her perceptiveness caught me off guard; I tried to counter it with a question: "In your letter you spoke of hard-hearted people who had no love for Edgar—"

"I scarcely know what I implied by that. You see, his death was such a shock, his failing so rapid, even though he had not been in good health—the circumstances so strange."

"I had an opportunity to read the venomous spouting of one of these hard-hearted people."

"You're no doubt referring to the 'Ludwig' obituary."

"Who is Ludwig?"

"The Reverend Rufus Wilmot Griswold. He revealed himself the next day. Eddie had appointed him his literary executor, and that was Griswold's first step—to malign Eddie's memory."

"I remember the name. Edgar referred to him once as an able editor."

"They were sometimes friendly, sometimes they quarreled. Clearly Eddie appointed him in good faith, without suspecting that Griswold would betray him. But to return—" She stopped while a servant brought in tea. She began to serve.

"Given the circumstances of Eddie's death," she continued, "the presence here of a famous detective from France can have only one meaning. But I must brace myself just to entertain such a possibility. What do you base it on, Mr. Dupin? What evidence is there?"

Her quick grasp of my purpose in coming here made me suspicious. I could have come simply to pay my last respects to my beloved Edgar and place a wreath on his grave. "A number of things," I answered evasively, my silver spoon making a melodious tinkle as I stirred my tea. "Last night, for example, I was shot at."

"Good heavens!"

I gave her a brief account. "I have little doubt that someone who was aware of my arrival was highly displeased with it." I sipped my tea and buttered a fragment of a scone. "Incidentally, how did you learn of it?"

"Lists of transatlantic passengers are published in some of our daily papers, as an extension of the society column. Perhaps you would have been wise to travel under another name. Except in that case I might have missed making your acquaintance."

It was her first suggestion that she liked me. "Do you think after receiving your letter I would have failed to call on you?"

She smiled. "Would you have gone all the way to Richmond?"

"Of course."

"It's fortunate I sent you a note. Imagine your sailing to Richmond and discovering that I was in Baltimore."

I stopped short of confessing that this almost happened. "How did you find out that I'm staying at Miller's?"

"I had a feeling that you would be in touch with Dr. Snodgrass, since he'd been so solicitous at the time of poor Eddie's death. So I sent word to his office and received an immediate answer."

"A brilliant piece of reasoning." Perhaps too brilliant. I was a touch uneasy with it. Could she have gotten her information from another source she did not wish to reveal? Still, I could not deny the attraction that was getting the better of me—nor the need to express it. "You can't imagine how pleased I was to get your note."

"I wanted very much to meet you. Eddie always spoke so admiringly of you. He said at one time that he and you shared one soul."

"I often felt the same thing." I drank my tea. "And you loved him—"

"Yes . . ." There was an almost imperceptible pause. "I loved him. Our first avowals when we were children were something unforgettable—even during our respective marriages. When Eddie walked into my house—good Lord, I can't believe it was less than four months ago—and said with a shy smile, in that rich, low voice of his, 'Elmira?' I felt a sudden revival of that first love." She held the teapot in a tremulous hand over my cup, then hers. "He proposed, but I could not give him an immediate answer. I wanted to think it over. This displeased him and we quarreled. But you see there were such obstacles. In my late husband's will I was named executrix and possessor of his estate only as long as I remained his widow. If I remarried I would have forfeited three-fourths of all control. Worse, my two children were against my marrying Eddie. It's not difficult to see why. They thought him unsteady, his efforts at abstemiousness unreliable, they didn't want him for a father. Yet even against these obstacles I finally consented—"

"Mrs. Shelton, when did you last see Edgar?"

"In the evening of the 26th of September. Early next morning he took the steamer for Baltimore."

"Can you be sure he was on that boat?"

"Yes. I spoke to acquaintances since, who had accompanied him to the wharf."

"Do you know when that boat docked in Baltimore?"

"I imagine the next day, or the day after. The boat I took made the voyage in thirty-six hours."

"You see, I'm trying to account for Edgar's final days in Baltimore. Have you any information about that?"

She shook her fine head and a silence fell. We were watching the dancing flames at several points of the log in the fireplace.

I had disturbing thoughts. I envisioned this lady, whose thin, patrician nose and high forehead and strong chin gave her a fine profile that I found so stirringly appealing—I envisioned her at the time of her final consent to marry Edgar, when she had perhaps deemed it too late to pull back yet feared her own decision, feared that she would regret it bitterly—regret hurting and alienating her children and diminishing her fortune, thinking perhaps that nothing could save her from the horns of her dilemma, except—oh, except—if Eddie should die—

Horrible, unkind, sinful thoughts against this lady whom I felt on the verge of loving myself. And yet such is our profession. No intuition is to be silenced, no evidence suppressed; all are suspect. Not that I deemed her capable of any coarse and violent act. But it took only money—of which she had enough—to delegate the execution of any act. Two persons seemed to have known of my arrival in Baltimore and my stay at Miller's. An apparent angel and an apparent devil. Was there any connection between the two?

*   *   *

I TOOK MY WAY SOUTH toward Baltimore Street, hoping to be able to see Dr. Snodgrass this time. The weather was dry and bracing and the streets were crowded. I couldn't help noticing a certain friendliness and openness about these Americans, now that I'd come in closer contact with them, even about the Negroes driving carriages or carrying enormous baskets or bundles on their heads. Many of them were free—I had noticed the city directory listing several pages of "Colored Households"—but many were slaves, which I had always thought incongruous: a people so proud of their freedom yet owning slaves. I remembered Edgar so brilliant, so sensitive, so compassionate, yet approving of the institution.

The contradiction in him was perhaps the contradiction in the land that had produced him.

In the light of day the red-brick building housing the *Visitor* revealed its quaint decoration of iron work and inviting storefront of a bookseller and stationer. I walked up and was soon ushered into the doctor's inner sanctum.

It was an appealing place—books in mahogany cases, leather armchairs, a Persian carpet on the floor, the aroma of good cigars. Dr. Snodgrass, rising behind a mountain of pasted-up copy, was about my own age, perhaps younger, with clean regular features framed by ear-length, light-brown hair. But my entrance, though he had expected it, had clearly unnerved him. His pale eyes stared, his lips parted, and his fingers froze on a vest button he was in the process of fastening. He looked as if he was seeing a ghost. In the next moment his face lit up in a smile and he came around his desk, one hand completing buttoning his vest, the other extended.

"Monsieur Dupin! I'm honored to make your acquaintance. Of course I feel I know you well—at least the intricacies of your thought. Won't you have a seat?"

I sank into a chair, while he sank into its mate, and I took a cigar from the box he held before me.

"When did you arrive?"

"Just about twenty-four hours ago."

"And you came to see me right away. I'm flattered, and I apologize for not being here. In fact, I returned shortly after you left and was given your card. Are you comfortable at Miller's?"

"Yes, perfectly." The investigator in me wanted to ask whether Mrs. Shelton had really gotten my address from him, but I was wary of such checking up getting back to her. Suspicion struggled in my mind with my deepening attraction.

"Edgar's tales in which you figure are among my favorites, you know. I had an opportunity to publish the one about Marie Rogêt, he offered it to me, but I didn't think it was quite up to the others and I procrastinated until it was snatched up by *Snowden's*. Then I was sorry."

His account revealed much about him. True, "Marie Rogêt" was not up to the others and the doctor-editor was afraid of taking a risk. He was cautious and conventional. He was a fine fellow—attractive, elegant, apparently prosperous. His well-tailored clothes and fine patent-leather boots reminded me of my own dandy days, but I could not see him squander a fortune. He was just the kind of friend Edgar needed at times—one to listen to him, encourage him, defend him, lend him money, and render him a final kindness. But I knew that if in the pursuit of my quest I had to take unusual risks, Dr. Snodgrass was not one to count on.

"Thank you for writing to me about Edgar's death," I said.

"It was a sad occurrence."

"I'll be direct. Did you at any time suspect that Edgar might have been poisoned?"

Snodgrass leaned back and blew a cloud of smoke toward the ceiling. Then he stood up and shoveled some coal into the potbellied stove. My eyes drifted over his books, mostly bound periodicals—*Godey's, Graham's,* his own *Saturday Visitor.*

He turned. "It did cross my mind. But what kind of poison would take three days to act? Take opium, for instance. If the dosage was so minimal that our poor friend fought for three days before succumbing to it, how can we call the act poisoning, rather than drugging?"

"Yes, there is that ambiguity about opium. But suppose someone gave him a corrosive or irritant, yet failed to make the dosage large enough—relying on a weak heart?"

"In that case there would be no question about evil intent."

"There is only one way to find out."

"Oh, Mr. Dupin, I know what you have in mind. But on what evidence would a coroner order a disinterment and a postmortem? No attending physician raised any suspicion of poisoning—even if I, privately and purely theoretically, agree with you as to the possibility. The coroner would need more to go on. Also I imagine the family—the few of them there are—would refuse to grant permission. To have your loved one's remains dug up and cut apart—what violation of the sanctity of the dead, especially to a believer."

"I know." I remembered my own thoughts at Edgar's grave. A postmortem would be a violation of *my* dead. And I was a believer in the immortality of the soul—and perhaps in more specific forms of survival, as Edgar was. "Ligeia," the celestial dialogues, "The Raven" flashed before me. And the more reverence I felt toward my dead, the madder my purpose seemed; and the madder, the more my will insisted, urgently, undeviatingly. I must carry out my plan against my own pain. I felt my soul in torment.

"Such a thing, you see, would create an unholy aura about Edgar—and he has been sufficiently diabolized."

"By Griswold?"

"Yes. Have you seen the despicable obituary?"

"I have. And it is despicable." But the question in my mind was whether I still considered its author, now that I knew more about him, my prime suspect. "Where does Griswold live?"

"In Philadelphia—at the moment."

I certainly wanted to meet him. But first things first. "I want to account for Edgar's days between his arrival in Baltimore and the time you found him at Gunner's Hall. Can you give me any information?"

Edgar's cousin, Neilson Poe, was at the hospital before Edgar died, but I don't know whether he had seen him previously. Then at the funeral I met an old schoolmate of Edgar, Mr. Zaccheus Collins Lee, the Baltimore D.A. He spoke of his wife's birthday party which Edgar had attended. I can't think of anyone else." He added, almost jocularly, "I doubt Edgar had any thought of visiting William Lummis."

I looked up from my note taking.

"Lummis is the brother of Elizabeth Ellet, a noted writer, who once sought to defend his sister's honor by going after Edgar with a gun."

"With a gun?"

"It was a very complicated business. Mrs. Ellet and Mrs. Osgood, the painter's wife and a charming poet herself, were competing for Edgar's favor—all this via poems—and apparently Edgar preferred Mrs. Osgood, so Mrs. Ellet did some bad things, including sending anonymous letters to Edgar's wife Virginia—hastening her death, as Edgar claimed. Edgar was driven to the point where he imputed that Mrs. Ellet had sent him some compromising letters, which then her brother demanded back at gunpoint. Ultimately the matter was resolved by Edgar apologizing and stating publicly that there were no letters."

"Was this about three years ago?"

"Yes."

"I recall Edgar writing to me that someone had threatened him. Does this Lummis live in Baltimore?"

"Yes, I met him once. Large, blustering fellow. Apparently as vicious and vindictive as his sister. I heard he once killed a man in a duel."

Not a poisoner type. Still, perhaps the matter had not been resolved in his mind—or in his sister's mind. I put his name down. "You mentioned in your letter that Edgar uttered the name 'Reynolds' as he was dying. Who is Reynolds?"

"J. N. Reynolds wrote a pamphlet, 'South Sea Expedition' which Poe reviewed many years ago. But why should he think of him at this time?"

"Yes, why should he? 'Reynolds' may be a significant clue. Tell me about this Dr. Moran you also mentioned in your letter."

"He is a young resident physician at Washington College Hospital. He became very devoted to Edgar. He and his wife were at his bedside day and night."

I was interested in Dr. Moran. He was perhaps my man.

5

I WOKE to the most difficult day of my life—for so I saw the grayness drifting through the shutters—in an appropriate state of lethargy and anguish. Between attempts to get out of bed I let myself slip into periods of sleep; I needed my utmost strength finally to pull myself up.

I was plainly afraid of my own plan. On my way to the Washington College Hospital I thought of Edgar with an intensity that made me think he was with me—and perhaps he was in some ghostly form. The feeling was familiar; there had been times, especially since his death, that somewhere within me I heard his voice as distinctly as if he were speaking from across the room. He believed in reincarnation himself. "You deny it?" he wrote. "Let us not argue the matter. Convinced myself, I seek not to convince."

But this experience had never come to me as tormentingly as on this day that I intended to open his grave. Again and again I had to remind myself that whatever lived on after us was not the flesh, that the flesh was food for worms, that cutting into the flesh with a scalpel had no bearing whatever on the soul's mysterious journey. It was superstition to think otherwise.

Ah but the uncanny, unreasonable power of superstition upon the mind . . .

My troubled thoughts accompanied me all the way to the hospital, where I was told that Dr. Moran was making his morning calls and his wife was with him. I was asked to wait in the small parlor of his residence, a cozy room with much red plush, petit point, and fringed throws. Finally the Morans came in. He was below medium height but had a strong, vigorous, tight-knit frame; he wore a full blond beard that emphasized his thoughtful hazel, unlined eyes. His wife was also young, quite pretty but dressed simply, with her dark hair pulled back. As I rose to introduce myself I saw them

35

as ministering angels from what I knew of their devoted care of
Edgar during his last days on earth.

"Are you a relative, sir?" he asked, no doubt struck by my facial
resemblance to his patient, but without recognizing my name.
Clearly Dr. Moran had not read Edgar's works extensively.

"No," I replied. "Edgar and I were close friends during his residence in Paris."

"You would no doubt like to see the room where he passed
away," Mrs. Moran said.

It was obliquely across the hall, a small, neat hospital room,
unoccupied at present, with a moderate amount of light coming in
from the small court that the window faced. I felt as if I was
surveying my own death chamber. On one wall I noticed an etch-
ing of a pleasant rural scene and I turned to it for comfort, as
Edgar perhaps had during his last hour on earth.

In a corner obscured by shadow, a cane was leaning against the
wall with a palm-leaf hat hung on it, giving the momentary impression of a small person standing there.

"Edgar's possessions?" I asked.

"Yes, they're all he had with him, besides the clothes in which he
was brought in. We have them."

I would ask for them later, for my investigation. "Did he have
his mother's miniature portrait when he died?" I asked.

The Morans looked puzzled.

"It was his most cherished possession. He always carried it
with him. Whoever robbed him of his decent clothes must have
taken it."

"Poor Poe," Moran said. "What you say explains his delirious
outburst one night: 'Mother where . . . ?' The rest was indis-
tinct."

"If someone wanted to make his last days on earth miserable, he
could do no better than to take that miniature from him."

We stood in silence for a few minutes, then left the room.

"You must join us for hot chocolate," Mrs. Moran said. "My
husband loves nothing better as a midmorning refreshment."

The hot chocolate, the cakes with it, and the conversation lifted
my spirits somewhat. The young doctor spoke of the difficulties of
medical practice in this country. Too many sick people relied on
patent medicines, questionable medical books, and plain superstition instead of calling a doctor. He and his wife asked many ques-

tions about Paris, which they hoped to visit as soon as the doctor could take some time off. Finally Mrs. Moran delicately withdrew and I had an opportunity to broach my subject.

We lit cigars. But as soon as I began to speak, a frown appeared and then deepened on the young physician's forehead.

"There was no indication of poisoning, Mr. Dupin," he asserted. "None of the gastrointestinal symptoms we associate with it, like uncontrollable vomiting, severe purging, burning pain in the throat and stomach, or insatiable thirst."

I had to smile, he was such a good student reciting. And of course defending himself for failing to pump the stomach as an extra precaution.

"In some rare cases of arsenic poisoning," I replied, "and I concede they're rare—the usual gastrointestinal symptoms are only mildly present, or even absent; in such cases the acute collapse occurs together with an anesthesia of the limbs, soon followed by coma and death."

"I admit I—and one or two other attending physicians, including Dr. Snodgrass—were divided in our opinion. We were all puzzled. A weakened heart, cirrhosis of the liver, brain fever were suggested. Your mention of anesthesia of the limbs and of coma does raise a query in my mind. But here is another factor. Poisons tend to act fast. Even if such a thought had occurred to me, each day, each night of Edgar's lingering death would have driven it further from my mind."

"They act fast as a rule, Doctor. But there are governing factors; whether, for example, the poison is in solid or liquid form, whether the stomach is empty or full. Much depends on the skill of the poisoner."

There was a sudden agitation in the young doctor. He rose, walked to the curtained window, came back, stamped out his cigar and stood staring at me.

"Good God, sir! What villain would have murdered such a noble soul as Edgar?"

"Alas, there are such villains."

He grew thoughtful, and I knew I was winning him to my cause. The analyst in me, who must put mind above heart, was meeting the scientist in him, the searcher after truth.

"There is only one way to find out," he said in a slow, troubled voice.

"And then we may not find out," I said. "Vegetable or animal poisons leave no trace. Minerals do. Of this group, I don't suspect a corrosive such as muriat of mercury, which devastates rapidly. Of the mineral irritants, arsenic is most frequently used because in powder form it is odorless and tasteless. If arsenic was used, we should be able to know."

"Your knowledge of poisons is impressive, Mr. Dupin."

"I have studied the subject. But you are the anatomist. Without your help I'd never be able to proceed. By the way, I understand we don't have much hope for official sanction."

"Indeed not. But there is a relatively easy and safe way to proceed outside the law. Medical colleges are forever in need of cadavers for their anatomy classes, and graves are habitually being robbed, to put it crudely, with the police instructed to look the other way. Is this the custom in Europe?"

"I daresay."

"We could stage a body-snatching. The important thing is to keep the identity of the body a profound secret. Here at the hospital the night porter will admit the coffin and there will be no difficulty in the dissecting room. How long do you think our investigation will take?"

"I estimate two or three hours. Then of course we need time to dig, to bring the coffin here, afterward to return it and restore the grave. The long winter night is in our favor."

We made an appointment for eleven o'clock that night. Meanwhile, Dr. Moran would see about a carter. But before I took my leave we had one of those silent exchanges in which we seemed to read each other's minds.

Finally he spoke. "I must tell you, Mr. Dupin, I have never attempted anything so difficult. I mean to make a cleavage in my mind between this scientific investigation and Edgar whom I grew to love."

"Yes, I feel the same thing. What we must remember is that Edgar will not be in the dissecting room. He is elsewhere."

"Ah, yes, in 'distant Aidenn.'" Showing that he knew at least some of Edgar's writings.

*   *   *

I LEFT the hospital in a troubled state—like a patient told to prepare for major surgery. I roamed the streets wanting to come in contact with Edgar—what I could summon up of him. I drifted south and east, into Mechanics Row, and stood before a mean little brick house on Wilks Street where he, a lonely, exiled youth in search of love and warmth, came to live in his aunt's already overburdened household.

How did I know this was the house? How did I know there had been six of them living in this tiny place: Mrs. Clemm, her son, her daughter, Edgar's brother Henry, the old paralyzed grandmother, and now Edgar? Had he ever told me? Written me? Or had some mesmeric message come, unknown to me, from Aidenn, the dwelling place of the angel Israfel?

How did I know that after Mrs. Clemm's son moved away and Henry died, but with the grandmother still living, they moved to No. 3 Amity Street at the other end of the town? I went there next—it was not far from my hotel—and stood once again before an almost identically mean two-story brick house with a dormer window projecting from the steep roof and three steps leading up to the plain front door. Here, after the grandmother's death, Edgar and Sissy lived, their souls married but not their bodies (this he told me), he writing, she playing and singing, while their Muddy went out daily with her wicker basket to borrow and beg for them.

I returned to my hotel ill with the burden on my mind, suffering from a kind of paralysis of the will. I was subject to such attacks. I was not entirely free of Edgar's spiritual maladies, or even physical ones. I sat in my room motionlessly with heightened pulse and senses, my eyes focused on a certain shuttered window across the street, listening to the silence which sounded like rainfall, conscious of a floral odor in the air—sweet? rank? My skin felt hypersensitive, trying to retreat from contact with my clothes, and my heart was pounding like rapid fire. Finally I pulled myself up to prepare fifty grains of laudanum. I sank back into my seat and soon my sense impressions became more harmonious and pleasurable. Mrs. Shelton's face appeared amidst luminous shapes and I heard her voice amidst organ music. She receded and I called out "Elmira! Elmira!" to bring her back. Slowly my mental balance was returning—I couldn't tell whether it was the drug or thoughts of her.

6

WE WERE TO MEET JOSEPH, the carter, at the northwestern corner of the cemetery at midnight. He had worked for the hospital before; he knew what to do and was reliable, Dr. Moran said. There was a partial moon, and as we approached along Greene Street we could see the cart and the nag clearly. Joseph was standing in the shadows, a fortyish man with a robust body and weatherbeaten face. On seeing us, he took a pair of shovels off the cart, flung them on one shoulder, grabbed a coil of rope, and we entered the narrow path leading to Edgar's grave.

I felt remarkably strong and in possession of my faculties, considering my state of nerves all through the day. It took the tension of doing to overcome fear.

We passed a couple of fresh graves that Joseph thought would do as well, but John Moran said there were good medical reasons why we wanted a particular one, and that seemed to satisfy him.

We gathered the flowers and wreaths—my own among them— and placed them carefully aside, then dug into the reasonably fresh but winter-frozen earth. Soon we hit the coffin, which by the light of the moon appeared to be a modest one made of pine boards. After clearing it of earth, we fitted the rope under it at each end and heaved it up.

Joseph was ready to pry off the lid and wrap the body in a blanket, but Moran told him that this time we'd take the body in the coffin, then after certain experimentation bring it back in the coffin and bury it again, once again offering medical reasons as an explanation. Joseph was puzzled, but he raised no objection to have his working time—and wages—doubled.

The operation proceeded smoothly, with disruptive feelings withheld on both our parts, and we carried our burden to the waiting cart. This time Moran and I rode along, perched somewhat precariously and uncomfortably on the narrow edges of the two sides, with the coffin between us, as the springless vehicle hit bumps and ruts along the way.

We had just turned into dark, deserted Fayette Street when a shot rang out. We hit the floor of the cart, but Joseph on the box was hit. A cry came from him and he slumped. Moran laid him back with some difficulty and tended to him while I grabbed the reins with one hand and returned fire into the darkness with the other.

"Hit in the shoulder," I heard from behind me. "Looks like a light wound, fortunately." I heard the sound of a shirt being ripped for bandage.

There were no more shots and we reached the hospital. Another physician on night duty saw to Joseph, while we carried the coffin into the dissecting room in the basement. We now had a moment to speculate about the attack on us.

"It was not unprecedented," Moran said. "The police may look the other way, but there are those who hold the sanctity of the dead higher than advances in medical knowledge."

"Or someone knows what we're about and tried to stop us— which would be an admission in itself of foul play. Someone shot at me two nights ago, too. Fortunately he missed."

"Fortunately, indeed. But it could be a coincidence."

"Could be."

We lighted lanterns which cast the remainder of the large room in lurid light. We tied handkerchiefs over our faces and commenced. The task was difficult for both of us, but my companion had at least seen Edgar in death, whereas my memory of him went back to those delightful days in Paris when he had been in full vigor. As we began to pry up the coffin lid, a musky, earthy smell hit us even through our handkerchiefs. We lifted the body out, placed it on a table, and began to unwind the shroud. I glimpsed at my beloved Edgar's shriveled, distorted face and went down in a faint.

I found myself lying on a cot, aware of a row of small, high, dark windows at the other end of the large room. Dr. Moran was standing at my side, passing smelling salts near my face.

"You were out for one minute," he said. "I saw you totter and I caught you and eased you down."

"I'm grateful to you."

"Will you be able to continue?"

"Yes, I'm sure of it. It was just that first glimpse of his face—"

It was more. It seemed now as if I had willed that faint in order to meet Edgar in the mysterious beyond. And perhaps I did meet him—unremembering. While I lay still for another minute or two gathering my strength, his words came to me about the two stages in coming back from a swoon: first, a sense of mental or spiritual existence, secondly, a sense of physical existence. "It seems probable that if, upon reaching the second stage, we could recall the impressions of the first, we should find these impressions eloquent in memories of the gulf beyond."

I now felt ready—in some ways reassured—to work on the long-abandoned shell of his being.

Still, I was a step behind my companion. When the shroud was off the chest, with its nipples and sparse dark hair between them, I felt a defenselessness emanating from the shriveled nudity that made me catch my breath. Then the exposed pubic region evoked a protest within me at our violation of its privacy.

"Let's push the body up," Moran said.

I helped him, in a strengthened state again, until the head hung down beyond the edge of the table.

"It stretches the neck," Moran explained, "which makes the task easier."

He made an incision behind the left ear and a shudder went through me.

But it passed, as I watched him bring the scalpel down the side of the neck, for there was no wincing, no movement in response, no cry of pain. Clearly the doctor was cutting up a *thing* upon the table. He made an incision behind the right ear now, continued down the side of the neck again, and connected the two cuts horizontally, under the clavicles. There was shiny, purple-black clotted blood wherever he cut through veins.

"We have an advantage," Moran said. "In a fresh corpse the frothing blood and other active fluids make a fearful mess." He now made a long incision from the neck down, past the navel, all the way to the pubis. We folded the flaps back, exposing the rib cage and vital organs.

"We want to remove the stomach and intestines in one piece," he said. "Would you kindly get that glass vessel, monsieur?" He pointed to a dark corner. "Also the cord you find on that shelf."

I did as he asked, then watched him reach under the lower ribs, tie the oesophagus a few inches above the diaphragm, then cut it. He cut away the gall bladder, the liver, and other impediments until we were able by gentle tugs to pull out the whole alimentary canal. Holding it over the glass vessel, we began to flush out its contents. There was considerable hardening of foul matter and repeated douses were necessary. The arsenic, if present, because of its greater specific gravity, would settle at the bottom.

Finally I saw something. "Look! That whitish powder—"

He saw it, too.

"It may be something else, of course."

We reached in with long-handled spoons and collected as much of the white powder as we could.

At this point I took over, for in my criminal investigations I had experience with this type of chemical analysis. I asked for a clean Florence flask and for a few ounces of distilled water. I boiled a pinch of the white powder and filtered the solution.

"I need sulphurated hydrogen gas, or sulphuret of ammonia, or hydro sulphuret of potash."

Moran handed me a small container of sulphuret of ammonia, and I made a highly saturated water solution with it.

"Now for the final test."

My companion knew what I was about. "We want to see a golden-yellow sediment," he said.

"Precisely." As I began to add the ammonia solution to the one containing the white powder, I noticed that my hand was tremulous. For several seconds nothing happened.

"A few drops of acetic acid as catalyst?" Moran suggested.

"Yes." I added them, and behold, a golden-yellow sediment fell to the bottom of the Florentine flask.

"Arsenic!" we both spoke together. Over our masked faces our eyes held each other.

"Edgar was murdered," I whispered.

"Suicide is still a possibility."

"An unlikely one, if the person who shot at us is the same as the one who shot at me two nights ago."

Moran said with a kind of American practicality, "We must protect our discovery from any doubt by anyone. We must sign affidavits to the effect. I'm going to ask Dr. Hare to be our third witness."

"Good. And of course we want to preserve the arsenic we found for any person's scrutiny. But I want to keep our discovery confidential for now. Can your colleague be trusted to be discreet?"

"Absolutely. I vouch for him."

"I'm determined to find the villain. And in investigating a crime it's best not to show all your cards."

His hazel eyes opened and I read in them the question: "Who are you?"

I smiled. "Read Edgar's 'Murders in the Rue Morgue' and 'The Purloined Letter' and you'll learn about me."

His eyes opened even wider, then he left the room to call in his colleague.

Dr. Hare, too, had a handkerchief tied around his face, but I recognized him by his tall, loose-jointed frame and high forehead. We had placed our carter, Joseph, in his care.

"How is the poor man?" I asked.

"Having the bullet removed from his shoulder was painful, but he is well bandaged and in good spirits. He says he knows his work is fraught with danger."

"We'll compensate him as best we can," I said. "Meanwhile, we'll have to use his cart to return Edgar's remains. By the way, I need the bullet. I might be able to determine the gun it was fired from."

John Moran explained to his colleague that we had performed a postmortem on the late Edgar Allan Poe and found arsenic in his system. Dr. Hare followed the report of our chemical analysis with great interest, and said he was willing to sign the affidavit.

A kind of belated reverence made Moran and me insist that we restore the emptied digestive tract to the body. He went so far as to stitch the incisions he had made, which touched me.

As we rewound the shroud around the body, he said offhand, "It's a nice one. My wife made it for him."

We replaced the body in the coffin and nailed down the lid.

Once again in the cold, refreshing night air, we began our journey back to the cemetery. We arrived without incident. If Edgar's murderer had tried to stop us before, it was too late for him now, unless he killed us both. It was close to four in the morning. We lowered the coffin into its grave, shoveled the dirt back over it and replaced the flowers and the wreaths.

7

THE EASTERN SKY was graying when I fell into bed, and sleep came quickly but I was beset by nightmares. I was trying to dig down into Edgar's grave to rescue him from having been buried prematurely. I heard his muffled moans but the earth was white marble, impenetrable to my shovel. At the same time I was dreaming his tale, "The Fall of the House of Usher," his moans becoming the shrieks of Madeline whom we had put living in the tomb. Then the dream turned into another one of Edgar's tales: we were cutting up his body at the Washington College Hospital, but his heart went on beating like a clock. I tried to cry out but was unable to take in enough air, for I was now enclosed in a tomb, slowly suffocating while my coffin was being nailed down. Some of the nails went in at an angle—a huge one coming toward my heart, but now changing into a loathsome worm. More worms coiled toward my face while the hammerblows continued relentlessly; they were now the tons of earth and rock piled upon my coffin. Part of my brain perceived the accruing weight as the dream itself from which I must wake myself or go mad. With my last remaining strength I pushed up against weight and darkness and terror with a howl that finally woke me.

I lay with pounding heart, for there is no clear demarcation between dream and reality, and fear still had a strong grip on me. It is one thing to be the analyst, the anatomist, the chemist, but sepulchral terrors haunt us still—as Edgar observed—even in so-called wakefulness.

My physical exhaustion soon pulled me back into sleep, and this time it seemed dreamless—if sleep is ever dreamless. What woke me now was a knocking on the door. It seemed well into the morning; the pale winter light came through the shutters, brightening the windowsill.

"Who is it?" I called out.

"Letter for you, sir."

"Slip it under the door."

I heard its rustle yet let it lie there, notwithstanding my curiosity. I could not get up. I felt ill, as if Edgar's corpse had infected me with its dissolution. I lay rigidly on my back with closed eyes, feeling the anatomist make incisions behind my ears, then bring his scalpel down on either side of my neck, connect the two incisions under the clavicles, finally cut me open longitudinally all the way to the pubis. I winced and moaned, feeling the pain. That was perhaps an illusion, but the weakness it produced was real. I wanted to be dead so as to join Edgar in a better world. Perhaps I should take measures. No, I must find his murderer. It was a sacred duty I owed him. I tried to lift myself up but my head was pulsating with a violent ache and chills went up and down my spine.

Then I could no longer withstand the call of nature and I clambered up and staggered behind the screen. On my way back, I bent down for the letter, carried it back to bed, and lay holding it.

My thoughts were chaotic; sometimes they cleared enough to indicate the series of steps I must take in investigating Edgar's murder. It would be helpful to know where he stayed in Baltimore, whom he saw. I needed to speak to the persons Dr. Snodgrass had mentioned: Zaccheus Collins Lee and Neilson Poe; they in turn might be able to provide further clues. Nor must I forget William Lummis.

But between these considerations and carrying them out, there appeared a gulf. Even in a more balanced mental state I considered meeting strangers and asking questions the dross of crime detection (though necessary); analysis of evidence in undisturbed solitude, the cream. Now as always when I was undergoing some crisis, I especially felt an aversion to society.

I broke open the letter in my hand and unfolded it. I looked at the signature first: Elmira Shelton. A thrill twisted into anxiety as I read her message:

> Dear M. Dupin: The Rev. Rufus Griswold is here from Phila-
> delphia. He is editing Edgar's writings and is coming to see me
> this evening at eight. Perhaps you would care to join us.

How could I? My head sank back into the pillow and my thoughts ranged wildly. I saw her face, heard her voice: "Mr.

Dupin, you didn't sail across the Atlantic just to grieve with me."
Pert almost, yet warm, enigmatic. Then suddenly a stab of agoniz-
ing doubt. Edgar's death had saved her from having to make an
impossible choice. Was she the guilty one I was after? It would
explain her opening her door to that maligner. Strange he was in
town just now, and so openly. But then he was no doubt cognizant
of what Edgar and I had once formulated, that placing an object
(in this case, oneself) in view was often the best way of concealing
it. I had to meet Griswold before his return to Philadelphia. I had
no choice.

Hours passed and I finally roused myself forcefully, and ordered
up strong coffee. Dusk was falling and I asked the porter whether
the nearby barbershop would be open. I was hungry now, but a
light meal was all I wanted. As I washed, then selected a clean shirt
to wear, I thought of Edgar who, unlike me, took such pleasure in
social gatherings. He once confided to me how much of an outcast
he felt himself to be, how much he needed to be with people who
admired him, flattered him, listened to him. He read to me a tale
he had just written about an old man roaming around the city,
seeking crowds in a descending order, finally mingling among the
most downtrodden in their world of alcohol, prostitution, and
crime. Because he could not be alone. Edgar looked up at the end
of the story and said: "I am that old man."

How happily we could draw on this difference in our tempera-
ments during our companionship in Paris, when day after day we
would see no one. He fitted beautifully into my solitude, and I
provided for him the company he sought. We were both gainers.

*   *   *

I ENTERED the Craigs' drawing room in more favorable circumstances than I had expected. I heard piano music. A young woman
was playing Chopin. The room was hushed; Mrs. Shelton glided
noiselessly up to me, took me by the hand, and led me to a chair.
Her smile, the music, the youthful beauty of the performer were
therapeutic. Chopin's music with its insistent passion that refuses
to let you go while it makes explorations into the soul to the point
of madness always reminded me of Edgar's writings. His recent
death—just eleven days after Edgar's, almost at the same age—
made my admiration particularly personal. And I had always been
affected by female beauty. The young lady at the piano—I assumed

she was Mrs. Shelton's niece—with her gamut of expressions and authoritative hands touched my heart, bringing me finally out of the day's illness. And yet the deepest thrill released by the music came not from watching her but from those occasional glances I cast at her aunt as she sat in her russet gown, her hands folded in her lap, her eyes resting on the performer. I gave myself to a reverie, that soon I would be given absolute proof of her innocence and I would feel free to love her.

Ah but there was still my enemy—by all rights, our enemy—to meet. Which one was he? I had noticed Dr. Snodgrass earlier—with pleasure, for I now thought of him as my friend; and there was a tall sixtyish man in a colonel's uniform, the lovely pianist's father, sitting near his wife, who seemed older, heavier, and more staid than her sister Elmira. Which left two strangers at the far side of the room, under a painting of a pastoral scene. One might be thought handsome, with a pointed nose and a beard, the other had a squarish face with pinched features and red hair. The two seemed to be friends, for they sat near each other, but it was always the bearded one who turned his head, leaned over, whispered a few words, whose light, curious eyes swept the room; the other seemed immobile, self-contained, silent. I thought the more expressive, flamboyant of the two to be Griswold.

After the applause, when Mrs. Shelton again took me by the hand to present me, I saw that I had been correct. The redheaded man, who was an inch or two shorter than I, was introduced as Harold Bradford Tyler, a name that sounded familiar, or perhaps merely historical.

"Ah, Monsieur Dupin," Griswold exclaimed. "I am editing Poe's works, as you perhaps know, and I must say meeting you brings some of his tales especially to life." He offered his hand.

I hesitated. Before me stood the man who had besmirched Edgar's memory. But I was an investigator of crime—perhaps his crime—whose method was conciliatory, not combative. I extended my hand—and felt his small, damp hand close around it.

"I am also writing a memoir of Poe, and if you have any anecdotes or letters to contribute, they would be most welcome. I've come to see Mrs. Shelton with the same request."

"Are you planning to write your memoir in the same vein in which you wrote your obituary, Mr. Griswold?" I asked in the mildest tone I could summon.

Griswold smiled—and there seemed to appear the tiniest smile on his friend Tyler's face also.

"You must not misunderstand the intent of my obituary, Monsieur Dupin," Griswold said, "as so many people have."

"Misunderstand your intent?"

"In one word, I raised Poe into a dark legend. I'm sure you know *Faust*, Monsieur Dupin. I'm sure you have read Byron. Or consider the violinist Paganini. Perhaps you have heard him play. Legend has it that he sold his soul to the devil who bestowed superhuman powers on him. Now I'm something of a publicist, too. I will soon publish four volumes of Poe's works. With my creation of him as a diabolic genius, his fame is established for ages to come."

I had to apply the most rigorous self-restraint not to thrash this impostor before me. I recalled my first reaction to his infamous obituary in Paris and was tempted to pull out my pistol again and fire it—now into his flesh. Diabolic genius? Twaddle! Yes, yes, Poe wandering in the night deliriously, muttering curses. Very romantic. But some other parts of that filthy piece of writing were simply paltry and mean: "You could not contradict him, but you raised his quick choler; you could not speak of wealth but his cheek paled with gnawing envy . . . No moral susceptibility . . . nothing of the true point of honor . . . hard wish to succeed that he might have the right to despise a world which galled his self-conceit." Should I quote his own words—more exactly words he copied from Bulwer—at him?

I saw no reason to revise my first estimate of him as a second-rate talent trying to make an impression before the world by pretending to be close to Edgar—now as his editor—secretly envying him and hating him. How I wished at that moment that I could prove him guilty of Edgar's murder and bring him to justice.

I turned to his friend. "I've been trying to remember why your name sounds so familiar, Mr. Tyler."

"We had a President by that name—no relation of mine. Or perhaps you mean my middle name. You are perhaps thinking of William Bradford of Plymouth Rock fame. I'm descended from William Bradford of Philadelphia. He was a printer who helped young Ben Franklin establish himself in our city. Those were good days, Monsieur Dupin. American life had tone then." He stood erect in his well-tailored frock coat, almost with a military bearing, his red hair brushed up to make him look taller. Griswold was listening to him attentively, fingering his beard. He seemed to hold Tyler in high esteem, was perhaps even dependent on him in some way.

"But you don't regret American independence?" I asked.

"No, no. Washington is one of my heroes. As are all the old Federalists—like John Adams or Alexander Hamilton. I can't say the same for Jefferson. He started the mischief. Jackson was unspeakable. His destruction of the United States Bank, which resulted in the states' flooding the market with useless paper currency, was sheer criminal folly. We live in degenerate times. We have put a Whig in the White House, General Taylor, but the mob still rules. And the Abolitionists want even more extensive mob rule. They want to destroy the South." A trace of a smile formed around his tensed mouth. "I would not want William Bradford of Massachusetts to be my ancestor."

"Poe had no great fondness for New England, either," I said.

"I don't know Poe," Tyler said dismissively.

That took me back. "Are you a literary man, Mr. Tyler?"

"No, I'm a lawyer."

"One who doesn't practice," Griswold put in. "Mr. Tyler is a legal editor. He has adapted such English classics as Smith's *Leading Cases* to American use." He put a hand on his friend's shoulder. "But I wish he were kinder to New England. I was born on a farm in Vermont."

"You are forgiven," Tyler said with a measured smile.

These two puzzled me. They seemed so antithetical to each other, yet they were intimate enough for Griswold to have made that familiar gesture. What was their friendship based on? Griswold was the open one, Tyler obviously the one with the hidden self. What was his business in Baltimore? Had he come just to keep Griswold company? More importantly, when did they arrive? In time to do some shooting on alternate nights? I engaged them in a chat about train travel. "Are the flying cinders as treacherous here as on European trains?"

"Indeed," Griswold said. "There was a high wind this morning; we scarcely dared to stick our heads out the window."

Sly dog. Or innocent.

The gathering was becoming festive. More candles were lit and a Negro servant brought in a silver tray laden with refreshments and moved from one little group to another. I walked across the luminous flowers at the center of the carpet to congratulate Miss Craig on her playing.

She was sitting next to her father with her hand in his arm. "Thank you, Monsieur Dupin." She blushed.

"You have a most talented daughter, Colonel."

"I'm not much for music, but she is a fine girl." He patted her large, capable hand with a larger, meaty one.

"Papa is a war hero, Monsieur Dupin. He led an army that captured Mexico City."

The colonel laughed, the furrows deepening in his face. "I think General Winfield Scott deserves some of the credit as well." He smoothed back his stubborn white hair.

"Maybe you should sit closer to the fire," his wife told him. "He has a bad leg as a result of that war."

"No, I'm fine, Lucy."

Looking into these two women's faces—the young one's cerulean eyes shining out of her alabaster skin, or her pretty little nose; or her mother's high forehead under her graying hair, or the shape of her lips—I recognized teasing touches, echoes, promises of the face of their relative, Elmira. I caught a glimpse of it then, the real thing, with mixed pleasure, for she was talking with Griswold. He was presumably pressing her for material for his evil memoir of Edgar.

"Would you grant me a few words in private, sir?" I asked the colonel.

"Certainly." He rose, towering over me, and led the way with a slight limp across the room to the adjacent library. It was a relatively small, inviting place with wood paneling, cushioned seats, books, and a large globe in one corner. I didn't want to call undue attention to the privacy of our talk by closing the door. We sat down.

"You no doubt know about pistols, Colonel."

"I know something about them, yes."

I took out the round lead bullet from my vest pocket. "Would you help me determine the kind of weapon this one was fired from?"

He held it between two thick fingers. "Thirty-two caliber. Do you know the exact weight?"

"Ninety-five grams. I had an apothecary weigh it for me."

"A bit unusual for thirty-twos made nowadays. They're mostly under ninety grams. The pistol is probably an older model." He turned the bullet back and forth. "With a smooth bore. Do you know the range and the accuracy?"

I was grateful to him for not asking who or what the bullet had been fired at. "The shot seemed fairly accurate at forty to fifty feet."

"Probably a fine dueling weapon of the late eighteenth or early nineteenth century. Something like these." He rose and unlocked a drawer of the heavy oak writing table near the window, took out a case, and opened it. The brace of pistols had ornamented barrels and pearl handles.

"They remind me a little of my own, but I think mine are more recent."

"These go back. I didn't carry them in the war, needless to say." He chuckled in a thick voice, the skin around his dark eyes creasing. "We used modern Colt revolvers." He returned my bullet.

"Your estimate corresponds with my own, sir. I'm grateful for it." I slipped the bullet back in my vest pocket.

"How are conditions in France?" he asked as we left the library. "I was always an admirer of the great Bonaparte. Does your President show any of his genius?"

"It's hard to say, since Napoleon's genius was mostly military. Louis Napoleon shows administrative skills, but he has not been tested in war. By the way, there are those who think that one of these days he'll crown himself emperor, as did his uncle."

The colonel laughed and smoothed back his hair. "I don't think that would be the best way to try to emulate him."

Miss Craig came toward us. "How about some port, Papa? Monsieur Dupin?" The silver tray had been placed on a side table and she handed us each a glass, also a plate of tiny open sandwiches of ham, cheese, and pâté.

"You're a most gracious hostess, Miss Craig," I told her, and she blushed.

I wanted to speak to Dr. Snodgrass, too, and the library was once again convenient. We sauntered in, sat down, and lit cigars. His good services to Edgar, our confident talk two days ago, and his friendly, open face, made me consider revealing to him the momentous events of last night. But perhaps it was wiser to wait. I asked him what he knew of Harold Tyler.

"Very little. I've met him maybe three times, always in Griswold's company. He comes from a distinguished Philadelphia family of lawyers; he seems to disdain court appearances or preparing briefs; he edits law books. He is erudite and has a fine mind, and is archconservative in politics. Yet he has certain public interests. During our talk just now, he said American museums should exhibit good copies of great European paintings rather than second-rate works by the masters." Snodgrass crossed his legs, projecting a fine patent-leather boot, and sipped his port. "That about sums up what I know about him."

"He is the kind of person," I said, "that one becomes curious about. There is something hidden there. What do he and Griswold have in common? I brought up Poe's name earlier and Tyler responded with an almost cutting 'I don't know Poe.' Something told me he was not telling the truth."

Snodgrass walked over to the wall of books and scanned them. He pulled out a volume. "One of Griswold's anthologies. He produces them by the drove. *Poets of America, Prose Writers of America, Female Poets of America,* on and on." He opened the one in his hand to the first page. I read the text in the middle: "To Harold Bradford Tyler this volume is respectfully dedicated."

"Interesting," I said.

"Griswold himself is an open book. Which you have barely dipped into."

"True, I just met the man."

Snodgrass replaced the book. He got momentarily lost in the yellow-brown globe in its wooden stand, scrutinizing it and turning it slowly. He looked up. "He is quite mad, you know."

"Mad?"

"He is an able editor, anthologist, even critic at his best—no one would want to take that away from him. That much even Poe recognized. Yet he is mad. First of all, he is an epileptic. He has seizures."

"I wouldn't call epilepsy madness."

"No, but listen to the following—"

A young Negro servant in a gold-braided green coat asked permission to come in to replace some candles and poke the fire.

Snodgrass waited for him to finish, then went on: "When Griswold was married to his first wife, Caroline—he is now married (I hear unhappily) to his second—he neglected her rather shamefully, living here, there, flitting about—oh, he is a great flitter. So when the poor woman died in childbirth and the infant, too, died, he apparently felt his sins catching up with him. He had a very pious mother, who kept asking him, 'Rufus, are you a Christian?' "

"Well, he is a minister, isn't he?"

"Yes, he was licensed as a Baptist minister, and he did some preaching, but his literary interests always outweighed his theological ones. Anyway, Caroline was buried in New York and Griswold returned to Philadelphia. Forty days after the funeral he went to New York again, gained entrance to the crypt, and removed the lid of the coffin. You can imagine the state of decomposition he found her in. Nevertheless, he started kissing her."

"Kissing her?"

"In the process he lost consciousness—or perhaps had one of his seizures. They found him at night with his face pressed against hers."

The candle flames, the firelight flickering against dark wood, dark volumes, and dark-red upholstery were just the setting for this story, and thinking of my own foray into the realm of the dead I felt shivers going down my spine.

"Do you think a capacity for remorse bordering on madness implies a capacity to commit a crime?" I asked.

He smiled. "I don't think Griswold killed Poe. I don't think anyone did."

Now was the time to bring up last night—if my purpose was to convince him. But I was newly taken by the good man's unsearching conventionality. Let him persist in his belief.

When we left the library, the guests were taking their leave. Griswold asked me again for material about Poe and gave me his Philadelphia address. I took it without making a commitment. I sought out Mrs. Shelton and told her in rather formal terms how much I had enjoyed her soirée.

"Stay awhile," she said softly.

I looked at her.

"I wish to talk to you."

The guests left, and the Craigs—first the parents, then the daughter—went upstairs.

Elmira Shelton indicated the pink sofa near the fire, and I sat down at one end. This time she took the other end, rather than a separate chair, as she had during my first visit. I looked at her expectantly, absorbing her lovely face.

"I want to explain to you that Mr. Griswold is not a friend of mine, that his presence here was not exactly my choice. He had requested an interview, he wanted materials for his memoir of Edgar. Actually, I had very little to give him. For over twenty years Edgar and I had not been in any communication."

"Where did you send your confirmation?"

"To the Fountain Inn where he is staying. He also asked whether he might bring a friend, Mr. Tyler. I knew you wanted to meet Griswold so I thought I might as well make an evening of it. I invited Dr. Snodgrass—he is a dear man—and I didn't think it would hurt to have someone on our side, so to speak." She smiled. "I know how you feel about Griswold's obituary—those of us who loved Edgar all feel the same way—I didn't want you to think I'm in any kind of alliance with him."

Tyler was probably staying at the Fountain Inn also. I wondered why Mrs. Shelton was so anxious to dispel the idea from my mind that she and Griswold were close. Did she feel herself to be a suspect? I studied her face—the firelight playing with her light eyes, the shadow of her hair falling over one cheek, her lips that could look severe now soft. All feeling in me was against considering her a suspect, yet I was duty-bound to.

Suddenly she rose, saying, "There is something I've been meaning to show you." She walked over to a secretary and took out a silver-framed picture. "It's one of my most cherished possessions." She handed it to me.

"Is this you?" The sketch portrayed a young girl; the gentleness of the face was perhaps its most salient feature, mixing with the gentleness of execution, the softened lines and shadowing, even of the dark bobbed hair.

"Edgar made it. I was fifteen, he was two years older."

It was a charming picture, done skillfully, and with love. "It says so much about you both." I let it hold me under its spell for another minute.

But then came the hard question. Why had she brought it with her from Richmond?

She answered it, as if reading my mind: "My niece had never seen it and I wanted to show it to her. It could be her portrait, don't you think?"

I was not convinced. More likely she had brought it to show me in order to build the case for her innocence. Her very presence in Baltimore—since she knew of my arrival—suggested that.

"Did Edgar ever tell you about our early love?"

"He spoke of it."

"We and the Allans were neighbors in Richmond, and Eddie and I would wave at each other from our windows. Then we began to take walks in our garden, or I played the piano and he sang. He had a lovely tenor voice, though his speaking voice was low. He was so talented in every field. He asked me if I'd marry him some-day. I said yes and we considered ourselves engaged. Then, while he was at Charlottesville at the university, we were betrayed."

"Edgar told me his letters had been intercepted."

"By my father. I thought Eddie had simply forgotten about me. When Mr. Shelton turned up, my father pressed me to accept his suit. My father was a very practical man. Edgar with his poetic ambitions, the son of actors, one who was not even legally adopted by Mr. Allan, did not seem to him a suitable son-in-law. Alexander Barrett Shelton came from a privileged family and had a promising future in the shipping business. Oh, he was a fine man. Do you know how he died at thirty-six?"

"No."

"One of his workers fell overboard. Alex dove into the icy river to save him. He did save him, but he contracted pneumonia himself."

"Did you love him?"

"It's not hard to learn to love someone who is good. Alex was a model father and husband—or tried to be. But I often asked myself whether I was happy. I kept thinking of the betrayal of my first love. I could never forgive my father for it. One time the question came most poignantly. Edgar had just married his little cousin Virginia and we met purely by accident. Maybe because the girl was so young, reminding me of myself at that age, I experienced a sharp pang of jealousy. I was a married woman by then with children, and I simply prayed to God to exile the feeling from my heart."

"Do you pray often, Mrs. Shelton?"

"Every day. And I go to church every Sunday." Her long, narrow hands folded in her lap as if she were praying now, and her face seemed transfigured by remembrance. "It happened to be a Sunday that Eddie came back to see me after twenty years. I was dressed to go to church. I bade him come back another time, telling him nothing could interfere with my going to church."

"Even though Edgar was the dearest object to you on earth—as you wrote to me in Paris?"

"He wasn't perhaps at that moment. But he certainly became that during our brief courtship."

Well answered. She had a shrewd mind. She was also exacting, severe. She accused Edgar at one time of wanting to marry her for her money and they quarreled. In a hurt, baffled letter to me last summer Edgar denied the accusation, though admitting that financial security for himself and for his aunt was not totally absent from his mind during his courting Elmira. But she also had a highly developed sense of duty. It's been said that her type is more prone to criminality than the easygoing, flamboyant type. I could see her being pushed into an intolerable situation, where crime might be the only way out. I recalled what she had said about committing herself to marry Edgar in face of financial loss and her children's displeasure.

"Would you have been happy to be married to Edgar?" I asked.

"I loved him. But happy? I don't know. Sometimes I think God did not intend that I should be happy on earth."

There it was. Committing herself to a course that would have brought misery from every direction.

And yet as I looked at the serenity in her face, with her gentle voice echoing in my ear, I felt my reasoning retreat like a nightmare before dawning gushes of love. Impossible! She was innocent! My hand made a move toward hers.

No! Someone had murdered Edgar, and this lady was not above suspicion. I rose. "I must go."

Intolerable forces battled in me. I felt like a husband suspecting his wife of infidelity, wanting proof in this direction, wanting stronger proof in the other direction.

She accompanied me to the door—so erect, so poised.

"May I come to see you again?" I asked stiffly.

"Oh, please do." She gave her hand.

I took it—and against my will I kissed it.

8

I HOPED that Griswold and Tyler would still be in town the next day. I was curious about them, especially about Tyler, since Griswold, to quote Dr. Snodgrass, was an open book. True, an open book could contain surprises. I decided on a beggar's disguise. I could not let myself be seen leaving my hotel wearing a shaggy beard, long greasy hair, and tattered cloak, so I carried my props in a canvas bag, then in an abandoned building effected the change. Within a short time I stood near the entrance to the Fountain Inn, extending a pitiful palm to passersby for alms. The weather was my ally, for after several hours it failed to freeze or drown me. At eleven-thirty Tyler emerged carrying a small valise and turned south on St. Paul Street, in the direction of the Baltimore & Ohio Depot just a few blocks away. To all indications he was leaving town; still, I followed him, now richer by half a dollar in change— which I handed over to the first genuine beggar I saw. My quarry was dressed in dove gray and black, with a gold-headed cane, as well as the valise, in his hand, his red hair curling handsomely under the rim of his silk hat. He was strutting with a kind of Napoleonic energy characteristic of small men, his homely, pinched face—what I caught of it—intense, his mien determined.

At the depot I loitered about, half expecting Griswold to show up so the two of them might travel together. But when the Philadelphia train pulled in puffing and squealing with its great funnel belching smoke, Tyler got on alone.

I thought I might as well shed my disguise, for if I was brought in contact with Griswold I could always say that I had material to give him about Poe orally. On my way back I stopped at a church and went in. It was fairly dark inside, with a handful of worshippers in deep prayer; in the back I effected my transformation back

58

into gentleman without notice. I returned to the Fountain Inn and asked whether Mr. Griswold was still registered.

"He checked out a little while ago," the clerk said, adding trustingly, "The reverend gentleman was on his way to Washington."

"When did he and Mr. Tyler check in?"

He studied the register. "Yesterday, sir."

Griswold had told the truth. Unless they changed hotels.

I returned to Miller's and set out again, now taking along the cheap alpaca coat and palm-leaf hat Edgar had been found wearing. I took my way to the Inner Harbor where the steamer from Richmond docked. I stood there imagining Edgar stepping off it in a troubled, nervous, even feverish state, anxious for affordable lodging. He stood perhaps on this very spot, fanned by the briny breezes from the sea, animated by the sights and sounds around him—the tall masts swaying against the sky and the steamers blowing their high and low whistles, and on shore the hubbub of travelers, the closed carriages and open lories carrying trunks; hoofbeats, shouts, the rattle of hard wheels on the cobbles. He knew the town, he could probably think of some small hotel in Mechanics Row, but the big sign of the United States Hotel just across the railroad tracks was inviting.

I walked toward it. The building was massive, built of inevitable red brick; it did not promise luxury, only decent accommodation, charging a dollar and a half a day for room and board. A block farther west, along Pratt Street, loomed The American; still farther west, The Washington. They all suggested similar accommodations and prices, and I tried the nearest one, The United States.

The clerk studied the names in his register.

"Poe, did you say?"

"Yes. Edgar A. Poe."

His forefinger ran across a line. "Stayed here from September 28th to October 3rd."

I showed him the daguerreotype I carried with me.

"Yes, that's the gentleman."

"Did you ever see him in anyone's company?"

"I can't say that I have, sir. He was always alone, he didn't go out until late in the day, sometimes steady on his feet, sometimes not so steady."

"Did anyone see him really drunk?"

The clerk had a young face and a ready grin. "Julius might have.

He sees a lot." He rang and a Negro porter materialized. He was tall and muscular and had graying hair.

"Come here, Julius. You remember this gentleman?" He pointed to the daguerrotype.

"Yessuh."

"Ever see him drunk?"

"Yessuh. Once. Pow'fully. I seed 'im reeling down the street."

"When was that?" I asked.

"In the mornin'. Mighta been a Tuesday or a Wednesday."

In other words, the 2nd or the 3rd of October. "Are you sure it was not Sunday or Monday?"

"It couldn't be no Sunday or Monday, suh. I's down with the fever on Sunday an' Monday."

"Was it the first day back on the job that you saw him drunk, or the second day. Try to remember."

The porter shook his head. He couldn't remember.

"How was the gentleman dressed, Julius?"

"Fine, suh. Sportin' a cane."

"Frock coat?"

"Yessuh. Light pantaloons."

"Hat?"

"A silk hat."

"Are you sure these were not the clothes he wore?" I opened my valise and let him peer inside.

Julius's grave features gave way to a chuckle. "No, suh, he didn't wear no such stuff. He looked fine and proper, even though drunk."

"Thank you, Julius. That'll be all." I gave him a coin.

I set out for the Law Buildings, where Zaccheus Lee and Neilson Poe both had offices. Charles Street as it ascended was becoming more elegant by degrees, with the wholesale establishments and warehouses giving way to fine stores. Here, equipages with proud horses drove by and I passed fashionable strollers with some beautiful women among them. Up ahead, the great column with George Washington's statue on top made me homesick as always, reminding me of Napoleon in a similar position in the middle of Place Vendôme. Before the street became more sedate, bordered by residences with their carefully cultivated front yards, I turned into Lexington.

This whole prosperous district of Baltimore, which the ordinary visitor would view with simple pleasure, evoked in me contradictory feelings. I saw Edgar wandering about here, ill, oppressed, miserably poor. As I entered Zaccheus Lee's stately complex of offices full of clerks and secretaries—as befitted the position of district attorney—I almost felt like a poor petitioner myself. Edgar with all his doctor and lawyer friends, I mused while waiting to be admitted. Poorer than the poorest among them, greater than all of them put together.

Mr. Lee was affable enough; he had prematurely gray hair, a creased face, and a politician's ready smile. When I apologized for imposing on him, he said he was only too glad to take a little time out to talk about poor Edgar.

"I attended his funeral. Our friendship went way back to our University of Virginia days. I was an upperclassman when he entered, but we often played cards together. He was a terrible player, God rest his soul. He could have the worst possible hand but he bet on it, thinking his next card would provide a miracle. No restraint, all emotion. He lost heavily and his foster father refused to pay his gambling debts. That was brutal of him. I think that's where all the trouble started, Mr. Allan's inability to deal with a sensitive boy."

"When did you see Edgar last, Mr. Lee?"

"Shortly before his death, on October 2nd. My wife had a birthday party and he was among the guests. He toasted her with a glass of wine, but that indulgence did not seem to affect him greatly. He left in what I would call a reasonably sober state."

Over the mantel, a picture showed a fox-hunting scene with red-coated riders and prancing horses and eager dogs. Lee followed my glance, then looked at me sharply. "Am I to attribute your visit to your suspicion that Edgar did not die a natural death?"

"I suspect he did not," I said cautiously. Zaccheus Lee was not someone I wanted to tell about the illegal postmortem we performed. Not just yet.

"I have great respect for you, Mr. Dupin. I read what Edgar wrote about your methods, but in this case you must permit me to be skeptical. Still, you bring me a good suspect—you and the police, I mean; you can't go far without the police—and I'll prosecute." He smiled.

I thanked him and left. If Edgar had been a guest at his house on the 2nd, it was unlikely that the porter at the United States

Hotel had seen him drunk on the morning of the same day. It was more likely the morning of the 3rd. And he still wore decent clothes. I now had a clear picture of Edgar getting drunker and drunker, and in that state being robbed of his clothes within hours of his collapse. This strongly suggested that his robber and killer were the same. If so, why didn't this person rob him of his Malacca cane as well (since he seemed to have robbed him of his mother's miniature), and use the more direct method of the knife or even a gun, instead of the subtle and sophisticated method of slow poisoning? Clearly his motive was not gain but mockery. Now who would want to mock Edgar and then kill him? Surely not some common ruffian or hired killer.

Neilson Poe, who practiced law, had offices in the adjacent building; but he was in court, I was informed by his secretary, a prim young woman with properly close-combed hair. She advised me to come back in the morning.

I planned to visit William Lummis next, but I needed a breather: I had had a full day and was tired. Also, the later I went, the more likely I'd find him at home. I had a great nostalgia for a Paris café where one could relax as in no other place in the world. The best I could find was a tea room on Charles Street overlooking the Cathedral of the Assumption. With its Greek portico and square towers topped by onion-shaped domes, it was a striking edifice, though a little too new for my European taste. Still, a kind of religious feeling came over me—a remnant perhaps of my old Catholic faith mixing with a longing to bring my soul into harmony with the great celestial Oneness—something Edgar had written about so profoundly in *Eureka*.

If I could call my mental state prayer, I was praying for deeper insight in trying to discover his killer.

It was time to go. I saw the visit as difficult, for I expected little from this gun-wielding, dueling man except unpleasantness. I turned into Saratoga and came to the house. It was modest, with the front garden small and unkempt, and when I knocked, Lummis came to the door himself. He was tall and beefy and he stood bending forward slightly, his hard face close to mine, his small eyes scrutinizing me unabashedly.

"You look like Poe. What do you want?"

"Just a few minutes of your time, sir." I held out my card.

He looked at it. "Dupin? From Paris? I thought I recognized that affected accent." He was still barring the door.

"I'd like to ask you for some information, then I'll be on my way."

Slowly he turned, presumably to lead the way inside. I closed the door and followed him into a small, dark, stale sitting room. He sat down and would have left me standing had I not simply taken the chair across from him at a small table covered with a greenish throw, on which an oil lamp was burning. It struck me that his rudeness was an attempt to show that he had nothing to fear from this interview.

"Poe died under mysterious circumstances," I said. "He may have been drugged and used as a voting repeater—and his clothing was taken from him. I'm asking everyone who knew him and may have seen him during his last few days—"

He didn't let me finish. "That scoundrel is better off dead. He tried to besmirch my sister's name, spreading filthy rumors about letters. To him? To that misfit? Ha!" His voice boomed. "I challenged the bastard—"

"Ah, you're a duelist. So am I." I took out my pistol, emptied it of ammunition and placed it on the table. "This is a French model—an excellent one. I recommend it—"

He looked at me suspiciously, then reached for it, showing a soiled shirt cuff. He examined it. "Mine are American. Smith & Wesson. Better than this one."

"Show me." Not that I expected to discover whether the bullet in my pocket had been fired by his weapon—he could have several but I was curious whether he'd want me to think he had nothing to hide.

He went to get his brace of pistols. They were thirty-twos, but my bullet came from an older weapon. I took one, checked the breech, cocked it and pulled the trigger. "Excellent workmanship."

We put our respective pistols away.

"He recanted rather than give me satisfaction, the base coward!" Lummis's voice rose with a violence that did not seem genuine. As if he were performing—rather amateurishly.

"Have you read any of his verse?"

"I don't care for it. My sister's verse is better." He strode to the rear of the room where a small fire was smoldering and returned with a thin volume. I read on the first page: "To my brother, William Lummis, this volume is affectionately dedicated."

"No, I didn't see that drunk during his last days—or I might've dispatched him before his time. May he roast in hell!"

Again I felt he was performing, not very convincingly. Was he trying to hide real hatred, real murder, under all these blustering noises?

*   *   *

IN THE MORNING I went to see Edgar's second cousin, Neilson Poe, in his elegant office in one of the Law Buildings. He was Edgar's age but in many ways his antithesis: easygoing, prosperous, open. He had a bland face with regular features and blond hair; we both remarked on my greater resemblance to Edgar than his, who was a blood relation.

"So pleased to make your acquaintance, Mr. Dupin." Soft handshake. "Take this comfortable chair. Cigar? I tried to see Edgar at the hospital but they wouldn't let me in, since he was in a highly excitable state. All I could do was to leave a change of clean linen for him. Edgar didn't like me, you know. He thought I was jealous of his literary fame."

I studied his eyes which were gray like Edgar's but rounder and not so thickly lashed. I remembered hearing Edgar voice that belief. Calling him, in fact, his worst enemy.

"Pooh!" he said as if answering my secret thoughts. "If I had to choose between literary fame and knowing where my next meal came from, you know which I'd choose—in fact, have chosen."

Meaning he had it in him to achieve literary fame. Had Edgar been right about him? Was there perhaps consummate jealousy under such pride? As I saw Edgar's murder now, literary jealousy was a likely motive.

"Not to take away any of poor Edgar's genius. There were times indeed when my heart went out to him. Like when I received the report that he was lying unconscious under the steps of the Baltimore Museum—"

That remark stunned me, pulling me away from my preoccupation with the man. "When was that, Mr. Poe?"

"On October 3rd, about two in the afternoon."

"On the same day he was found at Gunner's Hall?"

"Yes, maybe two or three hours earlier."

"Who reported this to you?"

"A young relative and partner in my law firm, Jacob Poe, Jr. Would you like to meet him?"

"Nothing would please me more, sir."

He rang and a clerk came in.

"See if Mr. Jacob Poe is about. If so, ask him to step in for a few minutes, if he would.

"Jacob was in a carriage on his way to court, so he had no time to stop and tend to Edgar, but he sent me word and I rushed out to the designated place, but did not find him. I didn't feel too terribly bad, because this sort of thing had happened before, Edgar falling into an alcoholic stupor, then coming out of it by himself. However, since he died so soon afterward, I confess the incident is still preying on my mind—"

A knock.

"Come in, come in."

Jacob Poe, Jr., seemed in his late twenties or early thirties; another Neilson Poe type, I thought as I rose and we shook hands.

"Mr. Dupin is here from France to look into Edgar's death," Neilson Poe said. "I told him how you found Edgar in a stupor and sent word to me."

"Oh, yes, it was a most painful business. I was on my way to face a judge who is known for his citations of contempt on the slightest provocation, and I could not afford to be late."

"Are you sure it was Edgar you saw, Mr. Poe?"

"Absolutely sure."

"What struck you most clearly about him?"

"Oh, his face, its pallor, its anguished expression, a lock of dark hair fallen on his broad forehead, his moustache, his slender hands clutching a cane. It took my carriage about sixty seconds to pass the spot but it was unmistakably Edgar."

"How was he dressed?"

"I didn't notice his clothes, I was so mesmerized by his face. I know one thing, he was hatless."

"Did you see his hat anywhere near?"

"I did not, which doesn't mean it wasn't there."

"Do you recall whether he had a coat on?"

"No, except it was a cold, dismal day. I'm sure I would have noticed the absence of a coat around his body."

"But you don't recall whether the coat he presumably wore was his own, or the cheap sack coat he was found in later?"

"No."

"Or whether he wore a vest and cravat?"

Jacob Poe shook his finely frisured head.

"He may have sold his clothes for a drink," Neilson Poe said.

"I doubt that," I said. "It is a known fact that he always tried to look respectable, even in the depths of poverty."

"Or someone robbed him of his clothes while he was drunk—maybe he hung on to his cane for dear life, or the thief was disturbed—and then poor Edgar bought whatever he could to cover his body, only to fall into the stupor in which you, Jacob, saw him."

I could not argue against this sequence of events as a possibility. I did not doubt that the poisoning occurred after Jacob Poe had seen Edgar lying under the steps of the museum, but the theft might have occurred earlier—which shattered the rest of the picture I had constructed in my mind. On the night of my arrival I could have been shot at by a thug who wanted to rob me; the next night, on our way from the cemetery, we could have been shot at by an opponent of body-snatching (with an old-fashioned pistol). Edgar could have been robbed of his clothes by a common thief; afterward he could have been poisoned by the agent of a woman with an insoluble dilemma . . .

I seemed to be going around in circles.

9

THAT AFTERNOON I went to see her in a mental turmoil, rushing against sudden gusts of wind until I became breathless, then standing still and panting, stunned by the magnitude of my suspicion. No, no, she could not be guilty of such a crime. Neilson Poe was a more likely suspect. Edgar had called him a jealous little man, his worst enemy. Had he totally misjudged him? Suppose after receiving word from Jacob Poe that Edgar was lying under those steps in a stupor Neilson Poe went out and found him and fed him arsenic?

Or Edgar could have taken arsenic himself.

But the case seemed stronger against her.

Perhaps I should not go to her. It would solve everything. Or would it? My kindled feelings? The agitation in my heart?

I turned my back sharply to my renewed suspicion; I locked it in the most secret chamber of my brain. I was going past a florist and I stopped abruptly. I bought a bouquet of purple chrysanthemums to take to her.

They helped to put me in a dream about her where suspicion had no place.

When I entered her sister's drawing room, she rose to greet me.

"How lovely," she said of the flowers.

"Not as lovely as you," I said. She wore a blue gown with lace trimming, which revealed the curves of her fine shoulders.

She had the flowers put in a vase, but then arranged them herself and placed them on the mantel with its garlanded frieze. "Edgar loved the color purple."

"The rustling of each purple curtain," I quoted.

"Ah, 'The Raven.'"

"I should not think of such a gloomy poem when I'm with you."

"Most of Eddie's poems are gloomy. They're not only about

death but the death of a beautiful maiden. I remember his saying that it was the most poetic subject he could think of. And now we have his own death. It's one thing to mourn him, though, another to imagine that someone actually— I can't even pronounce the word. What makes you so sure someone did, Mr. Dupin?"

"Oh, let's not speak of it, Elmira. May I call you Elmira? We have such little time. You'll be going to Richmond, I to New York and Philadelphia. Each day I can see you is precious."

A smile surprised her face and she cast her eyes down. But just then tea was brought in and she had it put on a small table close to the pink sofa where we sat. She dipped the silver pot over one of the fluted cups to test the strength, then poured. There were freshly baked blueberry muffins under a napkin and I took one, broke off a piece, and spread jam on it.

"When did we first meet, Elmira? Was it only two days ago? It seems much longer. But then the letter you wrote to me in Paris was more truly our first meeting. It seems I've seen you a hundred times since. Sometimes I suddenly hear your voice—see you walk across the room—'in your eye a kindling light,' as Edgar wrote of you."

"Oh, Auguste, what am I to do with your beautiful compliments? I don't want to marry again. My brief engagement to Edgar took a great deal out of me. I'll put on my widow's cap, wait for my children to marry and become a grandmother."

"Don't turn your back on life, Elmira."

"I've begun to think about eternal life."

"No, no, the time hasn't come for that—it won't for many years. Think of the joy that can be yours. You said yesterday that God perhaps did not intend that you should be happy on earth, but that's so wrong. God intended us all to take as much happiness as we can. Oh, Elmira!" I took her hand impulsively.

She looked up at me with a start. "You bring back Edgar so. He made these sudden moves, sudden declarations. It's a confusing sensation—I feel old stirrings, then the realization that you're not Edgar. Edgar is gone. Ah but you're here and these kindled feelings don't recede . . ." She extricated her hand and drank her tea.

I drank mine.

"You were never married, Auguste, were you?"

"No."

"But you had mistresses—"

"Yes."

"You're different from Edgar in that respect. I sometimes wondered if he and his little wife had any conjugality—and if we had married, how it would have been with us."

"He was pure spirit, pure intellect. The flesh was for him a kind of illness. Which it is not for me. We do differ in that. The joy I spoke of a moment ago is the kind you might not have had with Edgar, had you married him. I mean the pleasure, the fulfillment, the charm of closeness. Edgar said he could love several women at the same time. I was puzzled by that. For two faces may be beautiful, but each has its own individuality, and isn't that what we love? Not according to him. He loved the higher Beauty in each, not their mere fleshly manifestations. No one's flesh anchored him down. His spirit flowed freely as spirits will. All of which I can understand mentally, but my experience is different. I am not as pure a spirit. When I love a face I cannot think of any other. Since I met you, Elmira, how could I possibly envision another, feel love and express love for another?"

She was gazing past me, at the fire, as if trying to gauge the extent to which my words had moved her.

Then she looked at me and spoke remotely: "Some people thought him immoral for that reason. After we renewed our acquaintance, I received a letter from a Mrs. Ellet urging me not to have anything to do with him. She told me how while his wife lay dying he was courting Fanny Osgood, the painter's wife; then while he was trying to marry Helen Whitman, writing to her such things as 'the unutterable fervor of my love for you' and 'Helen, I love now for the first time and only time,' he wrote to Annie Richmond, a married woman, such things as 'I love you as no man ever loved woman, my pure beautiful angel, wife of my soul . . . why am I not with you now, darling, that I might sit by your side, press your dear hand in mine?' "

"Did you believe the woman?"

"She claimed she had seen the letters and copied those sentences from them."

"But you didn't heed her."

"I mistrusted her—not so much her veracity as her purpose in writing to me. There was something spiteful and vindictive about her letter. Afterward I found out that she hated Eddie, felt scorned by him."

"I know about Mrs. Ellet," I said. "Have you met her brother?"

"No."

Still, getting such a letter about the man she was going to marry—and how well she still remembered the quoted words it contained—had to intensify her dilemma, adding fuel to my suspicion of her. Except those words of love on her lips had the very opposite effect. Reverberating deliciously in my ears, they became her own, making an almost unbearable inroad into my heart. I moved closer to her and took both her hands in mine.

"It was so low to write to me in that vein," she said. "You had only to look into Eddie's eyes—" Here she looked into mine. "And hear his voice—and all evil tongues were silenced. Soul spoke, and your own soul responded. You were willing to think of marriage that way—perhaps not ultimately but certainly while you were under his spell—a 'marriage of true minds,' as Shakespeare wrote. And that feeling was remarkably free from jealousy. I knew about his recent engagement to Mrs. Whitman, but it did not matter. I felt pure and innocent with him, a kind of child. Do you know his last poem, 'Annabel Lee'?" She quoted from it:

> She was a child and I was a child
> In this kingdom by the sea . . .

"I first thought Annabel Lee was me. But now I think she is all women he ever loved."

We sat in silence, her hands still in mine, our gaze directed at the dancing flames.

"Yes," I said. "That was how Edgar loved and made one love him. But you and I are not children, Elmira, and my love for you is different." I extricated one hand and turned her face toward mine.

"No, Auguste."

"Come to me tomorrow."

"O God, how can I? You're like his ghost coming back to haunt me."

"His corporeal ghost. Come to me so we can love each other." I brought our faces closer and I kissed her lips.

A tremor passed through her and she stood up. "You must go."

"I'll go." I stood up and followed her toward the entrance hall. "But you must come to me." I caught up with her and took her in my arms. I kissed her again and now her lips parted.

"Edgar never kissed me like this."

I kissed her face, eyes, neck, what her gown permitted of her bosom. She was breathing hard.

"O God, deliver me from temptation. How can the Holy Spirit reside in us if we're subject to such unholy desires?"

"Ah, you desire me as I desire you. Yield, my beloved. Come to me tomorrow."

"I can't, I can't."

"In the afternoon. I'll be there waiting for you."

"Ah," she moaned softly, submitting to my wilder and wilder kisses, to my eager hands on her body.

"We must stop this . . . you must go . . ." she sighed, panted. Her eyes searched mine and her hand passed over my face. I took it and kissed the palm. Then her lips once more.

"Tomorrow, then," I said, already out the door, turning back as I started to walk across the garden.

She made no answer, merely stood in the open door, until I turned away from the garden gate.

*   *   *

IN THE MORNING I made a redoubled effort to discover something about the rags in my possession. I stood on the corner of Calvert and Baltimore streets, looking up at the museum building. On the Calvert Street side, a flight of steps led to the second-floor entrance. It was under these steps, apparently, that Edgar had lain in a stupor. Hatless, Jacob Poe had said. But from the window of a carriage going along Baltimore Street toward the courts, he could not have seen everything, the steps partially blocking his view. The hat had come off obviously and was lying on the ground. But the question still remained, which hat? Edgar's own silk hat, or the soiled, ribbonless palm-leaf hat?

I embarked on the task of combing the neighborhood, street by street, block by block, north-eastward, into the Old Town, in search of shops where used clothes might be bought. When I came to one I went in, opened my valise and asked, "Were these articles bought here?" I realized, as I received denials, shrugs, and shakings of the head, that my search might be fruitless. If someone had forced Edgar to change clothes with him, God only knew where these wretched clothes might have come from. They might have been acquired years ago and miles away. I needed a great deal of luck in my search.

"Good morning. Were these articles bought here by any chance?"

A quick examination. "No, sir."

Along Baltimore, Swan, Plowman, Salisbury, down to Pratt Street, then along streets intersecting these, Harrison, Front, all the way to East.

At the same time I was traversing, in a general way, the route Edgar must have taken from the museum to Gunner's Hall. If Neilson Poe's statement that at 3:00 P.M. Edgar was no longer under the museum steps was true, he probably met his poisoner in this area.

But now it was time to return to my hotel, and despair began to tug at me. Perhaps my search was futile. I had hard evidence that Edgar had been poisoned; I needed more hard evidence to track down his killer. My most interesting speculations about motive were useless without it.

I gave myself to thoughts of love, stopping on the way to buy a dozen white roses to proclaim my lady's innocence; then at a confectioner, a box of chocolates to match her sweetness; then at a wine shop a bottle of Cointreau to toast our passion.

It was a cold, drizzly day, the sky leaden, the fire in the room welcome, my purchases promising her arrival. Oh but she might not come. One-thirty became two o'clock, then two-thirty, then three. I stood by the window, watching for her. Sometimes I'd break into sudden pacing up and down, then return to my post.

Carriages passed, slowed down, moved on. Finally one drew up at the entrance. A woman in a long black cloak alighted. She! I rushed to the door, waited for her knock with pounding heart. It came. She entered and I took her in my arms.

"I almost didn't come," she whispered.

"I know. I felt your indecision. Thank God you're here."

"This is madness."

"Divine madness." I kissed her lips gently, breathing in her light perfume. "Your hands are cold. Come, let's sit by the fire." I threw some pillows down on the rug. I poured some Cointreau into two tumblers. "Let's drink to your being here, Elmira." We sipped the strong, sweet, aromatic liqueur. "Doesn't it warm you nicely?"

"Yes." She was still in her cloak, but now began to unbutton it. She stood up and I took it from her, also her bonnet. Her dark hair was smoothed back, held together with a clip. "What a nice room." She leaned toward the roses on the commode to smell them. "They're so bridal."

I went to her, undid her hair clip, and her tresses tumbled down luxuriously. I buried my face in them, my kisses roaming over her face, down her neck, to the softness of her breasts. She was panting, returning my kisses; we began to undress.

Edgar was in the room—somehow, in the unfathomable mystery of her being here. I think she felt him as much as I did—his presence not a jealous or prohibitive but a sympathetic one, watching this continuation of his wooing which had never gone beyond gentle kisses. I felt we were living through stories of his with the sexes reversed: a dead wife assuming life through another, in "Ligeia"; a dead mother living again in her child, in "Morella." I felt Edgar entering my body, becoming me, and I think Elmira felt him in me as we lay in our naked, passionate embrace. I drank deeply of her loveliness with every part of my own body, then we were anchored in each other and she cried out softly, shrilly, wildly, against my pervasive, ecstatic groans.

We lay for some time wordlessly and motionlessly as we clung together in the shifting shadows of the sporadically flaming log in the fire. Finally I reached out for the comforter and pulled it over us. We both seemed to be staggered by the momentousness of our union. It meant something beyond us. I found myself turning mentally to Edgar in an effort to understand it. Was she thinking of him?

She said suddenly, "It is fulfilled. It had to be."

I waited.

"What began with children betrayed and ended when he came back to die. Now I've tasted life after death."

I don't know why my suspicion began to plague me at this moment. It was perhaps a sudden remembrance of my disappointing morning, with the investigator in me growing impatient. I refused to attribute it to the satiation of desire. I tried to escape from it into whimsy, burying my face in her loosened hair, finding her ear and tracing its convolutions with my tongue.

"Sir, you tickle me." She laughed.

"What a heartwarming sound!" I cried. "The tintinnabulation of the bells! We have been too solemn." I sprang up, took some of the roses out of the vase and placed them on her body, one at each nipple, one at the navel, one at the luxuriant *mont de Venus*. Then I lifted each and kissed the spot underneath.

She seemed amused, though perhaps more shocked. "Is this how all Frenchmen make love?"

"Only those in the order of the *chevaliers d'amour*." I pulled her lovely thighs apart.

"I'm not sure I can follow you into all these refinements. I'm too set in the ways of widowhood."

"Cast them aside, my darling. Let Aphrodite reign." I entered her.

"Ah, my dear!"

"Do you like this?"

"Yes—ah, yes—"

I rode her hard, and when her little cries reached a crescendo I exploded. We lay spent with smiles on our faces.

But the question in the back of my mind was rattling chains, regardless of how much I tried to subdue it with playfulness and talk and chocolates and Cointreau . . .

"I don't want to go," Elmira said. "But how long can I spend shopping, yet return to my sister's house empty-handed?"

"Buy something on the way."

"Oh, Auguste . . ." she said with sudden sadness. "Why must all beautiful things end?"

"They need not end."

"I must get on my way tomorrow morning. My children are expecting me. They're growing up and are very severe with me. Come to Richmond, Auguste."

"I will, of course. But first I must go to New York. I expect to unearth a great deal there." I rested my hand on her bosom. Or should I go to Richmond with her? Stay close to her—get to the bottom of the terrible question the bloodhound in me was sniffing at?

She studied my face. "You're thinking of something you don't want to reveal. Something about Edgar's death."

I pulled her to me.

"You're trying to shield me from something. I'm a strong woman. I have stood up to a lot in my life."

"Very well. A young doctor and I opened Edgar's grave, performed postmortem, and discovered arsenic in his system." I watched her closely. She drew a sharp breath, her eyes dilating with horror.

"On our way from the cemetery to the hospital we were shot at, and our carter was wounded. It may have been some opponent of body-snatching, which we appeared to be doing, or Edgar's killer."

"It troubles me to see you expose yourself to danger." Her long, narrow hand caressed the side of my body.

"Which is less likely," I continued, "if he had been hired to do it."

"I don't understand."

"A hired killer is less likely to stalk investigators and witnesses—" I forced a chuckle. I was in this now fully, brutally. "Unless he has been rehired."

A frown on her face suggested that she still did not fully understand. Was it genuine or pretended?

"Suppose someone like Mrs. Ellet living in New York wanted to have Edgar killed in Baltimore—without involving her brother. All she had to do was to find such a person. I've known some. I'm thinking of one in particular. He had the blandest face and the coldest eyes I've ever seen in a man. Expressionless vulture eyes. I spoke to him, questioned him—this was about a murder case in Paris. He showed no human feeling whatever, no pity, no remorse. Killing a person meant no more to him than writing a letter means to a scrivener."

"Why are you telling me about such people?"

I tried to gauge her tone, its ingredients of displeasure and remoteness. "Someone may have hired such a person to kill Edgar." I kissed her face, her somewhat stiffened lips, gently. Not insincerely. I did not take our closeness lightly, I was deeply affected by it, and questioning her secretly in my own mind was a severe trial for me—far more severe than it might have been before. But I went on relentlessly, seeing her in a straight chair before me, the harsh, intensified light of a lamp on her face. *Were you glad when Edgar died? It saved you from a dilemma. Did you think, when he was still living, that if he died your problems would be solved? Did you think you could perhaps buy Edgar's death? Hire someone to carry it out in Baltimore while you remained in Richmond with a perfect alibi? Did you have Edgar killed, Elmira?* My interrogation was so vivid in my mind that a spasm passed through me and my hand resting on her breast contracted. I had to will it to stop short of giving her pain.

"What is it?" she asked.

"Nothing," I lied.

But she chose that moment to leave the bed, as if troubled by my questions. I saw for a brief moment her long nude form before it disappeared behind the screen. I heard water splashing. I assumed she was syringing herself to prevent conception.

I got out of bed also, draped myself in my shirt and poked the fire. "I could've gotten you hot water," I called to her.

She said nothing, only made shivering sounds.

Then as I took her place behind the screen, she passed me wordlessly like a shadow. I poured more water into the basin and washed. When I emerged, she stood in her hoops, lacing herself into her corset. She kept her back to me while she slipped on her gown. I watched her reflection in the mirror as she combed her hair and gathered it tightly at the nape of her neck, then applied a modest amount of color to her face.

She turned and faced me with that severity in her mien which I had found so enigmatically appealing, also disconcerting, at our first meeting. She pulled herself up to her full height and said in a calm, cold, queenly voice: "I did not have Edgar killed, whatever you think, Monsieur Investigator."

I went to her. "Good God! How can you think that I could ever—entertain—such a monstrous notion?"

In writing one of his tales, Edgar had me say that with respect to myself, most people wore windows to their bosoms. But this time my bosom had a window to this lady's gaze. I had never been so seen through by a woman in my life. I protested wildly, and she let me take her in my arms, but there was a stiffness in her, and when I tried to kiss her good-bye, her cheek was all she gave me.

"I love you," I called after her as she left my room. "Will you let me come to you in Richmond?"

She turned briefly. "Write to me." Then descended the stairs.

I watched her from the window until a carriage drew up and she got in. It struck me that perhaps she did not really believe that I suspected her of Edgar's murder, but pretended to do so in order to distance herself from me. She was passionate when aroused, but perhaps she now wanted to put an end to passion. I would write to her, go to Richmond, beg to see her. I did love her.

Meanwhile, she remained a suspect.

10

THE FLIGHT OF IRON STEPS under which Edgar had been seen delirious compelled me to return, now in order to comb the area in the opposite direction for shops where used clothing might be bought.

In one, just a block northwest of the museum, on Dana Lane, the proprietor scrutinized the soiled palm-leaf hat and said, "It had a ribbon."

"Hah, my dear sir—" I could barely contain my excitement. "The ribbon could have been easily torn off."

"True."

"Do you recognize this garment?" I spread the sack coat on his counter.

"Yes. It all comes back. The gentleman who bought them was well dressed. I couldn't imagine what he wanted with them. I assumed they were for a masquerade."

A disturbing thought crossed my mind, that Edgar had bought these objects himself for some weird purpose of his own. "Can you describe him?" I asked.

The man considered.

"Did he look like me?"

He studied my face. "I remember a full black beard. It may have been false. Put on a beard like that—I don't know. You might pass for the gentleman."

But why would Edgar go through all that? "Was he of my height? Taller? Shorter?"

"About the same. Maybe taller. Maybe even shorter. I'm short myself, as you can see, and everyone seems taller."

"Do you remember anything else about him?"

"His coat was of fine material, well tailored. He wore tinted glasses so I could not tell the color of his eyes."

"Would you by any chance remember the date and the time of day you made this sale?"

"It was around two o'clock. I had just come back from my midday meal." He took out a ledger and paged in it. "Black sack coat and palm-leaf hat. Sold on October 3rd."

"*Formidable!*" I exclaimed, involuntarily reverting to French. I gave the shopkeeper a gift of five dollars for his help and he thanked me effusively.

I didn't think the man he described would have resorted to selling the clothes he had taken off Edgar; more likely he had discarded them, which would make them impossible to find.

But where did a change of clothes take place? Hardly under the museum steps in broad daylight. Nor was any hotel or lodging necessary. A hackney coach was the obvious answer. One was just passing and I hailed it.

"Take me to where all you drivers congregate," I told the man, "where I can speak to several of you."

"There are a number of such places through the city, sir."

"I mean where I can find most of you who work in this area."

"I go to a place near the wharf, sir, at midday and at the end of the day."

"Good, take me there."

The ride took about fifteen minutes. We came to a line of hacks, the horses with feedbags on. It was a reasonably dry and windless day, and the drivers were sitting on a bench talking and smoking. Some were chewing and periodically emitting a rich stream of tobacco juice.

"I am investigating for the French police," I said, stretching the truth slightly as I addressed them. "I'm looking for someone who drove two gentlemen on October 3rd, Election Day, in the late afternoon or early evening, from the area of Pleasant Street to Gunner's Hall on Lombard Street. One of these gentlemen had a black beard, the other looked like me, except he had a dark moustache." I took out Edgar's daguerreotype and let the drivers pass it on.

Shaking of heads. No one remembered. Some of them returned to their horses, took off feedbags and blankets, and climbed on their boxes to continue working.

Two more hacks drove up. The driver of one caught my attention. He wore a silk hat which, from where I was standing, seemed to be of a better quality than one would expect a hackman to wear. I noticed it was somewhat soiled.

As soon as they were off their boxes I repeated my inquiry.

The one with the fine hat squirmed and shifted his eyes.

"I like your hat, my good man," I told him. "If it's the one I'm looking for, I'll buy it from you."

"It's worth a couple of dollars."

"Sure," I said. "Let me see it."

He took it off and I looked inside. The monogram stamped into the leather band read "E.A.P." My heart leaped.

"I'll give you three for it if you tell me how you came upon it. In addition, I'll buy you a meal."

I waited for him to put a feedbag and a blanket on his poor nag of a horse and we went into a greasy eatery not far. We sat down at a corner table and ordered soup, sausage, and beer.

He was in his twenties, with work-roughened hands, broad Irish features, and curly hair. His name was Dan.

"I wouldn't 'ave noticed them gentlemen, sir, but then as I's drivin' along I see this black coat flyin'. See it was a rotten day with the wind from behind, so when they threw it out the window it came flyin' forward. Otherwise I'd never 'ave seed it from my box. Then something smaller came flyin', like a vest, or a cravat. Then this here hat. I just had one thought, to take these crazy gents wherever they want to go and drive back and get hold of them garments. Well, someone got there faster for the other stuff, but I found the hat blown under a dray wagon."

"Did you notice anything else about those gentlemen, Dan?"

"One was sick or drunk, sir, the other holdin' him up. But I didn't see which was which."

"Where exactly did you pick them up?"

"In front of Kelly's Bar Room on Calvert, sir."

"And where did you take them?"

"To the voting place at Gunner's Hall on Lombard. I 'member it was Election Day."

"What was the time, do you remember?"

"Maybe two or three in the afternoon."

"Very good, Dan. You've been very helpful."

"Who were these crazy gents, if you don't mind me askin', sir?"

"The bearded one was a murderer; the one whose picture I showed you, his victim."

"Lord, deliver us from evil." He crossed himself.

"Amen," I said.

*   *   *

I NOW HAD THE OUTLINE of a picture, the parts beginning to fit together—somewhat in the manner of Edgar's own "Cask of Amontillado," which the killer perhaps set before him for a model. I saw him as a literary man, or one who had failed at being one, believing himself to be a victim of Edgar's injuries and insults and planning revenge; a man of high intelligence, one with a knowledge of chemistry, for to gauge the delayed effect of arsenic is a complex matter. Here the picture darkens. Edgar may know him well, or slightly, or not at all; he may have followed Edgar for days, or come upon him unexpectedly. Is the beard genuine or false? The tinted glasses suggest that it is false. If so, is he hiding from Edgar, or the world, or both? One way or another, seeing Edgar in a stupor under the museum steps he sees his opportunity. But the hate rising in him is of such all-pervasive magnitude that killing Edgar is not sufficient. He must humiliate him as well. The bearded, dark-spectacled man, with the vial of arsenic in his pocket, considers. His enemy is in a deep enough stupor to warrant a brief absence. He walks to nearby Dana Lane, where there are second-hand shops, enters one, and purchases the most disreputable coat and hat he can find. The cheap, soiled hat still has its ribbon, and he tears it off. He returns to his victim and starts to revive him.

"Oh, let me help you." He pulls Edgar to his feet, slips an arm under his. "You need some black coffee. Or perhaps some light wine . . ."

He leads him into Kelly's, they take a table in the back, and he orders.

The picture darkens again. If he is a stranger to Edgar he introduces himself—probably as Henry Reynolds. He flatters his victim, as in the tale Montresor flatters Fortunato as a connoisseur of wine in order to lure him to his doom. Perhaps he offers money to invest in *Stylus,* the magazine Edgar is anxious to start.

The picture clears. The killer watches the wine take effect. Edgar's voice booms out boisterously; in the next moment he is slipping back into his stupor. He does not see the vial being emptied into his glass. He drinks up, on his companion's hearty urging.

Outside, the killer calls for a hack, pushes Edgar into it, and directs the coachman to Gunner's Hall. The hack sways on old springs and the horse's hooves resound on the cobbles. Their tempo quickens; there is a strong, impelling wind from behind.

"Sir—" or, "Eddie—" as the case may be. "You're not well. Let us loosen your clothing . . ."

As cravat, vest, tailcoat, hat come off, the killer reaches behind him and lets each fly through the open window. Cane? He'll need it to lean on. Edgar is semiconscious. He cannot tell that he is being dressed in rags. His shirtfront is too white, and the killer smears it with mud from his bootsole.

At Gunner's Hall there is a hubbub of corrupt ward heelers trying to stretch the votes. The bearded man pulls the derelict out of the hack and leads him in, then retreats a few steps and watches him stand motionless, leaning on his cane.

What a sight. On his head a soiled palm-leaf hat with the ribbon gone, he wears no neckcloth or vest, over his muddied shirt an old, thin alpaca sack coat hangs grotesquely. Only the cane is fine—a Malacca, accentuating the rags.

"Hail to thee, king of poets!" the murderer intones under his breath. Then turns and walks out amidst gushes of voiceless laughter.

*   *   *

OH BUT THAT SUCH SUCCESS as I had met this day should be wedded to sorrow and repentance. I wished I could go to Elmira and fall down before her, proclaiming my conviction of her innocence. If she had only remained in Baltimore one more day! I considered sailing after her.

As I hurried along Pratt Street, with Edgar's silk hat in my hand, I sobered somewhat. An open apology would only affirm my previous suspicions, which I had tried to keep from her. Whether I had succeeded I did not know. Her words, "I did not have Edgar killed, whatever you think, Monsieur Investigator," uttered with such calm superiority, haunted me. Again I asked myself: had my bosom a window to her queenly gaze, or was she simply trying to distance herself from me?

It was even more upsetting to think so. A woman who loves you can always be pacified, however you might have hurt her; one who drifts away from you, nothing can bring back.

On my return to my hotel I wrote to her.

> My dearest Elmira:
>
>   I cannot tell you how painful it was for me to have you leave yesterday, to watch you from the window as you stepped into a carriage, then not to see the carriage any longer. I think of you now sailing southward, wondering whether you have docked in Richmond yet. The weather is cold but clear here: I trust you're having a good voyage . . .

I mentioned my discovery briefly—which should convince her I no longer suspected her. Should I allude to her words of denial? Defend myself once again: "How could you have even imagined . . ."? No, the less said the better.

> Baltimore is so empty without you. Is it not strange how such a brief period we spent together should affect one's whole life? Last night I woke up suddenly, whispering your name . . . To-morrow I'm leaving for New York; I will stay at the City Hotel, so please write to me there. I don't know how much I can accomplish in N.Y. and how long it will take me, but in any event I would very much like, in a week or so, to sail down to Richmond. I can't let too much time elapse without seeing you . . .
>
>   All my love, Auguste

Next I wrote to Charles Baudelaire. It was my second letter to him; in the first I had communicated the momentous results of our postmortem. This time I gave an account of my discoveries on this day.

> All evidence points to the killer and the person who deprived Poe of his decent clothing being the same—one the shopkeeper described as a "gentleman" with a black beard. I can think of no other motive than consummate hatred. I'm sure you will keep asking the same question I keep asking: what misguided soul could have hated Poe so? God only knows if I'll ever find him. So don't hesitate to write to me; by the time your letter arrives I may still be in America, investigating. Pity the transatlantic cable

everyone is talking about won't be laid for another few years. Here, there are now telegraph wires between a few major cities.

I hope your health is in a stable state. My respects to Madame. Yours as always,

Auguste Dupin

11

I LEFT MY TRUNK at the hotel and traveled with just a portmanteau, which made the trip more convenient, since I had to change trains in Philadelphia, then take a steamer in Perth Amboy. In the mad scramble for seats on the first train I managed to find one near enough the belching stove; in the second one the only seat I found was on the drafty floor. But the closed main deck of the steamer was well heated. As we approached New York, many of the passengers rushed to the top deck, weathering icy winds, to watch the big island city emerge from the twilight. Its growth was legendary. Within the last twenty years its population had more than doubled; it now boasted some half a million souls and was called the Empire City, the modern Tyre, great Gotham. The twinkling harbor lights amidst the vague shapes of masts and buildings excited me yet made me uneasy as well. Here was the future world—its commerce, shipping, banking—in the hands of the expanding, conquering rich. But oh, the dregs of humanity on whose bodies and souls this modern Babylon was being erected! As Tocqueville had written, the lowest classes in a great American city like New York were a rabble more dangerous even than that of European towns. The plight of the freed Negroes, condemned by law and opinion to a hereditary state of degradation and wretchedness, was the worst. But the plight of the European immigrant was nearly as bad. Thousands upon thousands had come to this great city in an attempt to escape from hunger and degradation in the Old World only to find hunger and degradation in the New. Lucky those in domestic service, who had decent food and lodgings; the vast numbers of unskilled Irish and German laborers lived with their families in unspeakable, overcrowded shanties—sometimes with their pigs—or in tenements, in disease-breeding filth, without daylight, without even water. In one of his letters Edgar had called my attention to Charles Dickens's account of his visit here, and as I stepped ashore, the English writer's description of these horrors came sharply to my mind.

As the hackney coach, which I directed to the City Hotel, bounced me over the dark, unpaved or ill-paved streets of the waterfront, my gloomy thoughts became a reality. The moment we stopped or even slowed down, we were surrounded by beggars— with maimed and malformed children among them that were heartrending. I passed out coins, until my coachman, no doubt inured to such misery, cracked his whip and we moved on. But then at one point there was a long delay, with flames shooting up ahead into the darkness and heavy smoke drifting through the air. It was one of the many fires that broke out here—with shanties going up like paper boxes or tenements trapping hundreds inside. There was a great crowd blocking our way, watching as volunteer firemen pumped water and directed sprays on the flames. God help them save some lives, I prayed.

Finally we moved on, but then stopped again to let a wagon piled high with coffins go through. My heart grew cold. Was this a sign of another cholera epidemic? The last one, some years ago, had killed thirty people in every thousand—mostly the poor of course, whose corpses were ferried to the potter's field on one of the islands in the harbor. By now some connection had been made between this deadly disease and foul water, and New York was building a system of water supply from the Croton River north of here, but it would take years to complete it. I leaned out and called to the coachman, pointing to the wagon with its dread burden, "Have you seen many of those?"

"Aye, I seen 'em. Lots of 'em."

But then Broadway! The contrast staggered belief. It was truly broad and well paved, with a profusion of gaslights, ostentatiously dressed crowds, newsboys running, crying a variety of papers hot off the press, vehicles of every kind—omnibuses, hackney cabs, gigs, phaetons, even carriages with liveried Negro coachmen. One was letting off two dandies before a restaurant; another a lady, bejeweled and wrapped in furs, on her way to a brilliant shop that held its doors open perhaps exclusively for her. Here was New York, transcending all human misery, throbbing with wealth and splendor, "the beautiful metropolis of America," as Mr. Dickens called it.

I secured a room, a rather palatial, ponderously furnished one, with a log sputtering in the broad marble fireplace, then went down to dine. Over the main course I began to feel the fatiguing journey; as I sipped my demitasse I nearly nodded off. I returned to my room and fell into bed.

In the morning I took the train to Fordham. The city seemed as various and congested as last night, but now a gray winter light pervaded all. As we left the last streets behind, numbered in the forties, patches of white appeared, and it struck me that the American genius was more rural than urban: the farms, the orchards, the neat white frame houses perching on snow-freaked hills warmed the heart and I thought of my countryman Crèvecoeur's *Letters of an American Farmer.* Sometimes the scenery was grand—sudden glimpses of snowy hills, vast valleys, the chiaroscuro of ancient forests, their winter bareness stark against the whiteness, or as we ascended an elevation, a sudden view westward of the Hudson.

On arrival I had to ask questions, go down snowy, wheel-rutted country lanes and brave barking dogs in search of information for the way to Mrs. Clemm's cottage. Finally, walking uphill along Kingsbridge Highway, I saw the kind of small rustic place with a long front porch and a lean-to a neighbor had described, set back on an acre of greensward. Was this it? I walked closer, past cherry trees, pines, and lilac bushes, with beating heart. There were asters in the window boxes and the path was shoveled free of snow. This had to be it—I knew from within; something unearthly had taken hold of me—as if I was Edgar coming back from the dead.

I knocked and heard heavy footsteps. The door opened and I saw her—a large, mannish woman, old yet erect, with kindliness and mournfulness but also something forbidding reflected in the broad planes of her face. She wore a black shawl over her crisp black dress with a small, blindingly white collar held together with a pin; her widow's cap was as white, and the hair peeking out from under it barely less so. She didn't think I was Edgar—there was something solid and prosaic about her; also I had written to her about my arrival in America. Still, she seemed moved. The shine in her gray eyes seemed saintly, or perhaps merely martyric, and a smile hovered around her narrow lips. Her two hands came forward and closed around my arms and her bosom was heaving. I could smell her clean, soapy emanation.

"Oh to have you here—someone who was so close to my Eddie!" She spoke in a low, mannish voice.

I felt something strange, a transformation. Perhaps there were ghosts, perhaps Edgar's had taken hold of me, for I felt a sense of belonging, of being home after an interminable journey. I felt almost as if I were being held by my own mother. "It's good to be here." Were these my own words? Or was Edgar speaking through me?

"Come sit here, dear friend." She pointed to the caned rocker close to the fireplace that gave off a little lingering warmth from ashes burned down some time ago. "I wish I could offer you a cup of tea at least, but there is nothing, nothing in the house. I have been selling odds and ends, that's why the room is so bare. But I'll go out later, see if I can scrape up something for a little repast."

How did she plan to do that, unless I gave her money? Ask for credit from the village grocer? Or try to borrow fifty cents from a neighbor on the way? I wondered how she fed herself when she had nothing more to sell—and fed her pets, a parrot in one cage, a bobolink in a smaller one, and the large tortoiseshell cat making her appearance in the doorway. I knew her, although I'd never seen her before.

"Catterina! Here, puss!"

She approached me slowly, looked up at me as if she knew me, too, and jumped into my lap.

Everything around me seemed strangely familiar—the small round table with two straight chairs, the ornate hanging bookshelf, the square table under the window covered with green baize secured all around with brass-head nails. Edgar had made it—though I don't know how I knew this. Nor did the general cleanliness surprise me. The gingham curtains were spotless and the wide floorboards were gleaming, as if the poor woman were trying to wash and scrub her way to total destitution. From where I sat I could see a tiny hall at the far end of the room, from which a spiral stairway led up to the attic rooms. Across from it there was a door.

"My precious Virginia joined the angels in that room," Mrs. Clemm said, making a move toward it. I put down the cat and followed her. The small room was almost wholly taken up by a bed and a little table with a half-burned candle on it. "First she and Eddie had the larger bedroom upstairs, Eddie used the smaller one for his study, and I slept down here. But when my poor darling became too ill to go up and down those steps, we brought her down."

We stood for a moment silently, looking down at her deathbed, covered with a faded brown throw. Then we returned to the sitting room.

"After I lost her, I had my Eddie to comfort and console me, but now I've lost him, too. I have the kindest, the best of friends in the world—they all want me to stay with them. I spent two weeks with the Lewises in Brooklyn, and soon I'll be going to Lowell to stay with Annie Richmond and her husband. After I lost my Eddie, she wrote to me so kindly, so movingly. She called me 'mother' in her letter. 'My darling Mother,' she wrote, 'if I could only have laid down my life for his, that he might have been spared you.' And how her own heart was breaking at the thought that she would never see Eddie again, never read one of his beautiful letters to her again." She sighed. "But none of these good people are my Eddie."

How was I going to tell her the circumstances of his death?

"I blame myself terribly for not going on his last trip with him, but I just couldn't scrape up the money. If I had been with him I could've saved him."

That was probably true. His murderer would not have found him in a stupor under the museum steps.

We were now sitting at the small round table, face-to-face, Catterina in her lap.

"Edgar was poisoned," I said.

"He was poisoned from birth on—when his father, my dissolute brother, ran off. He was no good. And his mother died on him— maybe that was for the best. You know actresses. They're an immoral lot. Then that brutal Mr. Allan. Eddie was poisoned by the world—the selfish editors trying to grow rich by paying him pennies, the small-minded, jealous rival authors, the literary women fawning on him just to suck his blood. I tried to protect him from the world—and from his own weaknesses. Most people are cold, bad, rapacious. The good ones like my darling Virginia, or Eddie, or our angelic benefactress, Marie Louise Shew, or the Lewises or the Richmonds or Mr. Willis, who put a notice in his paper appealing for aid to us—they're the exceptions. My Eddie needed protection, he was not equipped to face the world alone. He was a child, a prodigy with the gods speaking through him. Even in his weaknesses, his tantrums, his fears, a child—kind, loving, trusting, without a bad streak in him."

Yet his literary vision was dark. The yellow-and-blue talking bird interrupting us from time to time with an "Eddie" or "Sissy" or "Muddy" was metamorphosed into his raven croaking "Nevermore"; Catterina, lying safe and contented in her mistress's lap, into his tortured black cat.

"Edgar was poisoned," I repeated. "Physically. Someone fed him arsenic."

"Arsenic?" But she wasn't absorbing it.

There was no halfway measure possible if I wanted her help. She had to know everything. "A doctor and I opened his grave and found arsenic in his system."

"You what?"

"We opened his grave."

"You went to the cemetery—and dug up—his grave?" She gaped at me, her broad face ghostly white, her whole frame trembling. Suddenly she rose—large and menacing—making me stiffen in my chair. "How did you dare desecrate my Eddie's grave?" Her mannish voice broke into a wild moan and she took a step toward me.

"Calm yourself, Mrs. Clemm. Hear me out."

"What fiend are you?" she shouted. "What devil brought you here?"

"Please hear me out." I raised my hands defensively. "We couldn't risk prohibition—yours or the authorities'. We had to act. And we found that Edgar was the victim of a crime—"

"Yes, yours! Your unholy act—"

"No!" My voice rose. "He was murdered. Fed arsenic."

"How do you know? What abomination did you commit with his poor remains?"

"Only what was necessary. But we found arsenic in him. And now his murderer must be found and brought to justice."

Something yielded in her—perhaps she saw reason. She staggered back and sat down again, burying her face in her hands. She sat that way for some time, shaking. Then she looked up, her martyric eyes narrowed. "He did it himself." Her low voice trembled. "Oh, Eddie! Eddie! Eddie!"

She could accept the whole world poisoning him all his life

figuratively, but not his actual physical murder. I needed her on my side, I wanted to convince her that my investigation in all its frightening details was vital. I gave her details—how someone had dressed Edgar in rags, then discarded his decent clothes from the carriage window while driving him to Gunner's Hall where he finally collapsed. "He was mocked and insulted as the poison was working in him."

She finally faced it—the object of her anger shifting from me to Edgar's murderer. "Who? Dear God, who could have done such a thing?"

"Help me find him. You know so much about Edgar's life. Who might have hated and feared him that much? I keep coming back to the idea that some terrible jealousy was at work." I took out pencil and paper to write down names.

"Heaven help us," she wailed. "He had enemies—literary ones—those who hurt him, and I hate them to this day. Oh, Eddie was at fault sometimes, I won't deny it. He drank, acted crazy, said irresponsible things, wrote cruel criticism—" Her bosom heaved. "Oh if he were only here again to do those things, so I could give him love, and more love, and more—which he needed so desperately to set him straight.

"Dr. English, that terrible fellow, hit Eddie in the face. I don't know what their quarrel was about. But I can tell you about Mrs. Ellet, that vindictive busybody shrew—snooping and writing anonymous letters. She felt scorned by Eddie, and her brother threatened him."

"I've heard about Mrs. Ellet and I met her brother in Baltimore—an unsavory type." The pair remained on my list of suspects. "Is she in New York now?"

"Yes, she is married to a professor in South Carolina, but she is always in New York, stirring up trouble. Then there is Griswold, whom Eddie ridiculed, but he has already had his revenge."

"I met Griswold—I can't say I felt much liking for him."

"I gave him power of attorney—I had little choice, since Eddie had appointed him his literary executor and he is now editing Eddie's works. He assured me that after the expenses are met I would have most of the profits. But I don't trust him. Not after his treacherous obituary."

"I met a friend of his, Harold Tyler, as well. Do you know him?"

She thought. "No, I can't place that name—except for President Tyler."

"Tell me about Edgar's other enemies."

"Oh, he made so many when he published 'The Literati.'"

I knew that work in *Godey's*. Edgar had gone after a lot of writers, matching his sharp critiques with personal caricatures. He was unsparing with friend or foe—objecting to the shape of Willis's nose and forehead, remarking on Margaret Fuller's upper lip which habitually uplifted itself, suggesting a sneer, or on some editor's fidgetiness—his never knowing how to sit or stand or what to do with his hands. But these sketches hardly merited murder. Still, I wanted to make a careful study of them. Mrs. Clemm said she did not have a copy, but it should not be hard to find.

She gave me more names, some familiar to me, others not, people with whom Edgar had extensive battles like Charles Briggs and Lewis Gaylord Clark and Hiram Fuller.

"Mrs. Whitman's mother accused him of being after the family fortune in trying to marry Helen, and he accused Professor Longfellow of plagiarism, but I must say he took it like a gentleman. He has written to me kindly, saying he considered Eddie a great poet, and asking me to visit him. I think the villain may be someone whose name I don't even know. You must go among them, those literary people in New York, maybe the evil person will show up there. Maybe Eddie's cruelest criticism was about the poetry of the Rev. William W. Lord. But how could a man of God—?"

"How could anybody, Mrs. Clemm? Yet someone did."

"So few knew him as we knew him—as someone loving. I know you did, Mr. Dupin. He spoke of you as his closest and dearest friend, his other self, his soul. But these women he made love to— they were but poetic subjects for his great gift of words. Romance maybe, but not true love. He reserved that for us. I must show you his two dearest letters—"

She went up to the attic and came down with a box. "I have already started packing for my next visit." She pulled out a packet of letters, undid their pink ribbon. She quickly found the two she wanted. "He wrote this one from Richmond. We were living in Baltimore and Eddie's cousin Neilson offered to take Virginia into his family and educate her and give her some social advantages. She was thirteen. Eddie was frantic, as you can see. This one he wrote after they arrived in New York. They were both in such high spirits, so hopeful, my darling children—" She handed me the letters.

"What was Neilson Poe's claim to Virginia?"

"He had married her half-sister, Josephine. She is my husband's daughter from his first marriage."

"She had to be considerably older than Virginia."

"She was, by some fourteen years."

But now he wanted the younger half-sister. I did not find his noble purpose entirely convincing. "What do you think of Neilson Poe?" I asked.

"I never cared much for him. Eddie considered him his worst enemy."

"Because he wanted to take Virginia away?"

"That, too, besides being jealous of Eddie's genius. Neilson wanted to be a writer once. He edited a newspaper in a small town in Maryland but it didn't do well and he turned to law."

His trying to be a writer interested me greatly. I recalled his pooh-poohing literary success, which had struck an envious note. I unfolded the first letter.

"While you read them I'll do my errand," Mrs. Clemm said.

"May I be of help?" I took out some bills and pressed them into her large clean hand, which closed eagerly on them.

"God bless you, my dear friend. I will get some coal, too, for the kitchen stove. We'll make it nice and warm in here." She pulled on a pair of worn snow shoes, wrapped herself more tightly in her shawl and took her capacious wicker basket.

I sat down with the letters, gratified—also amused—that we were friends again.

Aug. 29th, 1835

My dearest Aunty,

I am blinded with tears while writing this letter—I have no wish to live another hour . . . My last my last my only hold on life is cruelly torn away . . . I love Virginia passionately devotedly. I cannot express in words the fervent devotion I feel toward my dear little cousin—my own darling. . . . It's useless to disguise the truth that when Virginia goes with Neilson Poe I shall never behold her again—that is absolutely sure. Pity me, my dear

Aunty, pity me. I have no one now to fly to—I am among strangers, and my wretchedness is more than I can bear . . .

For Virginia: My love, my own sweetest Sissy, my darling little wifey, think well before you break the heart of your cousin Eddy.

And so they were married. But how did Neilson Poe feel being thwarted?

I unfolded the second letter.

N.Y. Apr. 7th, 1844

My dearest Muddy,

We have just this minute done breakfast, and I now sit down to write you about everything. . . . The house is old and looks buggy but the landlady is a nice chatty old soul—gave us the back room on the third floor for 7 $ a week, the cheapest board I ever knew. . . . I wish Catterina could see it—she would faint. Last night for supper, we had the nicest tea you ever drank, strong & hot—wheat bread & rye bread—cheese tea cakes (elegant), a great dish (2 dishes) of elegant ham, and 2 of cold veal, piled up like a mountain and large slices—3 dishes of the cakes, and everything in the greatest profusion. No fear of starving here. . . . Sis is delighted, and we are both in excellent spirits. She has coughed hardly any and had no night sweat. She is now busy mending my pants which I tore against a nail. . . . Tomorrow I am going to try & borrow 3 $, so that I may have a fortnight to go upon. I haven't drunk a drop—so that I hope soon to get out of trouble. The very instant I scrape together enough money I will send it on. You can't imagine how much we both miss you. Sissy had a hearty cry last night, because you and Catterina weren't here. . . . We hope to send for you *very* soon . . .

Truly I had never known Edgar to be so ebullient, so hopeful, so happy. His devotion to his young wife seemed indisputable. My thoughts returned to Neilson Poe. Had he any intimation of this side of Edgar? Was he envious of his brief happiness with Virginia, as he was of his genius? I recalled his words on the subject of Edgar: "Edgar didn't like me, you know. . . . Not to take away from poor Edgar's genius . . . There were times when my heart went out to him . . ." So bland, open, easygoing. But Edgar had peered under that façade when he called him his worst enemy. Was the shadowy figure who revived Edgar, fed him arsenic, and dressed him in rags Neilson Poe?

12

CATTERINA WAS ASLEEP on the hearth close to the dead ashes, but the chill of the little house was getting to me, although I hadn't removed my outer coat. I stood up and wandered into the kitchen which hopefully would soon be made warm. Maybe I could lay kindling. The coal-and-wood bin was empty. I buttoned up my coat and stepped outside. I walked around the house and saw a wooded area not far and made my way toward it. I found some dead branches on the ground but most were wet with snow. I gathered an armful of the driest ones and went back to the cottage. There was a pile of old newspapers next to the stove, which would help. I crumpled up some, put them on the grate, and laid the kindling.

When Mrs. Clemm returned she was delighted by my preparations. We lit the stove, the branches sputtered but caught, and we piled on some coal. She took two chops, potatoes, bread, tea, milk, sugar, and a pie from her basket. She put up a pot of water over the starting flames and got a big frying pan ready.

"Those letters really touched me," I said.

"You see how much Eddie needed love. And how happy he could be made by the simplest things—a cozy room, a good meal. Everybody always thought of my Virginia as a child because she was small and in many ways simpler and much younger than Eddie. But he was more of a child. She was a tower of strength to him to the very end. If you had been with us during those last terrible days, you would have seen it. He seemed to be dying, not she. He was ill and distracted with grief, but she went bravely."

We sat at the kitchen table near the stove, she peeling a potato.

"She died on the thirtieth of January. On the twenty-ninth she felt a little better, she wanted to sit up. We had some wood and Eddie tried to make a fire but he wasn't functioning. His hands were shaking so that he couldn't hold anything. I told him just to sit while I made the fire. Previous to that, my darling was lying in that little room you saw, with Eddie's old army coat covering her and Catterina lying on her chest warming her. Eddie and I would rub her hands and feet for more warmth. She was so terribly thin by then, although her little face was still round. She was shivering, eaten up by fever. But even at a time like that her thoughts were with Eddie who needed her so much. 'Muddy, will you always take care of Eddie after I'm gone?' Her voice got husky with her illness. It used to be like a bell when she sang.

" 'Of course I will, dearest,' I told her. 'But you mustn't speak that way.'

"She knew she was near the end, but poor Eddie refused to believe it. 'Don't you feel a little better, my angel?'

" 'Yes, a little,' she said, mainly for his sake. 'Do we have any wine left?' She liked to have a little wine from time to time, although it hurt her to swallow. There were a few more drops in the bottle, which I poured out for her. As I held the glass to her lips she smiled.

" 'Louise will bring more,' Eddie told her. Mary Louise Shew was our good angel. Oh, she is worth more than all those flattering literary ladies put together. She is not as beautiful as she is strong and kind and capable. She comes from a family of doctors and she is a nurse herself, blessed with a truly Christian heart. She came every second day during my darling's illness bringing things— medicine, too—and ministered to Virginia, and to Eddie, too, who needed it as much as she did. Eddie never touched a drop of wine she brought, although I'm sure he was tempted to. It was medicine for Sissy, he said."

The stove was getting hot. Catterina came in, rubbed against the edge of her mistress's skirt, and received a bowl of milk. When the water began to boil Mrs. Clemm scalded the teapot, measured out the tea, and filled the pot. She greased the frying pan and put in the chops and the potatoes she had sliced. The kitchen was warm enough for me to take off my outer coat.

"I don't know if it was only for Eddie's sake she wanted to sit up, or she really rallied a little, but it was nice and warm by the fire and I put her in a clean nightshirt and combed her hair to make her pretty for our guest.

"There came two in fact, for Louise had met Mary Deveraux on the way. She's the beautiful one with her long blond hair. I wasn't very happy to receive her, although she was nice enough to bring a cake. She and Eddie carried on a flirtation many years ago in Baltimore—Virginia, then a little girl, used to carry notes from Eddie to her—and I thought what right had she to come here and flaunt herself at Eddie with my darling Virginia failing? I must admit she redeemed herself afterward by helping with the funeral expenses. They were bringing a huge bundle.

" 'Heavens, you ladies will hurt yourselves,' I said when I opened the door and saw them.

" 'It's light as a feather,' Louise said. It was in fact a down comforter from her own bed. It was so cheering, strewn with pink roses.

" 'God bless you,' I told her as I spread it over Virginia in the rocker.

" 'It's so wonderfully cozy. Thank you, dear Louise.' She was really grateful.

" 'You must be feeling better, to be up,' Mary said, taking her hand.

"Louise felt her forehead and took her pulse. Then she took Eddie's. 'It skips after every ten beats. You must try to be calm, Edgar.'

" 'I promise. You're the kindest, most unselfish woman in the world, Louise.' Then he turned to Mary. 'Dear Mary, it's so good to see you.' His voice was tremulous and he had deep circles under his eyes, and he kept touching his face, embarrassed about his two days' growth of beard. But he was in no condition to be let out to the barber, and I wouldn't let him use his own razor."

Mrs. Clemm turned the chops a couple of times, they were almost done, and she set the table as handsomely as poverty permitted: the tablecloth and napkins were freshly washed and the china matched and the silverware shone.

The food was excellent, the bread freshly baked, the tea full-bodied. "Everything is delicious," I said.

"It gives me much pleasure to serve this little meal. It reminds me of the times when things were going well and we were happy together. To think that after Louise and Mary's visit my darling had less than a day to live—it's unbelievable. She felt it. She made preparations—with Eddie in mind. She waited for me to be out of the room—I was cutting the cake and Louise was also here getting water for the quinine she was going to give her—but I overheard her say, 'Mary, be a friend to Eddie, don't forsake him. He always loved you—didn't you, Eddie?' I pretended not to hear and went in with the cake—a moment too soon, just as she was placing Mary's hand in Eddie's. She thought perhaps that I would be displeased because Mary was married."

"Or she was reluctant to display her unselfish devotion," I said.

"It was that certainly, a devotion that transcended all possessiveness or jealousy toward those who would live on after her. She had something to give Louise, too. She asked me to get her jewelry box from upstairs. It was a handsome object made of ivory and ornamented with inlay. It had been Eddie's mother's, she left it for him, and he gave it to Virginia. She held it in two hands, opened it, and took out a sketch of Eddie. Also an old, charred letter. It contained nothing else; her only jewelry consisted of a pair of earrings with tiny sapphire stones and a thin gold necklace which she had on. She kissed Eddie's picture and gave it to Louise. And then the box. 'I want you to have these, Louise, as a token of my thanks for your kindness.' Then she gave the letter to Eddie. 'Read it, Eddie.'

"It baffled him. He studied it, he looked up from it. 'I don't know—I don't remember—yes, I do—' His voice was pained, agitated. 'I received it years ago and I thought I burned it.'

" 'I pulled it out of the fire, Eddie. I want you to read it now so we can all hear it, and I want you to promise you'll always keep it.'

"He stood next to her with bowed head, murmuring, 'I promise, Sissy.' Then he read the letter in low, jumping voice. It was from Mr. Allan's second wife saying she was sorry for turning Mr. Allan against Eddie. 'I behaved in a small-minded, jealous way. I'd like to make it up to you somehow. I'd like to meet you—' But Eddie couldn't finish reading it. He burst into tears. 'It's too late,' he said amidst sobs. 'Don't you see? It's too late.'

" 'This letter vindicates you,' she insisted. 'No one can accuse you of deserving Mr. Allan's neglect.' She reached out to him and he came sobbing into her arms, and she held him like a child."

Mrs. Clemm collected the soiled dishes into a large basin and poured hot water over them. She served generous slices of apple pie and poured more tea.

"But then poor Eddie went out of control. Louise took out some money—it was sixty dollars—and said she'd helped to collect it from literary people who wanted to help us. Eddie stared at the bills and said, 'No, Louise, give it back to them. Thank you for your immense kindness but we don't want their charity.'

"I pleaded with him. 'Eddie, we need that money desperately.'

" 'No we don't, Muddy. Thompson wants me to continue my "Marginalia" series in the *Messenger*. He'll pay three dollars a page. If I just send him three pages a week we can live on that. I can turn out three pages in just a few hours.'

"Virginia, too, pleaded with him. 'Eddie, please accept it.'

" 'No, Sissy, it was doled out with contempt, like you drop a coin into a beggar's cap. I know those people—'

" 'No, Edgar, it was given in good faith,' Louise said. 'Everyone who gave feels kindly toward you.'

" 'Give it back, Louise!' He was so wrought up—trembling, his voice harsh. He was running out of the room, toward the staircase. Suddenly he stopped, turned back to us. 'Very well, I'll take it—as a loan. I want the name of every contributor and the amount, and I'll repay them to the penny. While you ladies are talking I will turn out three pages of "Marginalia" and ask you, Louise, to mail them from New York.'

"We were astounded. We remained silent. He was so obviously ill.

"A few minutes later he came down again. He said he needed a book. He took it, went up with it. He remained upstairs for a long time. Our visitors stayed until evening. When they were about to leave, he came down with some pages of manuscript for Louise to mail.

"By now my darling was back in bed again. Under Louise's down comforter she was warm enough. She slept through the night, but the next day she had trouble breathing. By evening she could only wheeze and choke—and bring up blood and sputum. Pain in her poor chest and throat was wracking her. She tried to scream but could only gasp and choke, her body in a convulsion. I gave her a few grains of laudanum to ease her suffering. Eddie was kneeling next to her bed, giving in to sobs, and when the pain let up a little she reached out to him, trying to comfort him. But we all knew the end was near. She stopped speaking, she spoke to us only with her beautiful feverish eyes. After an hour of choking and convulsions her breathing grew irregular, then fainter and fainter until no more breath came from her. She had no pulse. She was with the angels.

"Eddie broke down completely—moaning, crying, trying to shake her back to life. 'Sissy! Oh, Sissy! Why did you leave me?' Then he fell down in a faint. I had no smelling salts, only water with which to revive him—and get him somehow to the rocker where he slumped, sobbing, begging me for some wine. I couldn't say no to him and he drank a glass, then another, until he lay in a stupor."

Mrs. Clemm was sobbing herself now. I reached across the table for her hand and we sat in silence.

Then I asked, "What was the book Eddie took up with him?"

"I don't know. Maybe a copy of his tales or poems."

To help him write his "Marginalia"? I doubted it. His "Marginalia" were supposed to be jottings he made on the margins of books he was reading—books by other authors. I asked casually, "Have you sold many of Edgar's books?"

"No, they're all here as he left them. I haven't had the heart to sell them yet. There aren't many. He sometimes sold books."

I went in. There were no more than a dozen on the hanging shelf: Edgar's *Tales of the Grotesque and Arabesque*, in two volumes, early collections of his poems, poems by Robert Browning, Elizabeth Barrett, Longfellow, Willis, a collection of Hawthorne's tales. A thin book, called *Reflections*, bound in purple linen, showed no author. It was published in Philadelphia by Lea and Blanchard in 1836. The book was a miscellany of brief essays on history and art, aphorisms, thoughts. It seemed well thumbed. There were no marginal notations to speak of, but many penciled check marks and underlinings. One of these pointed to a passage about the Romans worshipping their standards, which kept me mesmerized. The more I pored over it, the more it struck chords of familiarity. My heart grew cold. Was this the book Edgar in his state of nervous illness and unproductivity had come down for? To lift passages from it for his "Marginalia"?

I turned pages ravenously for more, but there came a knock on the front door. Shutting the book, as if to protect Edgar's secret from intruders, I waited while Mrs. Clemm's heavy steps carried her across the sitting room to the entrance hall. I felt a blast of cold air and heard her voice resound with the name, Annie. Clutching the book, I went closer. She was in her twenties, tall and graceful, with whirls of light chestnut hair peeking out from under her beaver bonnet. It matched the trimming on her outer coat which below the suppressed waist spread luxuriously around her. Annie Richmond, of course, with "soulful gray eyes," as Edgar had described her.

"Annie, may I present the Chevalier Auguste Dupin."

She had a small mouth, which with her oval face and large eyes gave her a Madonna look. She saw my resemblance to Edgar, grew pale for a moment, and I noticed tears in her eyes. She made an effort to smile through them. "Edgar spoke of you, monsieur, with much affection. Did you attend his funeral?"

"I fear I didn't arrive in time," I said evasively.

"I didn't even know he was so terribly ill, or I would have gone to him. The first I heard—it was too late. And I live so far from Baltimore."

"I know you live in Massachusetts. Mrs. Clemm spoke of visiting you."

"Yes, and we want her to stay as long as she wants to." She turned to the old woman. "Dear Muddy, it will be good to have you. Carrie is so anxious to see you. She is my little daughter," she explained to me. " 'Don't forget to bring Muddy' were her parting words." She smiled. "When will you be able to leave?"

"I just need another day or two," Mrs. Clemm said. "I must wash things and pack, and I want to leave the house clean."

"Good, that'll give me time to do some shopping. This evening I'm going to the theater. As long as I'm here I want to take advantage of the wonderful things New York has to offer."

"You came just in time for apple pie and tea, Annie, but let's sit in the kitchen where it's warm."

Annie shed her coat, which I took from her, draping it over the rocker, and we moved into the kitchen. There was an airiness about her walk and I saw that "ethereal inner vitality" Edgar had remarked about her.

As we sat down I realized I still had the book under my arm, as if afraid it would vanish into thin air.

"Mrs. Clemm, may I borrow this book, *Reflections*, from you?"

"Of course you may." She was setting a place for Annie, her large, erect figure making slow, deliberate moves. The water on the stove was almost at a boil.

"Would you know who wrote it?"

"All I know about it is that Eddie had it for a long time. I never heard him speak about it."

"Or I could buy it from you."

"Yes, well—anyway you like." She served the tea; she urged me to have more pie and I compromised on a sliver. "Eddie had many more books," she said, "but when my darling became so ill he sold most of them to buy medicine for her."

A silence fell.

"Oh, Mr. Dupin, when I half close my eyes I think I'm sitting face-to-face with Eddie," Annie said.

I thought of phrases from his letters to her, as Elmira had quoted them: "Why am I not with you, darling, that I might sit by your side and press your dear hand into mine . . . ?"

"The pie is delicious, Muddy," Annie said.

"I can bake a better one, but Mr. Dupin's visit was so unexpected—" She smiled at me conspiratorially, meaning she couldn't possibly have afforded ingredients before my visit.

We stayed till after three. Annie said she wanted to catch the four-o'clock train and I offered to escort her.

"That's very kind of you, Mr. Dupin."

I asked Mrs. Clemm what *Reflections* was worth to her. She said she'd probably get seventy-five cents or a dollar for it, and I offered her two.

"Shall we make it Monday morning then?" Annie said. "I'll come for you."

"That's too much of a bother for you, Annie. Why don't we meet in New York?"

"No, I'll feel much better if I call for you—help you a little with odds and ends—hold Catterina. Or will you have a box for her?"

"No, she is a great traveler. She falls asleep in your arm right away." Mrs. Clemm walked with us to the door.

"Till Monday then, Muddy. I'll come with a carriage."

"That will be lovely, Annie. You're the kindest person in the world. And Mr. Dupin . . ." She hesitated; she seemed reluctant to speak before Annie. "If I can be of any further help—" Her voice grew tremulous. "God knows I want to be—"

I thanked her. The two women kissed.

13

IT WAS A TWENTY-MINUTE WALK to the station along Kingsbridge Highway, past snow-swept farms and orchards, the houses already showing lights against the descending grayness. It was cold and at one point Annie placed her hand on my arm.

"I hated to leave her alone," she said. "So isolated—with the weather getting colder every day—and so poor. But it'll only be for three more nights."

"Fortunately she is strong."

"Oh, yes, how would Eddie have survived without her? And face Virginia's death. As it was, he fell totally apart with grief—some people thought he became insane. I didn't know him then, I met him a year later, but he often spoke of the mental and physical devastation he'd gone through. He kept relapsing into that state. 'I'm so ill,' he wrote to me more than once, 'so terribly, hopelessly ill in body and mind—'"

I felt her hand clutch my arm as if she were responding to Edgar's plea, as we trudged on, taking small, careful steps, trying not to slip on the icy road.

"Are those boots of yours warm enough?" I asked.

"Feet do get numb, but we'll be there soon," she said with that pioneering spirit that I found so American.

The train had no stove, but we were at least protected from the elements.

"I must confess," I said as we rushed into the deepening twilight, "meeting you took my breath away. It was so totally unexpected. I knew about you a little, I knew Edgar loved you—"

"Meeting you gave me, too, the strangest feeling. I don't know if I can express it."

"Regret? The memory of love?"

She nodded. "He was so unlike any person I had ever known. I could not think of him as an ordinary being, or measure him by ordinary standards."

We rode in silence, looking out and seeing only the vague outlines of snowy hills. I needed her help, as I needed the help of anyone who knew Edgar, but with her I found it difficult to broach the subject. I wished she would ask me what Mrs. Clemm had meant when she offered to be of further help, but I knew she wouldn't.

"Mr. Dupin," she asked instead, "do you have plans for this evening?"

"Only to read this book." I pointed to it in my lap.

"I have a box at Burton's. Macready is playing Macbeth—"

"Is he here again? He is a brave soul. And you're brave to go to see him." I was referring to the Astor Place riot last spring, which shocked the whole world. There was of course more at stake than the rivalry between the rough-hewn American actor of the people, Edwin Forrest, and the aristocratic Englishman William Macready. In cultural matters America was still fighting its independence from England, but the sad thing was that the American cause should draw to itself the lowest elements such as the Bowery B'hoys, a gang of rowdies, who placed themselves strategically both inside the Astor Place Theater to interfere with Macready's performance of *Macbeth* and outside to shout such taunts as "Down with Macready!" and "Burn the damned den of the Aristocracy!" and throw rocks and paving stones. The riot was written up in the Paris papers in great detail. I admired Mr. Macready's insistence on continuing his performance, although some scenes could not be heard because of the taunts and hisses, and he had been warned of physical danger. After the last curtain he was spirited away in disguise by friends, but outside, the riot would not be quelled. Windows were broken in surrounding areas and people were injured. When the police arrived they managed to arrest a few rioters but the growing crowd responded with volleys of stones. The militia was called out, which only enraged the mob. The soldiers fired warning shots in the air, but they received stones in return that injured many, some seriously. Finally the command was given to fire into the crowd. But it still fought back. More troops were called—and even two cannons—before the riot was put down after midnight. The result was thirty dead and over a hundred injured.

"It was a terrible thing," Annie said. "That's why it can't happen again." She smiled. "Would you like to be brave with me?"

"With the greatest pleasure, Mrs. Richmond."

"Please call me Annie—and I'll call you Auguste, if you permit me."

"Then may I invite you to dine with me after the performance?"

"Oh, it will be a charming evening. In Lowell I get so hungry for such evenings."

After a period of silence I finally said, "Annie, when Edgar spoke to you about me, did he mention our solving crimes together?"

"Crimes? I don't remember."

"Did you ever read his 'Murders in the Rue Morgue,' or his 'Purloined Letter,' or his 'Mystery of Marie Rogêt'?"

She shook her head. "I only know his poetry."

"He wrote about our work in those pieces. You see, I am a detective. I am here for that purpose."

"To solve crimes?"

"To find—whoever killed Edgar."

"K-killed—Edgar?" She gasped. "What do you mean?"

"Someone poisoned him."

"Poi-soned him? Oh, Mr. Dupin—oh, no—" She began to tremble.

"I wish I didn't have to be the bearer of such news, but it's true. I mention it to you only because I think you might be able to help me. I have a list of people Edgar thought to be his enemies. Mrs. Clemm gave me some names. Perhaps you can think of others."

She looked pale, abstracted, as if she had thrown off all she'd heard. She didn't even ask what evidence there was for Edgar's murder. Finally she spoke. "I know Eddie had enemies—I met some—but I can't conceive of any of them in such terms."

"Who, for example?"

"Mrs. Ellet for one, and Dr. English, and Mr. Griswold, but it's absurd to think—"

"Maybe when you go back to Lowell you could look through Edgar's letters and see if he mentioned anyone he really feared—and if so, let me know—"

"Yes, of course. But people don't do such things—not the people I know. Not to Eddie—" She burst into tears.

"Most people don't. Yet even among such people there can be a rotten apple."

She sighed and wiped her eyes. My revelation had upset her terribly. She could not fully absorb what she was hearing. She was too ethereal. Edgar had been a kind of dream to her, his death an awakening from that dream. The rest she preferred to lock away.

I recalled how Elmira had immediately grasped the purpose of my visit, though no less horrified by the idea of Edgar's murder. She had of course known more about me. Also she was more ratiocinative—and ten years older than Annie. She had lived longer and suffered more.

*   *   *

IN NEW YORK we parted briefly. Annie took a carriage to Miss Lynch's house where she was staying; I directed one to my hotel. I had hoped that after changing into evening clothes I would be able to sit down with *Reflections* for a few minutes, but time was running short.

Burton's was a few streets up Broadway, through the evening crowd—and the peril at each crossing from carts, carriages, drays, and riders. Some of the shops were pulling in their merchandise from the sidewalk, but the street vendors were still shouting their wares. The theater was huge, ornamented with Greek columns; the square with the elegant eighteenth-century City Hall at the other end was impressive. There were military men posted everywhere, clearly in anticipation of another riot, but everything seemed peaceful.

I entered, joining the brilliant crowd in the foyer on its way to the auditorium. No, it was not quite like attending a performance at the Comédie Française, but almost. New York was rapidly becoming a sophisticated city, and American wealth was making great strides toward usurping the place of European nobility. It was something perhaps to fear, or to laud, depending on your political sympathies. You might think the display of jewels and gowns a touch ostentatious, or the dark-clad escorts a touch uninhibited, even vulgar, but you could not help feeling that the spectacle before you pointed to the direction in which the whole world was moving.

I mounted the carpeted stairway and entered Annie's box.

"There you are!" she cried. She looked lovely in her cream evening gown, which was closer-fitting and more décolleté than her large-skirted afternoon one. Her chestnut hair was combed tightly, and the light from a sconce played on her sapphire earrings and sapphire pendant adorning her bosom. "Did I give you the number of my box?" she asked. "I worried about you finding me."

"Of course you did. I could've found out in any case from the ticket office."

"Isn't this a splendid spectacle!" she exclaimed. The audience was piling in, and Annie was watching them fill the orchestra seats below and the circles of gilded tiers on our level and above, through her opera glass. She gave it to me and I took my fill of lovely faces, arms, shoulders, bosoms.

"Do you go to the theater much in Paris, Auguste?"

"I should go more often, but I'm such a recluse."

The lights in the great central chandelier were being lowered, the audience grew silent, the curtain was about to rise.

I knew *Macbeth*, having seen it in French; now hearing the English original was fascinating, although sometimes, admittedly, Shakespeare's complexities of language were lost on me—something I never had any difficulties with in the French translation. But what a splendid show! The illusion was most convincing; the witches made me wish I could consult them about Edgar's killer. Then Macready came on—in some ways unassuming physically, but all the finer an actor—though perhaps a touch cold.

There were short intermissions after the first and second acts, and no riot had occurred thus far. After the third act we took part in the general promenade through the halls of the theater which were lined with paintings of playwrights, actors, actresses, and scenes with an occasional bust in a niche. Annie rested her hand on my bent arm as we walked slowly, glancing at people and receiving their glances. Sometimes in response to a boldly admiring look Annie's small mouth would stiffen and she would color. Except for the wedding ring on her finger, she did not give the impression of being a wife and mother. When we got tired of the promenade, we stepped back into a recess.

"You see," I said, "this play, too, deals with murder—not by a thug but by a man in high position—someone you might know socially, with nobility in his nature—"

"Oh but it's only a play. And the wonderful poetry makes it all the more a play, all the less like real life."

Someone had spotted us and was coming toward us. A moment later I recognized the man's small, dapper, strutting form.

"Mr. Tyler," I said, instinctively looking around for Griswold. I presented him to Annie.

"Charmed," he said, then turned to me. "I hardly expected to see you in New York, monsieur." A small smile played on his tight, homely face—which was probably all one could expect of social grace from him.

"Nor I you, sir," I said.

"I go where Macready performs," he said. "It's rumored that this is his last visit to the United States. What do you think of his interpretation?"

"Excellent," I said. "Perhaps a little cold."

"I'm not surprised you should think so. You would perhaps prefer Kean in the role, but I think Macready is the more consummate actor. Kean commands the senses more, he overawes the fancy; Macready addresses the imagination and the intellect. He gives the unwritten portion of the character."

"Which is?" I asked.

"*Macbeth* is the one play to my knowledge in which Shakespeare heightens a criminal act to a tragedy. He could not do this without a highly sensitive perpetrator. Macready portrays his transformation supremely. At the beginning he shows us a man of sensitive feelings and at the same time of highly excitable fancy. Such a combination often leads to cowardice, and indeed as he hesitates, Lady Macbeth accuses him of that. Without her despotic nature and commanding intellect, he would never let ambition triumph over virtue. But she induces him to take the fatal step. And then, as we just heard in the third act,

> I am in blood
> Steeped so far that, should I wade no more,
> Returning were as tedious as go o'er."

At which—rather startlingly—the bell rang. Tyler bowed and walked away.

"That was some lecture," Annie said mischievously on our way back to the box.

"Especially from a nonliterary man, as he claims to be." I told her about our first meeting in Baltimore. "What do you think of him?"

"He is not very prepossessing."

"I almost asked him where he'd left his friend Griswold. You said you knew him."

"Mr. Griswold is more prepossessing than Mr. Tyler, and no doubt wickeder."

As we watched the rest of the play Annie showed signs of restlessness; at times she was almost fidgety. Shakespeare is of course long, complex, and taxing; and perhaps it took a Tyler to prefer an interpretation that I still found a little cold.

But we'd worked up a good appetite and I suggested Taylor's just a few streets up Broadway, a new, palatial restaurant everyone was talking about. But Annie said she'd been there and the food was second-rate and the service poor. She knew a place that was better and even closer, on Worth Street.

"Excellent," I said, confessing that Taylor's was the only restaurant I could think of, except Delmonico's, which was rather too far downtown. "Actually I don't like the newest, brashest, and showiest of anything."

"Nor did Edgar. Nor do I—except when you're not poor it's difficult to be an idealist, or a dreamer."

Worth Inn was a cozy place, divided into smaller rooms, with dark-wood-and-stained-glass partitions; a large fireplace was visible from our table. The maître d'hôtel recommended the lamb shank and we ordered it, with oyster stew to begin with, and I selected a good white Bordeaux I knew from France.

When our stew came Annie started to ladle it up with an ingenuous delight that intensified my own pleasure in it—if it needed intensification.

The main course was satisfactory.

"Excellent shank," Annie declared, slicing off a portion of the meat from the bone. "Does our cooking come anywhere near yours, Auguste?"

"It rivals it," I said politely, but managed only to make her laugh.

I poured more wine. "Annie, you spoke of Griswold as wicked. Did you have his obituary in mind?"

"Yes—and the probable cause, which was the revenge of a jealous man."

"How so?"

"He was in love with Fanny Osgood, who preferred Eddie."

"The painter's wife?"

"Yes. All this happened before I knew Eddie—while Virginia was still alive. I met Fanny Osgood recently—poor lady."

"Why poor?"

"She is ill—a consumptive. She's a small, sweet, eager person, pretty like a child. You wouldn't think just by meeting her that she is such a good poet. Charlotte Lynch told me that whenever Eddie recited at her gatherings Fanny would sit on a footstool and look up at him adoringly, suffused with tears. The closer Griswold tried to get to her, the more she doted on Eddie. Charlotte is having one of her gatherings tomorrow evening. Perhaps you'd like to come. It might surprise you that I'm staying with her, for she and Eddie ended up quarreling, but that wicked Ellet woman was at the bottom of it. She can poison the mind of anyone. Charlotte has been very sweet to me lately, asking me to stay with her whenever I come to New York."

"I'd like to come," I said. With luck I might meet Mrs. Ellet—and perhaps other suspects. I wondered how far Griswold's jealousy over a woman might take him. Was his obituary his worst offense against Edgar? Jealousy was a basic motive for murder. I wondered about the husband, too. "Was Mr. Osgood aware of his wife's doting on Edgar?"

"I think they were separated at this time. Afterward they got together again and she gave birth to her third child. Evil tongues whispered—Mrs. Ellet chief among them—that the father was Eddie. It was a laughable accusation."

"Why do you think it laughable?"

"Eddie—well—oh, Auguste, it's difficult for me to talk about this—" She lowered her flushed face, showing her lustrous curls to full advantage. "His love was not that kind—" She waited for our plates to be removed. "The kind of letters . . ." She paused, she took the last swallow of her wine. "The kind of letters Eddie wrote to me—they are the most beautiful, exalted, spiritual letters, as if an angel had written them from heaven. They are unearthly, untainted—Oh, Auguste, you deserve to see the one I carry around with me wherever I go. I never showed them to anyone, ever."

Then how had Mrs. Ellet gotten hold of the one she'd maliciously copied passages from to send to Elmira?

"Here, for your eyes alone." She pulled it, folded several times, out of her little beaded reticule and handed it to me. I read:

> My Annie, whom I so madly, so distractedly love . . . Oh to be with you now, so that I might whisper in your ear the divine emotions which agitate me . . . Do I not love you, Annie? Do you not love me? Is not this all? . . . Can you, my Annie, bear to think that I am another's? . . . I cannot live unless I can feel your sweet, gentle, loving hand pressed upon my forehead—oh, my pure, virtuous, generous, beautiful, beautiful Sister Annie . . .

I handed the letter back, meeting those large gray eyes Edgar had found so soulful, my gaze moving down her face to the sapphire adorning her bosom. Edgar's words had brought his feelings alive for me; I could almost share them. Still I found it strange, even in light of his total spiritualization of love, that he should write to Annie this way, and at the same time write similarly to Helen Whitman whom he hoped to marry.

"His letters made me love him—oh, with such pure love. When he appeared we would sit by the fire holding hands. He would talk, tell me of his feelings, recite—or we would sit in silence, the only sound the old clock's slow ticking in the corner. I felt so exulted, carried up, up—never daring to look down."

Because down below was the miasma of the flesh. "How did Mr. Richmond take these sessions?" I asked.

"He never objected to them—if he was aware of them. He liked to retire early, read, fall asleep. He trusted me implicitly."

But was she content—a young woman with a cold husband, merely holding hands with her lover? These Americans were strange. Though I had to admit that if there was one man in the world who could make a woman content that way, it was Edgar.

"Do you know his poem to me?"

"Yes. It's a famous poem and one of his best. He imagines himself dying in your arms:

> She tenderly kissed me,
>   She fondly caressed,
> And then I fell gently
>   To sleep on her breast—
>
>   . . .
>
>   She covered me warm,
> And prayed to the angels
>   To keep me from harm . . .

Whereby you change from sister to mother, although many years younger than he. For his mother was young when he lost her. Did he ever show you the miniature he had of her?"

"Yes."

"It was taken from him, apparently by his killer."

She winced. She didn't want to relearn what she had perhaps already forgotten.

Over the mousse and coffee and cognac, I asked her, "Do you think he loved Mrs. Osgood the same way?"

"I'm convinced of it. He couldn't love any other way. He loved Virginia, too, the same way, calling her 'Sis.' "

"And the women he tried to marry after her death?" Elmira's name was on my lips, but I didn't need to ask Annie about her. "Did he love Helen Whitman the same way?"

"Yes. He wanted to marry to put his life in order, to give it solidity—he told me so, and I said yes, he should marry her. He told me she had a weak heart and it would be a marriage without physical consummation—and he said it suited him—" Annie grew silent and cast her eyes down. "How did our conversation get so intimate, Auguste? It's all this wine and cognac."

Later in the hackney coach she said, "Edgar made such a difference to my life. He was beautiful, a great poet with an ardent soul. God, what a soul! I still can't believe what you told me. I don't want to believe it. No one could have intentionally—killed Eddie. No one could be that evil."

On Waverly Place I got out with her and accompanied her to the columned entrance to Miss Lynch's house.

"Thank you for the dinner, Auguste. I feel we have become such friends."

"Thank you for the theater. I will always remember this evening."

"Till tomorrow, then." She gave her hand—that narrow, delicate hand whose touch had been the climax of Edgar's love. I was not indifferent to it; how could I be, if there was any validity to Edgar's belief that we shared a soul? I even felt a secret urge to venture beyond the point where he had stopped. But I sobered, and after pressing the hand, I tipped my hat and returned to the waiting carriage.

* * *

MY ROOM, which I had nicknamed *le petit palais* because of its red carpet, silk hangings, huge gilt-framed mirror, and heavy mahogany furniture, seemed especially lonely. The day had been so rich with love—Edgar's and of those who had loved him—that my own soul felt sore and hungering. I pulled down the leaf of the secretary and wrote to Elmira. I told her about my day, of going to Fordham and meeting Mrs. Clemm and hearing her drenching account of Virginia's death, and of meeting Annie Richmond.

> She had a box at the theater and invited me to see *Macbeth* with her. We ran into Mr. Tyler during the intermission; I found him as strange as I had found him at your sister's house in Baltimore. Mrs. Richmond is charming, still deeply affected by Edgar . . . I think so much of you. How wonderful it would be to get a letter from you tomorrow, not to speak of seeing you. As soon as my plans crystallize, I'll let you know . . .

I sealed the letter, went down, and gave it to the night clerk with money for postage. Back in my room, I stood at the window looking down at the dark street. A carriage drove by, the horses' hooves resounding in the night. Another. Two drunken men arm in arm reeled along the sidewalk. Under the next gaslight a cluster of prostitutes—in the shadow of Trinity Church, whose slender Gothic steeple I had admired earlier. Beyond it, past the shadowy outlines of buildings, a darkness that was the sea. Here and there a faint glimmering coming from a lighthouse or ship in the distance. You felt America here more than in Baltimore, its brash newness, yet promise. I liked it. How could I not, since it had given birth to Edgar? No, Charles Baudelaire was not quite right about the *canaille*. It was more complex than that. Yet someone had killed Edgar. O God, I must find him or go mad.

I was very tired. I shoved a few pieces of coal into the stove and went to bed. I propped myself up against the monumental head-board and opened *Reflections,* but my eyes kept closing and my thoughts ranging. Suddenly I realized that it was dark, with the aroma of wax filling the room. I'd dozed off and my candle had burned down. I put the book on the nightstand, slid down and slept.

14

IN THE MORNING, with coffee and rolls next to me on a tray, I settled in the overstuffed chair by the window and opened *Reflections*. I immediately became absorbed in the heavily marked and underlined section entitled "Jottings." These were three- or four- or five-line observations, aphorisms, some of them quotations—very much in the manner of Edgar's "Marginalia" items. And, as I was quickly discovering to my sorrow, the unmistakable source for many of them. Edgar had been in the habit of sending me copies of his publications, magazines as well as books, which of course I left in Paris, thinking that if I needed them in America they would be easily available. I did not remember his "Marginalia" items word for word, but I remembered enough to recognize them in this anonymous author's book. For example:

"The Romans worshipped their standard, the eagle, as a god. Our standard, the dollar, is only one-tenth of an eagle, but we worship it ten times more."

"To villify a great man is the readiest way in which a little man can attain greatness. The Crab might never have become a constellation but for nibbling Hercules on the heel."

"That man is not truly brave who is afraid either to seem, or to be, when it suits him, a coward."

Some were quotations:

"Montaigne says, 'People talk about thinking, but for my part I never think except when I sit down to write.' "

"Mozart declared, on his deathbed, that he 'began to see what may be done in music.' "

" 'This is right,' says Epicurus, 'because people are displeased with it.' "

But had Edgar gone for these quotations to Montaigne, or Epicurus, or some book on Mozart? No, he culled them conveniently from here. And there were more. And each that I recognized gave me a stab in my heart. All I could bring up in Edgar's defense was that when he plagiarized these items he was distracted by Virginia's dying, sick in body and mind, and desperately in need of money.

The next section was called "Art in Europe." The author had apparently made the grand tour and seen much. There were brief descriptions of great paintings in the Louvre, in the Uffizi, and other places, with comments on the subject, sometimes on the elements of painting such as composition, perspective, color, and chiaroscuro. The comments on the cathedrals in England, France, Germany, and Italy showed an understanding of architecture, like the sentence, "In Rheims, the flying buttresses transfer the weight and thrust of the high nave vaulting across two aisles to the pier buttresses." But there was relatively little said about the effect of these masterpieces on the soul—yet the writer had to feel something; otherwise why would he be there making these technical comments? There had to be emotion lurking beneath the intellect.

The next section was called "The American Revolution" and consisted of tiny biographies. Washington got almost a whole page, his seventy-seven generals from one-third to a half page each. It was the strangest writing of history I had ever seen.

These two middle sections showed no markings; nor were the pages thumbed, which did not surprise me.

The last section was called "Tales from Bedlam" and consisted of miniature narratives, some marked with a small check on the margin. Reading the first one startled me.

"Once upon a time, a madman killed someone he believed to be in possession of the evil eye. He chopped up his victim and buried the parts under his house. Subsequently he believed he heard his victim's heart beating like a clock."

"The Tell-Tale Heart!" I exclaimed. In my momentary confusion I thought the passage before me was simply a summary of that wonderful story. A moment later I realized that Edgar had written it in the early forties, whereas this book was published—I flipped back to the title page to see if I'd lost my mind—in 1836! Edgar had gotten the idea for his tale right here.

"Once upon a time, a man unhinged by his wife's death insisted, as his second wife was about to die, that his first wife had come back to take possession of her."

Good God! The idea for "Ligeia," published two years later.

"Once upon a time, a lunatic who had brutalized and killed his cat believed, when a second cat followed him home, that it was the reincarnation of his first cat returning to bring retribution upon him."

The idea for "The Black Cat," published several years later.

"Once upon a time, a man on the verge of insanity became obsessed by the fear that the pendulum of a wall clock would come down toward him and decapitate him. To escape from such a fate he cut his own throat."

An idea used in "The Pit and the Pendulum," published six or seven years later.

"Once upon a time, a deranged man brooding about a crime he had committed with his twin sister hastened her burial; she returned from the crypt and brought him down to death with her."

The idea for "The Fall of the House of Usher," written just after "Ligeia."

And there were more.

The sheer impact of my discovery, its relentless accumulation, made me sink back in a swoon. I don't know how long I lay in that state against the cushions of my chair; I only know that my first conscious thoughts were words Edgar had written:

> During the whole of a dull, dark, and soundless day in the autumn of the year, when the clouds hung oppressively low in the heavens, I had been passing alone, on horseback, through a singularly dreary track of country; and at length found myself, as the shades of the evening drew on, within view of the melancholy House of Usher.

The passage was like a remembered melody haunting the mind, words, phrases coming to the fore in all their special wonder, then the whole replaying from beginning to end, again and again.

The total glory of "The Fall of the House of Usher," or "Ligeia," or "The Black Cat" was not plagiarized, or even derived, but Edgar's own. Just as *Hamlet* or *King Lear* or *Macbeth* was not plagiarized, or even derived, from Saxo Grammaticus or whoever, but Shakespeare's own. A tale or a poem or a play was more than an idea containable in a sentence or two. It was life in all its fullness, its pulsation, its wonder, its terror, its joy, its sorrow. Edgar had created that life—given it to the world as his legacy; where he had found the idea for a tale was less important.

But I had a strong feeling—a growing conviction—that the author of *Reflections,* if he was still living, did not think so. I had a mental vision of him reading one of Edgar's tales and seeing nothing in it except a sentence-long skeleton—pouncing on it as his own, condemning the whole as stolen from him. And I saw him reading another of Edgar's tales, and another, with the same reaction, his fury mounting, deepening into hate.

For the remainder of the day, there was forming in my mind a more and more distinct picture of the author of this miscellany. Anonymous, private, intelligent, even brilliant, with a wide range of interests, but with choked-off feelings. Troubled, perhaps not quite sane. The "Tales from Bedlam" section showed this best. He might have gotten these miniature stories somewhere, or invented them. No matter. They were not an author's notes; they did not suggest that he planned to expand them into full-length tales; he had published them; they each began with that traditional story-telling phrase, "Once upon a time"; he considered them complete. Nor was there any attempt at empathy with these embryonic characters. Their author could only think of distancing himself from them and thereby showing his own superiority. "Bedlam," "mad," "insane"—one read everywhere. The ego I saw looming behind his anonymity seemed monstrous and diseased. There was motive enough here, and I could see him kill.

15

IN THE EVENING I took a horse car to Waverly Place. Mounting the steps to the entrance of Miss Lynch's charming house just off Washington Square, I felt tense as always when about to meet new faces—the more so since my arrival in America. I never knew how people would take me here—Poe's double, his ghost, a noted detective, or varying combinations thereof. Conversely, I was never quite sure how to present myself, how much to reveal. What people knew of the three stories in which Edgar had written about me was of course an important factor. I braced myself and rang.

The spacious, elegant place with its inviting fire, piano, and gracefully hung curtains reminded me of the Craigs' home in Baltimore, except for the Grecian accent here: the entrance way to the library was flanked by two Ionic columns and the marble frieze of the fireplace was supported by a pair of caryatids. Miss Lynch, who came forward to greet me, had a sweet round face and her dark hair was combed in ringlets.

"Annie spoke of you, monsieur, and I'm glad you could come." Her manner was gracious yet simple, like her blue gown, with which she wore rose-gold earrings and a matching locket on a chain. There was a primness about her which I associated with her teaching English at the Brooklyn Female Academy.

Annie materialized at her side, her gown trimmed with lace, her garnet earrings sparkling as she turned her head. "It's wonderful to see you again."

"The pleasure is mine, Annie."

"Here you see one of Charlotte's famous *conversaziones*—or salons, as you would call it. She takes pride in refusing to take charge but letting things happen spontaneously. And they do, most satisfactorily."

Charlotte Lynch smiled and withdrew, and suddenly I felt uneasy, as if her manner toward me had been not so much simple as cold, as if I wasn't entirely welcome here. I could think of two good reasons: she perhaps did not relish the intrusion of the subject of crime (which I no doubt represented in her eyes) into her literary and artistic gathering; or her quarrel with Edgar still rankled.

"I'm going to present you to a few people, then I'll let you be on your own, as is the custom here," Annie said, taking my arm as we approached a circle. "Professor Longfellow, let me present Monsieur Auguste Dupin from Paris."

Meeting the famous poet took my breath away. He was in fact one of my tentative suspects, though I felt disarmed by the gentleness and kindness in his mien. He was fortyish, handsome, with resolute eyes, a sweetly shaped mouth, and a strong jaw that seemed to welcome the stiff collar with its sharp points like a calyx around it.

"I know you of course," he said. "I've read Poe. I was a terrible thorn in his side for some reason. Actually, the reason is fairly clear: his was the constant irritation of a sensitive nature, tormented by an indefinite sense of wrong. He must vent his anger, strike out, hurt, condemn—I was a convenient target partly because of my reputation, partly because I'm a New Englander, a 'Frogpondian,' as he liked to call us." He smiled.

I was a little embarrassed for Edgar, for his excesses.

"I will not speak ill of the dead," an intense female voice resounded next to me. I turned my head and was taken by the young woman's dark beauty. In that same instant Annie presented me to her and I learned that she was Mrs. Ellet. *"Enchanté, monsieur,"* she said in perfect French.

"Enchanté, madame." And I saw how terrible she could be. All that fervor in pursuit of literary success—hers was considerable—or love, or when scorned, hate. "I met your brother in Baltimore," I added.

"I know. I just got a letter from him mentioning your visit."

I would have given my eyetooth to see that letter. Not that I could envision Lummis as the author of *Reflections*—nor, for entirely different reasons, his sister; but *Reflections* notwithstanding, the Ellet-Lummis pair still figured among my suspects. I tried to draw her out. "He showed me a volume of poems you dedicated to him."

"We're very close," Mrs. Ellet said. The family resemblance was not obvious. Dark hair and eyes in both, a certain prominence of the jaw, but she did not have his beefiness or coarseness of facial expression, and her eyes were larger.

I turned to Annie. "Have you ever met Mr. Lummis?"

"No, I never had the pleasure."

"William is often in New York on business, for which I am grateful, since my husband seldom gets here from South Carolina and a woman needs a protector," Mrs. Ellet said.

I smiled. "Against columnators like Poe?"

"I repeat, I don't like to speak ill of the dead." She paused, smiled, waited for Annie to drift away, then continued. "But since you bring up the subject, Poe behaved abominably." She was apparently more wary of Annie's reaction than my own.

"Toward you?"

"He made the basest insinuations—that I sent him compromising letters. Good Lord! I sent him a poem—an admittedly coquettish one—which in fact he published in his *Broadway Journal*—"

"Give us a few lines, Elizabeth" came a man's high-pitched voice. He was young, tall, and jaunty, with a blunt, moustached face; Mrs. Ellet introduced him as Dr. Thomas Dunn English.

"How can I resist your request, Tom?" She threw her head back and smiled seductively. She recited:

> Ah yes—gentle sir—I will own
> I ne'er saw perfection till now . . .

Three stanzas enumerated aspects of addressee's perfection—eyes, voice, soul—and I had the uncomfortable feeling that the recitation was directed at me. Those intense eyes frequently met mine, until I found myself embarrassedly looking down. Each stanza ended with the refrain:

> But I mean to keep my heart whole—
> So away with your love-vows—away, I say, away . . .

I found myself mentally protesting: But I never made any love-vows, dear lady.

A little group had gathered around us and applauded her, and she beamed.

"Did you object to the poem's publication?" I asked.

"Of course not. Nor did my husband. But to send poems like that is a kind of game. You must carry on similar literary flirtations in France, Mr. Dupin."

"I daresay."

"But—" She drew closer. "To intimate that my sentiments ran deeper, that I wrote compromising letters to him—ah, the audacity of the wretch!"

I knew she was lying. I didn't know whether there were compromising letters or not, but I did know that her sentiments had run deeper than she claimed. Everything I knew about her—those phrases she had copied from Edgar's letters to Annie and to Helen Whitman—obviously without Annie's knowledge, and no doubt without Helen Whitman's as well—to send Elmira; everything I had heard from Elmira, from Mrs. Clemm, from Annie, about her made the same point, that she was a snooping, shrewish busybody, hating Edgar because he had scorned her. The question was only how deep her hate ran. Her brother had threatened Edgar, and Edgar had retracted everything. Lummis admitted that "the coward" hadn't given him the satisfaction he had sought. So, had brother and sister decided on harsher punishment? Had Lummis killed Edgar?

"I can give you further ramifications of that unfortunate business," English put in. "You've no doubt heard that I gave Poe a drubbing." He laughed. "Poor Poe. I no longer feel the slightest rancor toward him. I always liked him, although we quarreled—and in print—"

"Quarreled?" Mrs. Ellet said. "The names that devil called you, Tom!" She turned to me. "Tom English is a doctor, a lawyer, a poet, and an editor—and Poe spoke of him in his notorious 'Literati' as one without the commonest school education—oh, so patronizingly, suggesting that he get private instruction to improve himself at points where he is most defective—"

English laughed uproariously. "I answered in kind. I called him a drunkard, a coward, a liar, an assassin in morals, a quack, totally insane. So he called me a blackguard of the lowest order, an animalicula with moustaches for antennae—"

Laughter around us.

"A baboon, whose foul lies oozed through filthy lips—who had wallowed in hog puddles since infancy—how he gave me a thrashing I'd never forget—" He broke into laughter himself. "Poor Edgar, so much smaller than me. But I must say this for him, once aroused he didn't retreat—threw a few punches himself, though his nose was bleeding. But as I was going to say, the way this fisticuffs came about was that he came into my office and asked me for a gun to defend himself against this lady's brother who had threatened him about those letters. I advised him to remove the threat by simply telling Mr. Lummis and the world that he had no letters from Mrs. Ellet. At this, poor Edgar was beyond himself. He called me worse names than he ever had in print—finally he hit me. I suppose he felt insulted by the idea that there was one woman in this world who was not in love with him, who could not possibly write him love letters. So after bloodying his nose I immediately felt sorry for him—as one does toward a child one has chastised—"

I had seldom seen so much of a person in so brief a time. English was simple and homogenous. Somewhat on the rough side, but I doubted that he was a killer.

"Child?" Mrs. Ellet cried. "Rather the sinful begetter of one."

"Do you mean Mrs. Osgood's?" I asked.

"The father was Poe," she said. "The poor puny thing only lived three months—it was a judgment on her."

A severe and puritanical lady, I thought, in addition to her other vices.

"As a doctor who had observed Poe closely, I would say no," English said.

"The child was not Poe's." I heard a familiar voice behind me and turned.

"Ah, Reverend Griswold." I was really glad to see the miscreant.

"My pleasure, Mr. Dupin." His handshake was moist as always, and his bland, bearded face was screwed up in an oily smile.

"I saw Mr. Tyler at the theater last night."

"Yes, he came to see Macready, who is his passion. He mentioned that he saw you with a lady. Did you enjoy the performance?"

"Yes, very much."

"Poe and Fanny Osgood were together in Providence, in October of 1845," Elizabeth Ellet said. "She was at that time separated from her husband. In June next year, some eight and a half months later, she gave birth."

"Since she and her husband were subsequently reconciled," Griswold said, "I don't find it hard to accept that he visited her in Providence sometime in October."

"Except, Mr. Griswold, I saw a letter from her to Poe, intimating what I said."

"Ah, intimating," Griswold said.

"None of this matters any longer," English said. "Poe is dead, the child is dead, and poor Fanny is dying." He turned to Griswold. "Is she suffering much?"

"No, her spirit is good, and her husband is with her. I see her whenever I have a chance. She keeps writing and has pleasure in companionship. But her doctor doubts that she'll last beyond the winter."

There was such sadness in Griswold's eyes that it was easy to see he still loved her—a love that now made him defend her, a love that at its height had made him hate his rival, Edgar.

He repeated his request for information about Poe for his memoir.

"What he wrote about our relationship in the three stories is quite factual," I said. "I need only add that some of the brilliant ideas he attributed to me were his own. There were times when our minds were tuned in such harmony that ideas rose which could not be attributed to either of us individually."

"You no doubt have letters from him."

"Yes, a good many. On my return to Paris I'll be glad to go through them and copy out passages I think would interest you and send them to you."

"I would be most grateful."

"In exchange, perhaps I could make a request of you. Poe died under mysterious circumstances, which do not exclude the possibility of foul play. Can you think of anyone who hated him enough to kill him?" Ask a guilty person such a question, and there is a good chance that he will reveal something of the emotions that had led him to his crime. I watched Griswold's face—beads of perspiration on his high forehead, a troubled expression around the eyes, a twitch.

"Lots of people hated Poe." He burst into a small, explosive laugh. "I meant what I wrote about him, that he had few or no friends—"

"That view has been challenged by Graham, by Willis, by Neal, to name only three," I said more impetuously than wisely.

Griswold smiled. "I may have been guilty of a hyperbole, but that still leaves plenty of those who hated him."

"Did Neilson Poe hate him? Edgar thought him his worst enemy." I could see Neilson Poe as the author of *Reflections.*

"I don't know. I met the man maybe twice. How can I give you names, Mr. Dupin? It would be tantamount to making unfounded accusations. There are people in this very room, people you have talked to—and I am one of them—who had little love for Poe. Murder—good God! That's something else again."

"Let me ask you one more question. Have you ever come across a book called *Reflections?*"

He thought, then shook his head. "What kind of book is it?"

"A miscellany. Published anonymously in 1836. It deals with European art, also the American Revolution, among other things."

"It rings a distant bell. I may have seen it at the time, but I haven't seen it since. Why do you ask?"

"I came across it and it interested me. Anonymous books have a particular fascination for me."

"Ah, forever the detective," he said with a laugh. "In any event, I did not kill Poe." Still laughing, he walked away.

The room became animated—conversations rose and settled, people moved about, extra chairs were brought in. Professor Longfellow was going to recite passages from the epic he was working on called *The Song of Hiawatha.* Eventually all twenty-odd people found seats, some perching on sofa arms, others on footstools, and Longfellow stood before the fire, handsome and perfectly tailored. His public voice was smooth, though lacking some of the richness of Edgar's which I remembered.

"My Indian Edda, if I may so call it, is based on the legend of a personage of miraculous birth sent among the tribes to clear the rivers and forests and to teach them the arts of peace. . . . Here are some lines from a section I will call 'The Peace-Pipe':

> On the Mountains of the Prairie,
> On the great Red Pipe-stone Quarry,
> Gitche Manito, the mighty,
> He the Master of Life, descending,
> On the red crags of the quarry

Stood erect, and called the nations,
Called the tribes of men together.

I have found the unrhymed lines in the Finnish epic, *Kalevala,* an ideal measure for my poem. My material comes from Mr. Schoolcraft's study of Indians. It will be a long poem, with twenty or more sections, with various Indian legends woven into it . . ."

He recited more lines. Then after the applause—and some eager questions about *Hiawatha,* tea and cookies were served and the room resounded in general talk.

A young woman approached me, unshyly, offering her hand. "I'm Margaret Fuller."

I had heard of her as a noted feminist and Transcendentalist, friend of the Concord sage, Emerson. She was attractive, with well-defined angular features, her eyes deep, her dark hair worn longer and more loosely than fashion dictated just then. Her face shone with intelligence.

"Did you like the lines you heard?" she asked.

"They were pleasant," I said somewhat diplomatically, "evocative, the rhythm haunting."

"But imagine that same rhythm going on for six or seven thousand lines." She smiled, her upper lip rising a little strangely, giving the suggestion of a sneer—something Edgar too had noticed. But O God, to write about it publicly! How could he? Just thinking about it made me color with embarrassment.

"Trochees are not the most suitable for a long poem in English," she went on. "Iambs are better. Longfellow's vast knowledge of foreign literatures may be a problem here."

"Poe used trochees," I said.

"Yes, but he kept his poems short—which was his philosophy. I miss Poe's intensity in Longfellow."

Charlotte Lynch stood next to us, her sweet, round, prim face turned to her friend.

"I had my quarrels with Poe, like everyone else," Margaret Fuller said, "but I can't entirely condemn him for going after Longfellow."

"Oh, but he was so unfair," Charlotte Lynch said. "Accusing Henry Wadsworth Longfellow of plagiarism and keeping it up, and keeping it up!"

"Poe may have overstated it," Margaret Fuller said, "but

Longfellow is derivative. He is too much of an idol for too many people, but he falls short of being a great poet."

Then something unexpected happened. Someone sat down at the piano and started to play a quadrille. The center of the room was cleared of chairs and the whole company divided into groups of four couples. I asked Annie to be my partner and we danced, the gathering becoming a whirl of delight. As the line snaked along to the music, smiling faces kept coming into view—Margaret Fuller with Longfellow, Elizabeth Ellet with English, Charlotte Lynch with Griswold—with literary rivalries and quarrels reconciled in joyous, animated movement. For the first time today I felt my spirits lifted. Yet underneath, the gnawing question still: Who killed Edgar? Was he here among the dancers?

16

THE NEXT DAY was Sunday and I took my way to St. George's Church on Sixteenth Street, where the young clergyman William Wilberforce Lord was assistant to the senior rector. I was aware of the devastating review Edgar had written of Lord's poems and wanted to leave no stone unturned.

He was holding service when I entered the massive pile with its Romanesque arches and I sat down in the back. Lord was a thin, nervous-looking man with hollow cheeks and watery blue eyes; the surplice seemed a touch loose on him. As he held up the Sacrament his hand seemed tremulous, and the voice in which he intoned the Credo, impassioned.

Afterward, in the rectory, he told me with a smile that he had seen me enter the church and thought God was visiting Poe's ghostly presence upon him. "Oh, yes, he was very hard on my poems. Did you read his notice of them?" I shook my head and he rose, stepped to a cabinet, and pulled out an issue of the *Broadway Journal.*

"It's my own private bloody scourge," he said with another smile—behind which I detected a real need for self-torture. I recalled that Edgar and I had often spoken of this perverse human tendency, which he developed in several of his writings.

Mr. Lord read the whole lengthy review aloud to me, with the eloquence of his profession. When he came to a particularly brutal part he slowed down, emphasizing each word, his voice becoming as impassioned as during his service:

> The only remarkable things about Mr. Lord's compositions are their remarkable conceit, ignorance, impudence, platitude, stupidity, and bombast . . .

I winced at each word. He read on:

> Mr. Lord is of a very ordinary species of talent, without any
> indication of genius. No man is entitled to the sacred name of
> poet, because from 160 pages of doggerel may be culled a few
> sentences of worth . . . When amid a Sahara of platitude, we
> discover an occasional oasis, we must not fancy any latent fertil-
> ity in the sands.

The one emotion I was in search of during my investigations, hatred toward Poe, seemed to be singularly absent in the young clergyman. Or perhaps he was a consummate actor.

"Why," I asked him after he finished reading, "do you dwell on this devastating review—almost lovingly?"

"The idea of self-flagellation—physical, mental, or spiritual—is to descend all the way. Once we are down at the very bottom of the pit, which is our own personal hell, we are in a position to understand our need for God, without Whom we cannot rise."

His mysticism was somewhat beyond me. "Are you writing more poetry?" I asked.

"Oh, yes."

"Poe was so destructive in his review, saying you were without genius, or even latent fertility. Surely you must disagree with him if you haven't given up writing."

"He may have been wrong on that point—I pray that he was. Meanwhile I place faith in his phrase 'occasional oasis' taking it not as an aberration but an indication."

"Did you meet Poe after he wrote that review?"

"No. But I heard how much he suffered—losing his wife, hover-ing on the brink of mental and physical collapse. I had always thought highly of him. I prayed for him."

This man was either a saint or a deep-grained villain. I left the rectory brooding about the pit he had spoken of, that personal hell, which had led someone not to God but to murder.

Fifth Avenue was busy in spite of the cold, people parading up and down in their Sunday best. I walked toward Washington Square. I wanted to see Annie once more, for tomorrow she and Mrs. Clemm would be going to Lowell.

At 116 Waverly Place a maid admitted me, I sent in my card, and Annie appeared.

"Auguste! What a pleasant surprise. Do come in."

"I hope this is not an inappropriate time."

"Oh, no. We just came back from church." She had that spiritual look lingering about her; perhaps it was her simple, white-trimmed blue gown, her plain hairstyle, and that she wore almost no paint or jewelry.

"I would have felt badly not to see you once more," I said.

"I would have, too. I thought of sending you a note."

Charlotte's widowed mother was in the room, a quiet, gray-haired lady, whom I had met last night. She had seemed a little bewildered by all the literary people swirling around her, though she remained staunchly at her post as senior hostess even through the quadrille.

"It was a delightful evening," I told them both.

But now Mrs. Lynch confessed she was exhausted, and excused herself.

Charlotte was behind the closed door of the library preparing for her classes tomorrow, Annie said, so we sat alone in the large, elegant room whose vista of floral rug and unoccupied sofas and chairs seemed strangely empty. There were ashes glowing in the fireplace flanked by the caryatids, and from the opposite side a pale winter sun slanted in between the graceful satin drapes.

"I want to modify the term 'delightful' about last evening," I said. "It was extraordinarily useful to me—I wouldn't have missed it for the world—and I owe it all to you, Annie. But it pains me to hear people speak ill of Edgar."

"Hah, why do you think I retreated the moment Elizabeth Ellet started on the subject?"

"I'm not blind to his faults—he had many—but I keep feeling only I have the right to speak about them." I gave a small laugh. "Of course I never do."

"I may be more blind to his faults than you are," Annie said. Hot chocolate was brought in and she served.

"I thought about our conversation two nights ago. I still find it strange that your husband didn't object to your being so close to Edgar."

She grew thoughtful. "I sometimes wondered whether he was more resentful than he showed. But you see Edgar was close to us all. He adored my little girl, Carrie. In his letters he wrote affectionately of my husband and my brother and my mother—sending his special love to my sister Sarah."

"How old is Sarah?"

"She will be thirteen."

"The same age Virginia was when he married her."

"I used to think it strange that Eddie married a child, but when love is pure, what does the age of the beloved matter? It is said that Beatrice was even younger when Dante fell in love with her."

It was time for me to go. I finished my hot chocolate and rose. I didn't want to suggest that the main purpose of my visit was a reminder, so I said as casually as I could, "You will look through Edgar's letters for anything that might be useful to me?"

"Yes." But as we walked toward the entrance hall she suddenly stopped, a sob breaking from her. "To think that anyone could have—"

I handed her a silk handkerchief and she daubed the corners of her gray, thickly lashed eyes.

At the street door she said, "We must meet again, Auguste. You must come to Lowell, or I must go to Paris. Write to me." She threw her arms around me and we kissed on the cheek. "Good-bye, dear friend."

"Good-bye, dear Annie."

As the door closed behind me I felt her good-bye was not even addressed to me so much as to Edgar.

*   *   *

I WAITED EAGERLY for Monday, which announced itself with the sound of a letter being slipped under my door. From Elmira? I leaped up from bed and tore it open, more excitedly than efficiently.

My dear Auguste:

Your letter from Baltimore, which came soon after my own arrival, brightened up the melancholy which had been weighing on me ever since our parting. I found it confusing—and I still do—to have known you so briefly yet so well. I don't know how it all happened, I keep thinking it shouldn't have; at the same time another part of me keeps reassuring me that I have nothing to regret. I confess there were moments when I wasn't sure I'd hear from you again. How wonderfully your letter alleviated such a fear . . .

Oh, yes, do come as soon as you can. I'm anxious to see you, my very dear friend . . .

Elmira

It was so much her voice that when I closed my eyes I heard it— saw her walk across the room, sit on the edge of my bed, place her hand on my forehead. Not passionate but warm, with that private sorrow about the heart which perhaps nothing could alleviate. Not a word about the hurt which my suspecting her had caused her—if she had fully recognized it at the time—for which I was grateful. I folded the letter and held it close to me as I tried to wake up better from my deep sleep.

Coffee helped, and I set about answering Elmira's letter, telling her how happy hers had made me. "But oh, Elmira, how cruel of you to think that you might not hear from me again?" I wrote about last night:

> It would have been a charming evening except for having to listen to some of Edgar's enemies. Mrs. Ellet sounded as she did in her letter to you—a handsome woman but apparently as wicked as you suspected her to be. Now I am about to meet more of Edgar's enemies—not a pleasant prospect, but carrying your letter next to my heart will make my day far more endurable . . .

I dressed and went out, leaving my letter at the desk for immediate posting. I wondered, as I headed north on Nassau Street, to what extent I thought of the remaining names on my list as suspects. Less than before. But I could not consider my work in New York completed without talking to them.

It was never quite clear who had committed the first offense, but as soon as Edgar drew brutal caricatures in "The Literati" his targets shot back with double venom. So the war went on. In some ways I had my fill of it listening to Dr. English on Saturday evening; still, as I entered the old, bleak four-story building housing the venerable *Knickerbocker* I was painfully conscious of the editor, Lewis Gaylord Clark, calling Edgar "a wretched inebriate, a jaded hack without principle, unworthy of scorn." I felt belligerent, I disliked Clark sight unseen, I was not sure I would be able to be civil. Not that Edgar might not have been in the wrong. It was a question of loyalties. I had to force myself to be impartial, to be concerned with only one question: how much of this vituperation had been spent in words; how much, if any, lingered on?

Clark, a tall man with a high forehead and blue eyes, seemed, however, more bland than violent. He came forward from behind his overcrowded desk to shake my hand and offer me a comfortable chair.

I told him I was investigating Poe's death and would appreciate any information he thought might be useful to me.

"I don't know, Mr. Dupin, if I can tell you anything you don't know. Poe was quarrelsome, he made many enemies. He and I quarreled—bitterly at times."

"Is it true that he once physically threatened you on the street?"

"It appeared so. He was terribly drunk—reeling—and he lashed out at me for having attacked one of his reviews. Honestly, I had not known the review was by him; at the same time aren't we supposed to be free to express our opinions? Poe always did. Fortunately his friend Chivers, the poet, was with him and he drew him off. Then I was of course critical of his doings in Boston—"

"The lecture he gave there?"

"Yes. Promising a new poem and reading one of his juvenilia, and then ridiculing the audience for not noticing the hoax. That was Poe at his worst. So we exchanged insults. It all seems trivial now—and so long ago."

As I was leaving I asked him whether he had ever heard of a book called *Reflections*.

His hand went up to his high forehead as he thought. "I don't recall anything by that title. It's not a very good title, is it?"

"I suppose not. It's a miscellany—aphorisms, a section on art, one on history—published anonymously by Lea and Blanchard thirteen years ago."

"Something is glimmering before me about such a book. We may have even reviewed it. But I just don't remember—"

I thanked him for his time and left.

I retraced my steps along Nassau. As I came to Ann Street, where a similarly old, bleak, four-story building housed the *Mirror*, I had the feeling that I was being followed. Just then, two overladen wagons were trying to pass each other on the narrow street and I joined the pedestrians who stopped to watch them, giving myself an opportunity to look carefully around. The drivers cursed each other and people laughed. Finally one drove his team up on the sidewalk with the huge crates on his wagon dancing dangerously and causing a commotion. I watched faces as I went into the building. Perhaps I had been wrong.

I walked up, sent in my card, and was admitted to Hiram Fuller's inner sanctum. He was in his overcoat, on his way out for a morning snack. He was a heavyset man with a gentle face; Edgar had called him a fat sheep in reverie, something less than a man for standing calmly by while his father-in-law publicly punched his daughter for marrying him. I didn't know whether the story was true—and was not going to ask him.

"Come along, Mr. Dupin," he urged.

Sandy Welsh's wine cellar was just down the street—a cheerful, noisy place redolent with the sour, teasing smell of barreled wine and beer, mixing with whiffs of frying food and stew. The walls were dark with smoke, with pillars supporting a vaulted roof and gas flames flickering in lanterns. We passed the bar, and Fuller surveyed the crowded dining room. He spotted a friend and led me to his table. I was at once uneasy and pleased to be introduced to Charles Briggs, another Poe enemy I had intended to see. He was a small man with quick, nervous movements, with the long hair, pointed beard, and flowing neckcloth of an artist. In fact he wrote novels.

"Do you really think Poe was murdered, Mr. Dupin?" were his words of greeting.

I smiled, saying "Possibly" while I tried to recover from his question. Apparently there was more general awareness in literary circles about me and my doings than I had realized. I tried, while we ordered sandwiches and beer, to determine in my own mind to what extent I considered these two men suspects. Again, there had been the usual insults exchanged; Edgar had gone so far as to sue Fuller for printing English's libelous attack—and won over two hundred dollars in damages plus court costs. That was the sort of thing that might rankle for years.

Yet Fuller, after gulping down half his stein of beer, said, "But who could've done such a thing? Poe's battles were with literary people."

"I could've done such a thing," Briggs said—either naively, or very slyly—and I doubted that he was naive. "The time he squeezed me out of the *Broadway Journal.*" He shifted in his seat, his small hand playing with his black flowing neckcloth. "And then he attacked me for no reason I could think of."

"Insult upon injury," Fuller said. "That was old Poe's forte."

I tossed my beer down to numb the pain their talk gave me.

"But after you used him up in your fiction you no longer needed to kill him," Fuller said, laughing at his own wit, his belly straining the buttons of his vest.

Briggs nodded. "Time was the chief factor. Time, my friends, is the great healer."

Our sandwiches came—ham and cheese and roast beef and turkey in fresh, home-baked bread.

"Food is the great healer," Fuller said, spreading mustard on his sandwich, then biting into it.

With my third beer I began to feel friendlier toward them.

I noticed a youngish man with a blond beard standing at the entrance to the dining room looking in our direction. Had he been following me? No, he hadn't. He was coming to our table.

"Hello, Walt, sit down," Fuller said. He introduced him to me as Mr. Whitman. He had light, dreamy eyes.

"Any relation to Helen Whitman of Providence?" I asked.

"No, but I've heard of her. She writes verse, doesn't she?"

"Poe was supposed to marry her," Briggs said, "until she came to her senses."

"Mr. Dupin is investigating Poe's death," Fuller explained to Whitman. "We've been very hard on him—because we've been hard on Poe. They were very close."

"I met Poe once," Whitman said. "I'd written something for the *Broadway Journal* and I went up to collect my fee. He was perfectly courteous. I found him pleasant in looks, voice, and manner—very kindly, very human, but subdued, maybe a little jaded." He took me in and there was something melting in his expression. "You remind me of him strongly." He corrected himself with a small laugh. "I don't mean you're jaded—I mean in looks."

"No," Fuller laughed gustily. "I see nothing jaded in Mr. Dupin."

We ate and drank and lit cigars, and the mood became mellow.

Still, Briggs's saying that he could have killed Poe preyed on my mind. Could he have, under his levity? Could Fuller have?

"I miss the sunlight and fresh air and health in Poe's writing," Whitman said.

"Are you a poet?" I asked him.

"I'm trying to be. I want to write the kind of poetry that's large, all-inclusive, ultimately joyous, in spite of life's tragedies. We have a great country—it should be sung in a corresponding way. Emerson said these things so well. A poem like that should be about the people who make up America. I like to ride the omnibuses and talk to the drivers—oh, they're such fine fellows. I want to write about them. I want to write about myself—frankly, about my body as well as my soul—yet I want that to be about you and you and you as well. I want to make the grass a symbol of the humanity in my poem. How common and cheap it is, yet how each individual blade is a miracle of creation."

We all listened. There was something mesmerizing about him.

Finally we asked for our check. I said, "Gentlemen, have any of you heard of a book called *Reflections*?"

Heads shook.

"Wait," Briggs said. "Does it have something to do with art?"

"Part of it does. It's a miscellany. Published anonymously in 1836. I'm trying to discover who wrote it."

"Art is all I remember about it," Briggs said, "and I haven't seen it or heard of it since."

Outside on the street we said cordial good-byes and went our separate ways.

Feeling a little unsteady, I decided to walk rather than take the omnibus, expecting the cold, dry air to clear my head. I went up Broadway to Houston, turned east, and continued north on Lafayette, sometimes taking a sharp look behind me but seeing no one suspicious. The new Astor Library loomed ahead. It was built in the Italianate style, with a rose brick façade and graceful mullioned windows. The building was not quite completed—I saw workmen at one side mixing cement—but it was open to the public. I went in.

"Do you have bound issues of magazines?" I asked the young man at the desk.

"Some of the older ones. The newer files have yet to be collected; a few are at the bindery." He directed me to an elegant room containing paintings and busts and books on mahogany shelves. Readers sat at long carved tables under crystal chandeliers.

But first I looked in the catalogue for *Reflections*. Library listings sometimes gave the author of an anonymously printed book. I did not find it. The library apparently did not have it.

I found the shelves containing leather-bound, gold-tooled volumes of such publications as *Graham's, Godey's,* and the *Gentleman's Magazine.* I pulled out a couple bearing the date 1839 and 1840, just to see Edgar's name as editor and to greet some of his tales and poems. But I was after something else. I was particularly interested in the years before 1836, for miscellanies such as *Reflections* frequently had previous partial magazine publications. The tables of contents and indices were helpful. I was scouring them for anything having to do with the American Revolution or great painters or cathedrals, or for such titles as "Jottings" or "Tales from Bedlam" or anything similar to these.

After hours of research, half an hour before closing time, I struck gold. The October 1834 issue of the *Gentleman's Magazine* contained an article on Leonardo da Vinci. It sounded familiar and I read on with mounting interest. The following paragraph made me sit up:

> In the museum at Basel there is a head of John the Baptist after it was cut off, ascribed to Leonardo. It is of a greenish-olive and white color and bears a strong resemblance to the portrait at Abbotsford of Mary Queen of Scots, after decollation, in the manner in which the features are collapsed and in the sickly softness of expression.

They were the same words I had read in *Reflections*! When I turned the page I cried "Eureka!" The name of the author was given as H. Reynolds.

The library was closing and I rushed out and broke into a fast walk down Lafayette. In my feverish state of excitement I gave no thought of being followed.

17

I WAS BARELY CONSCIOUS of my physical movements; I was thoroughly absorbed in the scene in my mind: the killer reaching for his early pseudonym, Reynolds, as he introduced himself to gain Edgar's confidence. Nor was I conscious of the darkness of the street, or the cold, or the paucity of pedestrian or vehicular traffic. Suddenly I fell forward, realizing only in retrospect that I had been tripped. But by then they were on me. I tried to reach for my pistol but my arms were pinioned and twisted back, while the point of a knife was trembling near my eye. Past it, a coarse, pitted visage. In the overpowering stench of stale liquor, tobacco, and sweat, I felt ropes cutting into my wrists, and my sight was cut off by a foul-smelling cloth being tied over my face.

"Who—? What—?"

The answer was a blow against my mouth and I tasted blood. I kicked back impulsively but made no contact; I was answered by a sharp kick in the ribs.

Rough hands going through my pocket, seizing my pistol, billfold, watch, and other belongings. Maybe now they'd let me go—or leave me here to the pity of a passerby. There seemed to be two of them—presumably robbers who found it more expedient to tie me up than to kill me. It was all happening so fast that my fear had been delayed. But now I was trembling, with cold sweat breaking out over me.

I heard a carriage draw up, and when they pulled me to my feet one fear replaced another. They were doing more than robbing me. They were taking me somewhere. Hired to do so. They were giving me shoves ahead on the unevenly cobbled street—I could smell the horse—forcing me up into the carriage. As we began to move there was one thug next to me on the seat, pressing the barrel of a pistol—I assumed my own—against my temple; the other on the box, driving.

"Who—?" I tried again to ask, but was answered with a slurred "Shut up!" and a blow with the pistol butt against my jaw. If I could somehow free my hand, make a grab for it—

The horse trotted on, making several turns. There had to be people on the street, perhaps even a policeman. At a right turn, as I was thrown against the door, I gave it a powerful kick, it snapped open, and I shouted, "Help!" But my captor clamped down on me in a stranglehold. The door kept flapping, until a sharp left turn and the wind made it shut again. When I thought I had no more breath in me, the thug let up on his grip. These devils probably had instructions not to kill me.

After what seemed like a mile, the horse stood still and I heard the driver jump off. As he opened the carriage door I leaped out with enough force to shove him aside. I broke into a run, shouting, "Help! Help!" But I could not see and immediately they were on me again, pulling me down and hitting and kicking me. Held by iron grips, I was made to stumble along, into a house smelling of garbage and urine, down rough stone steps into a cellar. Here the faint light my blindfold had admitted dissolved into total darkness. But now a candle seemed to be lit somewhere behind me. I heard a heavy door creak open and I felt dankness and cold hit me. My blindfold was torn off and I saw a dismal windowless wall. Near it, the floor was broken by a large gaping hole. My wrists were un-bound, but in that same moment I was shoved forward with such force that I landed on one knee. I swung around to get a look at my assailants in the distant candlelight: the one with the pitted face was gigantic, the other wore a sandy beard and was sinuous like a snake. But at that moment the door shut with a heavy metallic ring. A lock snapped into place, and I clambered up painfully and stood in total darkness.

Terror made me break out in cold sweat and my heart was rac-ing. In the next moment a dizziness came over me and I thought I would faint. Gradually my body took cognizance of its abuse—aches in my jaw, my face, my ribs, my legs. My wrists were numbed by the ropes and I tried to rub them into life so that I might extend groping hands to explore my dungeon in search of a possible means of escape. This hope, however faint, kept me from going insane.

Of my clothing, only my hat was missing, though my shirtfront was broken and my neckcloth and trousers torn. That the thugs hadn't taken my outer coat supported my belief that they had been hired to bring me to this hell. Perhaps their employer had watched their operation.

"Who are you, you fiend?" I shouted with a trembling voice into the darkness.

Silence.

"Are you Reynolds?"

Silence.

I retraced my steps to the door and felt it. Yes, it was made of iron, with a row of studs at the top and bottom. It had no window or grating, not even a keyhole, only a handle. It seemed to be secured entirely by a padlock outside, which allowed it to give about half an inch. But under it there was a space of about two inches. Dreams of digging myself out. But the floor was cement.

I heard scurrying—rats probably coming out of that hole at the other end of my cell. I shivered with fear and disgust. I needed a weapon. I must see if I could loosen a brick from the wall. I explored the left side of the door, feeling rough bricks up and down, the mortar between them. I turned the corner and went on examining the adjoining wall for some ten or twelve feet before coming to the next corner. Here I hesitated. I feared the hole in the floor—I didn't remember its exact location except that it was two or three feet in diameter. God knew how deep it went. I proceeded cautiously, taking half steps, keeping close to the rear wall. There was no window anywhere—something I had noticed during the single glimpse I was permitted of my prison. When I turned the next corner my fingertips were raw and sore, but I was coming away from the area of the hole, which was the focal point of my horror.

Coming to the front wall again, on the right side of the door, I found the mortar on the bottom side of a brick considerably receded. I probed it with my nail and retrieved some dust and small fragments. My pocket knife had of course been taken, but in the depth of one trouser pocket I found a quarter and three pennies. The quarter was better than my nail, and I dug in with all my strength, loosening a few more fragments of mortar.

I worked on for what seemed to be hours, until I was able to push my finger under the brick, feeling its whole width. I pushed on.

At one point an overwhelming fatigue seized me: it was sometime in the middle of the night. I needed sleep, but the moment I considered stretching out on the floor I became conscious of the distant scurrying. And then I heard them closer—saw several pairs of phosphorescent eyes just a few feet away. Or perhaps they were the trickery of my own eyes. But the sound was real enough. I leaned back against the wall and let sleep come, trying to keep it from becoming deep sleep. Even so, I dreamed: the hole in the floor was expanding, covering more and more of my prison, coming toward me, closer, closer, about to engulf me. I woke with a cry.

I didn't know how long I slept intermittently on my feet, but the moment I felt at all refreshed I continued my digging, now along the left edge of my brick.

Would dawn ever come—and would it bring any light? Would I be given food and water, or was I condemned to die of hunger and thirst? The house in whose cellar I was confined was no doubt abandoned. Still, if I were to shout for help someone might hear me.

I worked, I slept on my feet, I worked—and now the total darkness seemed to lift ever so slightly. When I passed my hand before my face, it seemed almost to have a vague outline. Perhaps the street door had a window and light came through it, trickled along the hall, down the steps, under the iron door. Yes, my hand began to have the shape of a hand. I ventured slowly toward the hole, hoping to see its shape and location emerge. The floor did seem darker in one area, but no distinct contour could be discerned. An hour later I could see no better.

For some reason this disappointment touched off a hysteria. Sleeplessness, fatigue, my still-aching body, my terror of death all came tumbling down about me and I shook and sobbed and rattled my prison door, crying out, "Help!" The desolate walls echoed back my voice. Then again, "Help! Help!"

Gradually I calmed down and returned to my digging. I could now push my finger in along two sides of the brick and I tried to grab it and pull it out. It needed more work and I dug with my miserably round, edgeless tool, then pulled, dug, pulled. Finally I felt the brick move. I dug on with renewed energy until I could move the brick more, still more. I pulled with all my might. The brick came out with an impact that made me stagger back.

It didn't surprise me that I hadn't made any breach in the wall, which seemed to be about a foot thick, with two more layers of bricks behind the one I held in my hand. Could I dig them out, then widen the hole enough to crawl through? It would be Herculean labor for weeks, maybe months. Could I expect to be allowed to live that long—and work undetected?

Meanwhile, I had a weapon against any rat that ventured near.

Overwhelmed by fatigue, I leaned against the wall with the brick in my hand and closed my eyes. I was thirsty and my stomach was growling, yet I was able to doze off. I woke to a sharp thud and an ache in my toe: I had dropped my brick.

Leaving it at my feet, I dozed off again, but was soon awakened by a noise that sounded like scurrying. Under the door the darkness seemed to be congealing. Movement. Something coming through. I went closer, looked, bent down, smelled. Bread! I pounced on it before any rat could. A quarter-pound piece cut from a loaf with a crisp crust. My mouth was watering, but what if it was poisoned? I would have to take a small bite and wait for any adverse effect . . .

I was on my hands and knees trying to see under the door—and thought I made out a pair of shoes, just as something else was being pushed through. Water? O God, make it water. Yes, apparently, in a flat flask that grated on the cement floor. I grabbed it, pulled out the cork and smelled. Summoning all my self-control, I took a minuscule amount in my mouth, let it roll around to taste it, then swallowed it.

As I stood up, still looking down, mesmerized by the strip of grayness under the door, I heard a voice that made me jump. The looseness of the door allowed it to come through relatively well, yet it sounded distant, distorted, unrecognizable even if I had heard it before—produced, I suspected, by ventriloquism.

"Tomorrow before you get water, you will return the empty flask. Or you get none."

"Who are you?" I called out in a loud, desperate voice close to breaking. "What do you intend with me?"

No answer. Footsteps receding.

"Monster!" I shouted, rattling the door. "Bastard! Devil! Did you kill Poe? Did you put arsenic in this bread and water?"

Silence. He was probably gone.

But his word "tomorrow" preyed on my mind. If there was to be a tomorrow, then perhaps the bread and water were not poisoned. Still, I resolved to be cautious. I took a small bite and one gulp and waited. The brick below the one I had removed formed a ledge, a place to keep my precious provisions. Except I recalled that some rats could climb a brick wall—the black ones that grew to eight inches. The brown ones that grew to ten inches were good swimmers but bad climbers. Which ones were these? It was too dark to tell either color or size, but the fact that I had been able to snatch minutes of sleep leaning against the wall unmolested suggested that these were the brown variety. Still, I decided to keep the bread in one pocket of my coat, the flask in the other.

The dark emptiness around me was seeping into my mind, and I groped for constructive thought. Perhaps I could continue my investigation into Edgar's murder mentally; or try to compose a poem; or find some diversion—recite, sing, think up some puzzle or cryptogram, such as Edgar and I used to amuse ourselves with. I could not even keep my mind on Edgar long, or on Elmira, before the dull, gray lethargy descended, dissolving my mind in the blackness around me. Paper and pencil and a little light would have helped: Montaigne said he could think only when he wrote. Then this tasty morsel of thought too dissolved into nothingness.

The night had been better. Digging out the brick had given purpose to my existence. So man lived until death canceled his greatest as well as most trivial purposes. Another thought, then my mind relapsing into blankness. I found myself back at the wall on the right side of the door, trying to dig into the mortar around the three remaining sides of the next brick.

I felt something brushing past my shoe and I swung around. Those phosphorescent eyes again out of the dimness. No mistaking them this time. More than one pair. Some four or five rats venturing closer, closer, excited by the smell of the bread in my pocket. I snatched up my brick and raised my arm. Closer. I hurled it. Wild squealing reaching the register of screams: I might have killed or wounded one. The rest ran.

I groped my way to the patch of darkness on the floor, feeling with the toe of my shoe for my brick. Softness. Yes, a dead rat. I found my brick and kicked it away from the corpse, then bent down for it and held it gingerly, rubbing it against the wall in the hope of removing blood or fur from it.

I felt a pull on my trouser leg. I kicked out wildly, but before I got the rat off it sunk its loathsome teeth into me. The sharp pain made me wince, and reaching under my trouser leg, I felt blood.

More came back, and I hurled my brick again, scattering the rodents but not killing any this time. I recovered my weapon and hurled it again, apparently wounding one, for it leaped up at me with wild ferocity. My brick was on the floor, all I could do was step back and give a hard kick. It connected and the beast fell back.

I had to eat my bread as soon as possible to put an end to this horror. Holding the brick in one hand and sometimes hurling it and making a kill and recovering it, I ate with the other—in quick, large bites.

I tried to mark the passing of time by the hunger pangs that began. I knew this should be two and a half to three hours after eating. Soon they receded, then started again. I drank water. Meanwhile, I worked on extricating the second brick. I had learned how useful it would be to hurl one while holding the other for close combat.

My battle with the rats endowed the hole in the ground just a few feet away with renewed terrors, and before the onset of total night I went toward it slowly, counting my steps, always tapping the floor with one foot before bringing up the other. The floor now seemed darker just ahead, my exploring foot felt no solid ground, and I knew I was at the edge. I heard squealing sounds as if from below, but I had purposely left my brick behind, not wanting to be tempted to throw it and thereby lose it. I continued my exploration in what I hoped to be a circle, counting my steps in order to calculate the size of the hole. Yes, it seemed to be from two to three feet in diameter. When I saw the vague outline of the door ahead, I knew I had come to a full circle. I wished I had some heavy object to throw in to see if it hit anything, but all I had to spare were three pennies. I threw in one and listened carefully but did not hear it hit anything. Perhaps the hole was bottomless, perhaps it was an abandoned well with water at the bottom. The thought of going down and trying to dig myself out that way gave me shivers. I'd be eaten alive by rats. And dig with what? My brick? My quarter? My nails?

The darkness was getting deeper—soon I would not be able to

see even the vague outline of my own hand—and I broke down again. I threw myself against the hard door, rattling it, crying, "Let me out! O God! Let me out!" I trembled with rage and sobbed like a hurt child.

*   *   *

So THE NIGHT WENT, and the next day, and the following night and the following day—tormented by exhaustion and aches and hunger pangs, snatching up my bread before the rats could get at it, fighting them, trying alternately to catch a few minutes of sleep on my feet and digging out my second brick, the darkness and the silence broken only by the horrible squeaking and squealing invading my mind until I was being shaken by something close to raging insanity.

On the third day—if I had calculated them correctly—I heard the loathsome voice again outside the iron door. It now had a certain urbane lightness, but it sounded as alien and distorted as before.

"Have you gone mad yet, Dupin? Do you recognize the tale I cast you in? It's one your double stole from me—"

Reynolds! It was Reynolds standing out there. The confirmation of my discovery excited me, giving me new strength, even if I had to die before I could tell the world. But who was Reynolds? Why the altered voice unless I knew him?

"You'll have to do without a pendulum and moving walls, but there is a pit and there are rats, as you've no doubt discovered." His laugh was high-pitched, cold, a hyena's. "You must agree I have a sense of humor—also a sense of the theatrical, in dressing my victim in clothes that expressed what he was—a shabby outcast and a thief—before avenging his crimes against me."

Hearing Edgar's killer confess stunned me, awed me. "You beast," I hissed. Then in a sudden rage: "Murderer!"

The same laugh. "You will die, Dupin. But as we read in 'The Cask of Amontillado,' another tale the thief stole from me, the avenger must punish not only with impunity but also by making himself known to the offender. So I am making myself known to you."

"Poe wrote those words—like five thousand others in that tale—not you!"

"You will die, Dupin, but you will not know when or how. I

have you totally in my power like a noxious insect I might hold over the flame which I will let fall whenever it pleases me."

That proud boast gave me hope. He could have killed me by this time if he wanted to—his hired thugs could have. He wanted me alive, at least for a while longer. We reckon life in years, but life can be reckoned by days also. A day of life is a great gift; it can be given a purpose—like digging out a brick, or investigating a murder. The detective in me put urgent, anxious questions to him.

"What other names do you go by? Have I seen you face-to-face?"

"You will know before you die. At which time your possessions will be returned to you intact—perhaps placed next to your body. I don't stoop to theft."

His promise sent a shiver through me. "You accuse Poe of theft, but are you blind to the masterpieces he created out of your plots?"

"My tales are parables. He stole them and cheapened them—and with them he stole my reputation, my fame. He fattened on my literary corpse. I will tell you this, because you'll soon take it to the grave—" The voice became lower in pitch, rapid, compulsive, with a strange echo to it. "Until I'm ready to burst upon the world in full greatness, no one must know I write. But I must write. Under my mask of unassailable professional dignity, behold the artist—brooding, tormented, vulnerable."

"What is your profession?"

"You will find out in the hour of death. Which may be imminent—or whenever I choose. For I am your god, a suffering and jealous god. Nothing has given me greater pleasure since ridding my life of that devil, than to watch you wriggle on a pin—"

He was interrupted by a distant scream. Then immediately another louder one. They seemed to come from street level.

I heard footsteps receding. Reynolds was fleeing, not wanting to get involved with whatever was happening above. Was someone being murdered? Would that bring the police? I stood still, with my ear pressed against the edge of the door.

A long time passed. Maybe hours.

Now I heard something. Voices? I waited for them to grow distinct, then I began to rattle the door and call out "Help!" as loudly as I could. "Help! Help! Help! Help!", shouting myself hoarse.

Footsteps. Unlike those of Reynolds, which were sharp, rapid, and light, these were slower and heavier. Police boots? I felt my heart hammering at the mere thought of freedom.

"Help!" My voice was almost gone.

"Who is in there?"

"The victim of a crime." I stood with my forehead pressed against the cold door, listening to them probe the padlock.

They weren't making much headway. I wished I could be outside with them, take their skeleton key and give it a try.

Finally a snap—similar to the one with which the lock had been shut, ages ago. The door gave, opened, and I fell into the arms of one of the policemen. Another held a lantern to survey my dismal prison, the sudden brightness making me shut my eyes. Bit by bit I opened them, squinting.

"You look sick, sir." They led me to the steps and helped me sit down. "How long were you in there?"

"Three days—if I count correctly."

"Who imprisoned you?"

"Two thugs. They robbed me." I thought it best to keep Reynolds out of it. At this point there was nothing the police could do about him.

"Why did they lock you in there?" The policeman's yellow eyebrows knitted suspiciously across his broad red face.

"I don't know."

"They usually kill their victims, like the man up there." He tossed his head. "They didn't take your clothes—that's strange, too. Can you describe them?"

"One was gigantic with a pitted face, the other thin and sinewy. He wore a sandy beard."

The second policeman with the black waxed moustaches wrote.

"I have a rat bite. I want a doctor to see it."

"We'll take you."

I felt so weak that I needed help up the steps to the street level. I recognized the garbage and urine smell. Here there were two more policemen in the entryway, standing around a dead man. He lay in his underwear in a pool of blood, his face covered with a handkerchief. One of the policemen took it off.

"Have you ever seen him before, sir?"

The face was thirtyish, freshly shaven, well tended, the one visible hand clean, the underwear silk. Probably dragged in here, then killed. Robbed of everything, clothes, too. "No, I haven't," I answered. The thought that I owed my freedom to this man's murder canceled the joy I was trying to feel. Forgive me, my unknown friend.

"Maybe the two that locked you in there did this job, too."

"Maybe."

"We're in Five Points, the toughest district in New York. Murder a day."

I had heard of it. A logical area to be kidnapped to.

We went out. In the late-afternoon light, the street seemed particularly sinister, with the houses dilapidated, some with missing windows, the frames blackened by fire. I was helped into the police wagon, and as we bounced along I would nod off and wake, incorporating into my half dreams the misery and filth around me, the people ill-clad and emaciated, the children, some of them barefoot, playing around mounds of garbage speckled with snow. A group of them with sticks were chasing a rat amidst howls. Two men in a doorway quickly stepped back when they saw us. One burned-out building seemed to house Negroes. Groups of them were out in front; perhaps their hovels were colder than the street. A woman passed us pushing a cart filled with rags; a man emerged from a gin shop reeling.

At the infirmary on Chamber Street, a young physician examined the wound just above my ankle. He thought it looked normal enough, but you could never tell with rabies and it should be cauterized as a precaution.

"Fortunately the bite came through the trouser leg," he said, "which probably acted as a screen against the animal's saliva, which usually carries the disease into the human body."

Each time he brought the red-hot needle to my wound I sucked in my breath, mauled my hands, cried out; finally I fainted. Had I been in better physical condition I would have stood the pain better. But then, revived and bandaged, with the physician's advice to eat a good meal and get plenty of rest, I was discharged.

Barely able to stand on my feet, I hailed a hack and directed it to my hotel, falling asleep on the way. I explained to the clerk that I had been robbed and the driver should be paid and the amount put on my bill. I ordered a bath and a five-course meal to be sent up to my room: oysters, soup, capon, salad, and apple tart, with a bottle of Chardonnay. After eating, I fell into bed and slept fourteen hours.

But I could not throw off my ordeal; it haunted me with sudden flashes of memory so real that though my eyes were open, I felt as if I was in total darkness, fighting off rats, waiting for my executioner to step at any moment through the door.

It was close to noon; Reynolds no doubt knew I had escaped, and what was his next move? What was mine? We both wanted a confrontation—he to kill me now probably as quickly as he could, I to capture him and hand him over to the police. He had the advantage: he knew me. I knew much about him but only internally; I didn't even know whether I had ever seen him face-to-face.

There were immediate tasks before me, since Reynolds's eerie promise was of little help to me for the nonce—to transfer some funds from my Baltimore account to a bank in New York, to replace my personal possessions, to have my soiled clothes cleaned and laundered, to buy a new hat. Fortunately my set of scarce skeleton keys, the bullet from Reynolds's gun, and Gaston's letters of recommendation were safe in a drawer. When I went out, I carried my remaining pistol cocked in my pocket, my finger on the trigger.

Since I did not know Reynolds's true identity, I had no means of pursuing him. I must let him pursue me. To Richmond, if he cared to. For I did not want to postpone seeing Elmira any longer. I made arrangements at my hotel and consulted my travel guide. Then I walked over to the telegraph office and wrote out a message: "Taking the steamer to Richmond, should arrive Thursday afternoon. Love, Auguste."

I suspected Reynolds was monitoring my moves.

18

As we sailed out of the docks the air was almost balmy for December, with a pale sun reflected from the windows on shore and the water itself. There were many people on deck, wrapped in coats, their scarves blown by the breezes, watching the harbor teeming with crafts large and small, high and low—sailing ships, steamers, tugs, ferries, freighters—with the buildings of the city behind them, now the green expanse of Battery Park, all converging in the shimmering distance, growing smaller, soon to disappear. Fascination on arrival, regret on leaving—New York produced that particular effect on the traveler. But I was giving only partial attention to the view, as I shot subtle glances around me, sometimes going to another part of the railing just to survey the crowd better. Had I seen that face before, however fleetingly? Or that one? Any man appearing to be in his thirties or forties was suspect. At the same time I was fairly certain that if my enemy was on board he occupied a private stateroom.

Of these there were four on board, the rest of the passengers berthed in large dormitories called "gentlemen's saloon" and "ladies' cabin," equipped with tiers of bunks, washstands, and pegs to hang clothes on. While I was careful to observe faces and to guard myself—carrying my pistol at all times—I tried to appear unsuspecting. In the dining saloon I did not choose the very end table; in the lounge I played chess with my bunkmate, Mr. Webber, a large sixtyish man from Ohio, with pretended absorption. Our ship, the *Georgia,* carried close to a hundred passengers; of these a quarter or a third were women, children, and elderly men, which allowed me after a few hours to recognize most of the men who interested me: I had of course long cultivated the art of capturing facial features upon the briefest observation, as if I were a portraitist.

If I had met Reynolds before, he would have to put on an elaborate disguise before showing himself; several passengers made me wonder whether the beard they wore was real or false.

And then I began to wonder whether the voice outside my dungeon had truly belonged to Reynolds. I remembered calling out the name Reynolds, which he did not contradict. But that did not prove that he was Reynolds. Why should a killer object to being taken for someone else? In this case, someone would only have to be acquainted with *Reflections* to pretend to be its author, to pretend outrage at Edgar's "thefts," with the rest of the mad tirade to follow. I had no doubt that the voice belonged to Edgar's killer, who intended to kill me also, but he might have killed Edgar for some other reason. Of the enemies Edgar had made over his reviews, verbal caricatures, rivalries, love affairs, I had met a good number; and however pleasant, casual, or forgiving they seemed, any of them might have a dark, murderous side. Even the Reverend W. W. Lord. For sometimes the devil appeared in the most pleasant guise. The murderer did not even have to be a literary man to pretend to be one. He might be avenging a wronged literary sister. My list of possible suspects overwhelmed me. I was back where I had started.

I let it all go for the nonce. My mind was as exhausted as my body after my recent ordeal. I needed such respite as the sea voyage could offer. I tried to let the casual, relaxed mien I was projecting take hold of me within as well. This was not difficult; actors often become the role they play. By the end of the day, with the pale sun disappearing westward over the invisible land and darkness falling, my tenseness had let up. I ate supper with good appetite, thinking more and more of Elmira, whom I had scarcely let myself think of all this time. In less than two days I would see her.

I went forward to the crowded bar, ordered a cognac, and listened to the hubbub of voices. One rang out: "A great little ship." He seemed to mean ours, the *Georgia*. "She may not be as luxurious as some of these riverboats with their million-dollar saloons and crystal chandeliers and all that junk, but she is sturdy, with a cedar hull and copper sheathing and a deep draft—she's made for the sea—"

"Do you own a share in her, sir?"

Laughter.

"I wish I did. You know, gentlemen, some of these money-hungry owners will put a riverboat out to sea—then you better watch out. That's how the *Home* was wrecked in a gale off Cape Hatteras, with eighty lives lost."

I studied the faces, listened to the voices.

"Or they'll put in inadequate boilers. Nothing's worse than that. Remember the *Medora?* Suddenly a blast and fifty people blown into the air. 'Course pilots can make mistakes, too, especially on a moonless night, like passing a ship on the port, instead of the starboard side, against her expectations. That's what happened when the *Gibbons* got sliced in half—"

Finishing my cognac, I realized how tired I was. At the exit I spotted Mr. Webber making his way out from the other end of the bar. He said he was calling it a day. My berth was over his and I told him I would follow him soon so as not to disturb him.

But first a brief stroll under the stars, if there were any—or if the air was not forbiddingly cold. I stepped out, pulling my tailcoat tightly about me. I braved the cold well enough, but the sky was overcast and the moon the palest glimmering. I walked the length of the deck and paused for a minute—long enough to realize that a section of the railing seemed to be missing. Actually, it was a gate that a sailor had apparently failed to secure properly, for as the ship rolled, it swung outward. I waited for it to swing back so that I might grab it and secure it—my mind at that moment on nothing else in the world. As it swung back and I reached out for it, I felt an enormous shove from behind, making me half crash against it, then fly past it, past everything into the darkness. Came a blow, and an icy wave caught me, threw me, sucked me relentlessly under. Ice was penetrating to my bones. I tried to swim, flail, as brine filled my mouth, my nose. I rose to the surface through an eternity of breathlessness, my lungs at the bursting point, but my water-logged clothes and shoes pulled me down again. I breathed water. My last coherent thought was that I was drowning.

Yet there was a rope that I had grabbed—perhaps in an unconscious death struggle—apparently holding on long enough for a boat to be lowered and rowed to me. From that point I remembered nothing until I felt powerful hands squeezing me from both sides to induce breathing. Water was pouring out of me and I was shivering, yet my lungs felt on fire every time air was forced in or out of them. I didn't know where I was—still in the rescue boat, or on deck, or below. After another blackout I realized that I was in a berth with blankets piled on me and a doctor taking my pulse. There were others that I could see, the captain with his grave face and gold stripes, Mr. Webber in a brown dressing gown, men in nightclothes and slippers.

"Fortunately a sailor saw the attack on you," the captain said. "Otherwise I doubt anyone would have spotted you in the water."

Reynolds, or whoever my enemy was, had counted on that. "I—appreciate—" It hurt my throat and chest to talk.

"The boy saw a dark figure who immediately vanished. Of course his first priority was to send up an alarm for a rescue team. Have you any idea who might have wanted to kill you?"

I shook my head. I did not want to involve the authorities as yet. It would impede my own investigation. "Could the sailor give— any description?" I brought out painfully.

"I questioned him myself, but all he saw was a dark figure. We were about to dock at Toms Landing and we screened all the passengers who were disembarking but found no grounds to detain anyone."

He had been too clever for them. And for me. I felt rage and shame. How could I have been so off my guard? Had I been so tired, my senses so dulled by one cognac, that I couldn't feel anyone lurking behind me? Oh, Edgar, you would not be proud of me.

"He's probably gone," the captain said. "He knew you'd been rescued, but he didn't know how much anyone had seen of him."

That was true. He would probably lie low for a while.

The officers left, and my visitors wished me well and returned to bed.

"You must not try to move," Mr. Webber said. "I'll take your bunk." There were three on top of each other.

"You're—most kind. What time is it?"

"Half past midnight. It took them over two hours to bring you around." He climbed up heavily, making the spring and mattress groan overhead. New snores broke out around us.

On the brink of sleep, I had a vision of a black beard. But how could I possibly have seen him? Was I sure I was not fantasizing on the strength of the shopkeeper's description in Baltimore? I did not think so. This was a real memory flash, still hovering in my mind. Could I recall anything else about him? Stature? Clothes? Nothing else came, only his presumably false black beard.

*   *   *

IN THE MORNING my chest and throat felt better and breathing was easier. But the ship doctor ordered me to stay prone as much as possible. The purser brought in the contents of my pockets. My new billfold was ruined, but the money in it would dry out and other documents I carried, such as my bank record, remained legible. My new watch had been opened and dried out, but it needed the services of a watchmaker. The purser knew nothing about my pistol; it had apparently been lost in the sea. I was weaponless, which troubled me. I would have to purchase a brace of pistols as soon as I stepped ashore.

I asked the purser about the passengers in the private staterooms. He pulled out some folded sheets and consulted them. In one there were newlyweds, in one a sick old lady and her nurse, one was empty, No. 4 had been occupied by a gentleman who disembarked last night at Toms Landing. The purser knew nothing about him.

The steward brought in my dried-out, cleaned and pressed clothes. My shoes were ruined, but I had another pair with me. I asked him about the man in stateroom No. 4. He tried to remember. "Did he have a black beard?" I asked.

"I think so, sir. I don't recall much about him—except he was laid up and had to be served his meals in bed."

This strongly suggested that he was afraid I'd recognize him even with his false beard. "Did you serve his meals?"

"Yes, sir."

"Do you remember whether he was young or old?"

"No, sir. I put the tray down and went out without looking at him much. The same when I returned to pick up the tray. He had that dark beard—and I think something on his head. Kind of a nightcap—"

After breakfast I went in search of the sailor who had witnessed the attack on me. I was told that he was on duty on the afterdeck and I went up—still weak on my feet—and we stood in the wind, he with wet, reddened hands. He was young, maybe sixteen.

"Thank you, my lad, for saving my life. Did you notice anything about my assailant?"

"No, sir. My eyes were on you as you leaned out toward that swinging gate—"

"Which the villain had probably opened himself—"

"Then I saw you being pushed and flying through the air. I called out, 'Man overboard!' and he was gone."

For most of the day I rested in the lounge or on the main deck where I could watch the white furrows churned up by the side paddle, or in the distance, the changing colors of sea and sky. I measured time by estimating the hours still separating me from Elmira.

Off the coast of Delaware we ran into heavy fog. The mournful steam whistle blew continually and the sea was a mass of grayness—but for the grace of God and an alert young sailor, my own watery grave. I saw sharks in my mind's eye gliding with open maws, nosing the depths, searching for me.

19

I WOKE TO THE GROANING of the ship's timber amidst wild rolling and pitching. It was still night; a voice from another berth said we were passing through the Horseshoe, where the ebbtide runs counter to the gentle sou'wester from the land. But it promised that once we were past Old Point Comfort we'd enter the calmer currents of the James River, and soon I slept again.

The morning gave me several more hours to regain my strength, though as I reclined on the closed deck each mile of the wooded shore made me more impatient to see Elmira. I envisioned her like a jewel in a lovely setting, for Richmond was also Edgar's city. He had grown up there and, in spite of his troubles with his foster father, always spoke of it fondly. It was built like Rome on seven hills, a passenger said; appropriately, as the city came into view I caught sight of a classical temple on one of them, its white marble columns gleaming under the bright sky. It was the state capitol, built by Jefferson, the gentleman explained. I recalled Harold Tyler saying that with Jefferson all the mischief had started—something that irritated me at the time, for we in France admired Jefferson. Yet he, too, kept slaves. As we sidled up to the wharf and ropes flew out, a gang of them came on board with their overseer to get the cargo. Every time I saw Negroes owned like chattel I shuddered a little. I wondered if Elmira kept slaves.

Leaving the boat with my valise—through the very gate of my rude ejection—and walking down the gangplank I looked excitedly for her.

There she was, tall, elegant in a mauve gown and a rich, lace-edged shawl and matching bonnet, smiling. I ran to her and we embraced.

"How long has it been, Auguste? Two weeks? It seems much longer."

"An eternity," I said. "It's wonderful to be with you."

"Did you have a good voyage?"

"Ah," I tried to laugh. "I'll tell you about it later." Her gray-haired coachman in handsome livery took my valise with a complaisance that eased my mind about his status. He hurried ahead to haul it up on the box of the meticulously polished carriage. A pair of fine palominos tossed their heads. He opened the door for us and we got in, then he sprang up on his box and we began to move.

I had been waiting for my first opportunity to take Elmira in my arms and kiss her, but now I felt shy of her. I succeeded only in taking her long, narrow hand. I peeled the glove back and kissed the perfumed wrist under the lace cuff.

"You will of course stay at the house," she said.

"Oh, dear—I don't know—"

"There are rooms in my house for my guests to stay in," she said haughtily, as if answering someone else's objections.

Still, I did not envision this as a purely brotherly visit, and how would we manage it with servants and slaves around—not to speak of her two undoubtedly inquisitive children?

She pulled down the window slightly to let some air in—which was balmier than in the North and had an enticing sweetish tobacco fragrance. Then as we turned into Grace Street lined with elms that seemed profuse even in their winter bareness, the fragrance was more foresty. The horses were trotting uphill, chasing their shadows in the intermittent afternoon sun.

"This is Church Hill," Elmira said. "My house is just about across from St. John's. Convenient for a churchgoer," she added with a smile.

"St. John's in Richmond—it rings a bell."

"Edgar's mother is buried in the yard."

"Yes, of course."

"You can imagine how that preyed on his mind during his last visit to me. 'I feel her spirit in your house,' he kept saying."

The coachman reined in the horses. The well-kept garden, the evergreens, the summer pavilion, the graceful driveway all spoke of prosperity; yet the house itself seemed less friendly than somber, perhaps because of its unbroken three-story red-brick façade. Mr. Shelton had built it, and Elmira had not been happy in it, and his legacy protecting it had been severe on her.

But she was obviously proud of it in many ways, smiling as we entered the drawing room which was more luxurious than her sister's in Baltimore, with the ceiling loftier, the sweep of the satin curtains more majestic, the paintings larger, in richer gold frames, the candelabra more ornate. The fireplace was pink-and-black marble and the furniture was in the heavy-footed, gold-ornamented Empire style. Ordinarily it would have been less to my taste than the Sheraton pieces I remembered seeing in Mrs. Craig's house, but when you're transported by angels from hell to heaven, taste is of little importance. The horrors of my dungeon, my near-drowning still lived in me agonizingly, and everything around me was glorious, unbelievable, a dream from which I was afraid to awaken. My room, to which Elmira led me by way of a gracefully curving staircase, then a straight, shorter one, was a wonder. The four-poster bed, the cornflower-strewn counterpane and curtains were warmth, hominess, and ultimate comfort. My valise had already been brought up and placed under the window which looked down at the quiet residential street.

"This room will surely tempt me to outstay my welcome," I said.

"How could you possibly?" She turned to me, the smile receding on her face, her features softening. Her pale-blue eyes flamed up, overcoming my shyness and I drew her to me and kissed her— lingeringly, feeling her mouth open and her arms holding me hard against her. "You made me miss you so," she murmured.

But then she extricated herself. "Have you had lunch?"

"Yes."

"Then we'll have tea." We went down again and she gave orders to have it served in the sun room. It had a picturesque view of the old churchyard beyond a moldering ivy-covered wall.

"Can you see Eliza Poe's grave from here?" I asked.

"Not quite."

"Still, I can imagine what an effect sitting here must have had on poor Edgar."

"I think it made him look for her in me—which I found somewhat disturbing."

"Consider how young she was when she died, how young she remained for him. That lost miniature showed her like a child almost. For him, child and mother kept merging into one." I relapsed into silence.

She touched my hand. "You're so subdued, Auguste. I remember you as more high-spirited. Did something bad happen?"

Tea was brought in with freshly baked muffins, and I waited for her to serve, with that grace I remembered about her. Then I said, "Two bad things happened, one following on the heel of the other—but I don't want to bring them up and spoil all this loveliness."

"You must tell me, you promised." She handed me a cup.

"I don't know which to start with. The first was in many ways worse, but I'm still feeling the physical effect of the second." I told her about my near-drowning.

She gasped. "Oh, Auguste!" Her eyes dilated with fright and horror.

"I was lucky a young sailor saw it happen."

"The Lord be praised for that." She felt my head, my face. "Any sign of fever? Or a cough?"

"No, I just feel weak."

"You will rest. I lost a husband that way—after a plunge into icy water. And he wasn't pushed, either, and it wasn't the sea."

"I'll stay with you a couple of days. Then I'll go on. I can't let him escape."

"Who is he, Auguste? It's so frightening to think that someone really killed Eddie—and now wants to kill you."

I waited until she swallowed the last bite of her muffin, then began to tell her about my imprisonment. What I hadn't counted on was the effect on me of my own telling, with the experience and the remembrance becoming almost indistinguishable, as if I were now, this very moment, leaning against that brick wall in total darkness, exhausted, starving, dozing off, hearing the rats. My voice faltered and I was trembling and felt clammy, close to passing out. My weakened state from my near-drowning did not help. Elmira was horrified. Tears came to her eyes and she broke out in sobs and clutched my hand. Then she looked up to heaven and cried, "O God, why do you take the best and let such monsters live?"

We sat for some time hand in hand, she wiping her eyes, I my forehead, drinking our tea.

"I think he is someone I know," I said then. "Before he pushed me into the sea he had kept himself out of sight, even in disguise, pretending to be ill and having his meals sent to his stateroom."

"Whom do you suspect, Auguste?" she asked with a sudden sobriety in her voice.

"Someone who once used the pseudonym Reynolds, first of all. Edgar uttered that name on his deathbed, and Reynolds is the author of an anonymous book, *Reflections,* from which Edgar took certain things—ideas mostly—which Reynolds in his diseased mind magnified into total theft and avenged by killing Edgar. This comes from that ventriloquized voice outside my prison: 'He stole my tales, my reputation, my fame. He fattened on my literary corpse.' Now if I have met Reynolds, and I think I have, there are some nine or ten possibilities of his true identity, taking into account the fact that the best disguise is often made up of elements of the real personality underneath. Thus any of these literary enemies of Edgar, who supposedly have long forgotten their quarrel with him and can laugh about it and be perfectly pleasant toward me, may be a murderer. Reynolds may be Griswold; or Neilson Poe, that complaisant prig whom Edgar considered his worst enemy; or Charles Briggs, who claims Edgar squeezed him out of the *Broadway Journal;* or Lewis Gaylord Clark, who says Edgar came close to attacking him physically on the street over a review; or Hiram Fuller, whom Edgar sued and won a judgment against; or Dr. English, with whom Edgar exchanged insults and fisticuffs; or Griswold's friend Tyler, that secretive man who disclaims any knowledge of Edgar; or the Reverend W. W. Lord, whose poems Edgar destroyed in a review; or even Longfellow, who Edgar insisted was a plagiarist. Then the murderer may not be Reynolds, simply using Reynolds as a double mask, so to speak; he may not be a literary man, which would put Mrs. Ellet's brother Lummis, who tried to engage Edgar in a duel, too, among my suspects."

"Perfectly pleasant toward you," she repeated in a bemused voice. "Yet torture you and want to kill you—"

"Yes, because he knows I'm trying to get him. It's like an extended duel we're fighting in the dark. By the way, I don't think he has followed me to Richmond. He doesn't know how much he revealed of himself on board ship, as the captain wisely suggested. I think he is lying low. Still, it makes me nervous to be unarmed. Can you recommend a reliable gun shop in town?"

"Tomorrow we'll drive to one if you like. Now I want you to rest. I'd better not ask you if you're up to going to a ball tomorrow night."

"Oh, do ask me. What ball do you have in mind?"

"A ball to benefit our volunteer firemen. I was asked to be a chaperone, and it would be delightful to show up with an escort. But you need your rest more."

"A ball may be just what I need."

"We shall see."

We were still in the sun room when young voices came from outside, interspersed with a mammy's scolding. I stiffened, remembering Elmira's saying that her children had disliked Edgar.

"They're home from school," Elmira said. "I told them we'd be having a house guest—they should not be so obstreperous."

On bursting in, they immediately quieted down—puzzled by me and shy of me. Elmira presented them as Master Southwell and Miss Ann, and me as Monsieur Dupin from Paris. I felt two pairs of blue eyes, light like their mother's, studying me avidly. They were no doubt thinking of Edgar. They had the Royster patrician nose and narrow lips as well—both attractive; she seemed in her early teens, he about twelve. Had they been older, I might have considered them suspects.

"Did you just come across the sea, monsieur?" the boy asked.

"Not quite. I just came from New York."

"I'd like to go to New York," he said.

"I'd love to go to Paris," the girl said dreamily, then giggled.

"Someday you'll both go to both places," Elmira said with an easy laugh, but with a note of dismissal in her voice.

They took the hint; he bowed his head and she curtsied.

"It was a pleasure to meet you both," I said. "I suspect we'll see a lot of each other in the next day or two."

But I hadn't quite been able to reconcile myself to their dislike of Edgar. Perhaps if they hadn't put up such a strong objection to him, Elmira might have married him—and saved him from disaster.

Later I had an opportunity to hear Ann on the subject. Elmira had prescribed an hour of rest for me and I was reclining in my room, paging through some magazines—with an eye to finding something I could attribute to Reynolds—when I heard piano music. It enticed me and I rose, knotted my cravat, slipped on my coat, pulled a comb through my hair and went downstairs. I could see from the foot of the stairs that Ann was alone in the drawing room, playing what sounded like a sonata by Haydn or Mozart. Catching a glimpse of her lavender dress as she swayed on the bench, I waited for her to finish the movement, then walked in.

"Do you mind if I listen to you?"

She seemed a little confused. Maybe I was being too formal. "It's all right. I must get used to people hearing me play."

I took a chair—not too close, but so that she could see me if she turned slightly. She played nicely, but hitting a wrong note affected her visibly. She would sigh and throw her head back. "Oh, darn!" she said at one point and played the phrase again. Yet when she finished she was able to turn to me with a smile. "Was it *effroyable, monsieur?*"

"No, it was splendid—like your French pronunciation."

"I get so upset when I make a mistake." She was fingering one of the lace insets of her dress.

"You need not be. It's human to make mistakes. You play very well. Did you ever accompany Mr. Poe? He had a fine tenor voice."

She shook her head. She grew thoughtful. "My mother did in the old days, she told us. Are you related to him?"

"No, but I knew him well."

"Southwell and I didn't care much for him."

"Why is that?"

"He wasn't very—reliable. People said he drank. My wicked brother—" She giggled, losing all self-consciousness. "He liked to imitate the way Mr. Poe walked." She showed me—without getting up, simply raising one pretty shoulder and jerking her torso a little in slow motion. A child's spontaneous sense of fun. In the next moment her demonstration embarrassed her and she blushed. Then she grew soulful. "Maybe if it wasn't for Southwell I would've liked Mr. Poe more. He was so against our having him for a father."

I wanted to defend him somehow. "Did you ever read any of his poems?"

"I heard him recite 'The Raven' once. It was a fine performance. I almost liked him then."

*   *   *

WITH THE CHILDREN long in bed and the servants in their quarters, I lay in bed, with a streetlamp yellower than the moon creating soft, blurred contours around the furniture and the rectangle of the door. I listened with bated breath for the faintest footsteps outside, but I heard only the thumping of my own heart. Would she come? I thought back on the kiss we exchanged earlier in this room, her

parted lips, her pressing hands—would she want to stop there?
Since we had already experienced more together?

I waited, my body waited—sometimes with sudden eagerness,
then with a resigned wisdom of its own, beyond my will. Oh,
Elmira, come to me. Come. You couldn't have wanted me to be a
guest in your house just to bar us from the joy we've known.

I heard nothing for a long time, but now the outline of the door
seemed to shift. It was opening, revealing her standing figure. It
closed behind her as soundlessly, until I heard the faint snapping
of the lock over my heartbeat. She came closer. I could distinguish
her tall, slim figure in an elaborately ruffled, wide-sleeved dressing
gown, her loosened hair, but not her features. She sat down on the
edge of my bed and bent toward me, and now I could see her eyes
as we began to kiss passionately. It took but a moment to shed my
nightshirt and for her to throw off her dressing gown and we
embraced naked. "Oh, my love—my love—" I whispered, seeking
new places on her face and body to kiss. She was passive at first;
she was basically less sensual than severe, puritanical, but there was
a deep-lying passion in her and soon she began to writhe, reaching
for me, wanting me in her. She choked off a cry—we could not
afford to emit loud sounds. I had to move little; I felt myself a kind
of axle to her center as we soared higher and higher. Our climax
shook us to the heavens, then we lay still, panting, in each other's
arms.

"Did you think I wouldn't come to you?" she asked.

"I was afraid you might not."

"It was not easy for me. Suppose one of my children wakes up
sick and calls for me? Also, I'm sinning. I keep thinking the Lord's
most appropriate punishment would be to render the precaution I
take ineffectual—"

Women sometimes syringed themselves with alum, or phos-
phate of zinc, or chloride of soda, or even vinegar, to prevent
conception.

"It would be the end of me. How could I face my children? How
could I hold up my head in the world?"

She could do both as my wife, but I was not ready to say this. At
the same time I knew I would not abandon her.

"Pray that the Lord spares me. I must go now." She got up,
wrapped her dressing gown around her, kissed me and left as
soundlessly as she had entered.

* * *

AFTER BREAKFAST THE NEXT DAY, while Elmira was busy with household tasks, such as ordering the menu for the day, I set out to do my errands. I assured her that I felt strong enough, and she wrote down the names of a watchmaker and a gun shop.

But I hesitated to go out unarmed. "Do you have a pistol in the house I can borrow?"

She showed me her husband's old pair in a cushioned box—German-made, a little like my own. I cleaned one, loaded it, and put it in my pocket.

"Will you be careful?"

"Yes."

Main Street was only two blocks away, and after less than half a mile downhill it got busy with carriages, drays, and horsemen, with shops and stalls lining the sidewalks. I found the watchmaker soon enough. He turned out to be a French-speaking Swiss, who opened my Omega with respect, scrutinized it under a magnifying glass, and concluded that though some corrosion by the brine had set in, he could clean the watch and put it back in working condition by tomorrow.

"*Magnifique*," I said.

"*Je vous en prie, monsieur.*"

At the gun shop I was shown several pairs; one highly recommended was a .32 caliber Smith & Wesson model—ironically the type Lummis had shown me, as I recalled. Having been attacked several times, I might as well provide myself with the best defense. As I made my purchase, a feeling of restlessness took hold of me. It seemed as if I'd been on this delightful visit much longer than one day. My work was waiting for me. Tomorrow I must kiss Elmira farewell and go.

It was more laborious to return to the house, having to walk uphill with my package, but I was essentially back in my stride. Nor did I feel that I was being followed. At one of the last stalls on Main Street I bought a bunch of roses to take to Elmira.

She placed them in the sun room where we had lunch—cheese omelet with stewed okra and corn muffins, followed by fruit tart. I spoke of my decision to leave tomorrow. She put down her fork and looked at me with the particular restraint she was so adept at, but her eyes seemed moist.

"You just came. If I promise not to make a fuss, will you come again as soon as you can?"

"Do you have any doubt that I will?"

"Can you possibly come for Christmas? Or perhaps I could take the children to Baltimore, if it's any easier for you."

"I want to see you again as soon as possible. The trouble is I can't make any predictions."

"I understand. I'll try not to think of the danger you'll be constantly exposed to." She let out a sigh.

We continued to eat in silence, with the fragrance of my roses wafting over us.

In the afternoon we went for a drive, Elmira directing old Luke, her coachman, to go west, past Capitol Hill, to Franklin and Second streets. She was going to show me what I wanted to see most, the two neighboring houses where she and Edgar had first known each other. The carriage stopped and we got out.

The two frame houses both showed their age; both seemed lonely somehow, though people lived in them.

"I think it was those two windows from which we waved to each other," Elmira said, pointing. "After twenty years my memory is a little vague. Oh, but how well I remember our enchanted garden." It was across the street and she led me to it.

"It still seems enchanted," I said as we took a curving path, although the dominant note was a winter bareness, with only some pines and perennial hedges and bushes green under the white sky, and birdsong reduced to the chirping of sparrows and the cries of jays.

"It was better tended then," Elmira said, "even in winter."

I felt no jealousy, only a kind of remembrance, as if she and I had walked here once as young lovers.

"Being here with you makes me think you're my lost Eddie," she said at that very moment.

We stopped and I pulled her to me and we kissed.

"I will miss you," she said.

"And I you."

We walked back to the carriage.

*   *   *

IN THE DRAWING ROOM some candles had been lit and a great log was burning in the pink-and-black fireplace. I stood in my dress coat, waiting for her to come down, sometimes walking up to one or another of the gold-framed paintings hanging in deep shadow. Some were landscapes, others family portraits, mostly going back to wigs and ruffles; one youngish man in modern dress I recognized as the late Mr. Shelton. His face seemed unobjectionable enough—his expression rather imperial like the furniture around him. I felt our affinity. In some ways I was more his successor than Edgar's: he had known her intimately, as Edgar hadn't. I dreaded parting from her tomorrow. That I might never see her again was a possibility I did not care to think about, much less mention to her.

I heard her come down and I turned. My breath caught, she looked so queenly. She wore a dusky-rose gown—muted enough to be matronly yet light enough to be youthful—modestly décolleté, revealing but a small portion of her shoulders, bosom, and arms above the elbows. Her hair was swept back to form a tight chignon, showing her long neck and garnet earrings to advantage. Her face bore a minimal amount of paint that gave it a serene beauty. Her eyes shone wonderfully blue, barely lined. The skirt of her gown, adorned with overlapping layers of delicate lace, billowed over her petticoats enticingly.

Her personal maid came down after her, crouched low and adjusted a fold in her skirt.

"Thank you, Melantha."

"Perfect," I said. "You look absolutely lovely."

She smiled.

The ball was held in a mansion on Clay Street, a short ride away. But we had to wait in line behind other carriages as they moved up to the front entrance. Finally we could alight, a liveried footman helping us out, and we walked across the Greek portico. Inside, more liveried footmen took our wraps and carried them into an anteroom on each side, one for the ladies, one for the gentlemen. A pair of elegantly curving staircases led to the upper ballroom, with music seeping down. A little committee of matronly women in sedate gowns received us; Elmira presented me as a dear friend from Paris. No one seemed surprised by my looks; I was not in Poe territory. As I caught names as old as names could get in this new country—Lee, Byrd, Hamilton, Newport, Davis—I noted young faces everywhere as beautiful, pert, pampered, or as handsome and insolent, as faces could get. There was a preponderance of light eyes and blond hair.

In the ballroom with its fretted ceiling, glowing chandeliers, huge mirrors in ornate frames, a Virginia reel of many couples was snaking along the highly polished floor, to the tune of a Negro orchestra in brilliant uniforms seated on a platform, playing strings high and low, banjo, accordion. Elmira and I moved along the side, past velvet settees, to a corner where most of the chaperones seemed to be sitting—more matronly ladies, a couple in mourning, some with husbands next to them. More introductions. Elmira seemed to know all the people worth knowing in Richmond. Meeting them, I thought of huge plantations of cotton and tobacco worked by "darkies" as they were called here, far less kindly treated than their brothers and sisters in fine houses.

The next dance was a waltz and a shout of enthusiasm went up from among the young people. "Shall we?" I asked Elmira.

"I never danced it."

"It's not hard. One-two-three, one-two-three. Come, I'll show you."

After the first few steps she got into it well; she had much natural grace. We swayed and dipped and turned smoothly among the young couples, for whom the waltz was a great opportunity to hold each other close. To our comfort, there were a few older couples on the floor, as well.

"What a charming dance," Elmira said, flushed like a young girl.

In an adjoining room, a lavish buffet was set with sides of beef, turkey, ham, various fishes, potatoes done in every way, salads, fruits, cakes. We took a table and a servant appeared with champagne in a silver cooler.

We ate and drank.

"I want to make a contribution to your volunteer firemen," I said. "How do I do it?"

"You see Mrs. Newport. You met her earlier."

"The lady in the bombazine gown?"

"Yes. Poor woman recently lost her husband in a fire."

I took Elmira's hand and kissed it. "Oh my dear, I'm not happy to go from you tomorrow."

"I'm not happy to have you go."

"Even when I come back—however soon, say by Christmas— we'll just have to part again. There is only one way out. Yet I would be presumptuous to suggest it. I'm poor. I dipped into just about the last of my resources to make this trip possible. How can I offer to marry you and take you to Paris, where I live in a small, gloomy apartment in a decaying house?"

"Your poverty would not be an obstacle if by marrying you I wouldn't make myself poor also. You know what strictures my husband's will have put on me."

"I know."

"True, I almost married Eddie—but it would have been a mistake. I've learned that much from that experience. So this is the best we can do. I'm waiting for my children to get a little older, then I want to travel abroad—to Paris, of course." She smiled. "Will you show me Paris? Now I want to dance with you again. I want to enjoy our last hours together."

We tossed our champagne down and went into the ballroom and joined the young people in the polka, making glorious hops, giggling all the way.

That night she came to me and we made long, passionate love.

In the morning we went to get my watch, then drove on to the harbor. The packet for Baltimore was loading.

We stood at the gate, our hands in each other's. "Let's aim for Christmas one way or another," I said.

"You will be careful, won't you?" she said. "I'll pray for you every day."

How much warmer our parting was than it had been in Baltimore. As we kissed, there were tears in her eyes, and as I walked up the gangplank, I felt a choking in my throat. I stood on deck smiling and waving to her on shore. She took out a handkerchief and I whipped out mine, and as the steamer belched out a hoot and the wheels began to churn the water, we waved to each other and kept on waving until wharves, buildings, other craft, and a turn of the boat blocked her out of view.

20

IN THE DINING SALOON that evening I noticed a man looking at me with more than casual interest. I had noticed him before—a man of medium height, sixtyish, with a round face, white hair and goatee, and small, dark, inquisitive eyes. Now from three tables away he was taking long, observant glances at me. That kind of scrutiny was not unfamiliar to me either, on the part of those who had known Edgar.

Later in the lounge he came up to me.

"I beg your pardon, sir. You cannot be Poe. He died."

"No, I am not Poe. And you are correct—he did die."

"Remarkable resemblance. Of course I never saw Poe during the last years of his life—I knew him in his youth. Allow me to introduce myself: James Ewell Heath."

I gave him my name and we shook hands.

"Auguste C. Dupin," he repeated. "Auguste C. Dupin. Where do I know your name from?"

"Poe mentioned me in some of his tales. We were friends and associates in Paris."

"Yes, of course. I confess I don't know Poe's tales too well— except a few early ones. We were both editors of the *Southern Literary Messenger* in its heyday. I fear that magazine has declined in recent years. Under Mr. White's proprietorship it was excellent. And young Poe is so clearly before me, walking down the street with a nervous, rapid, almost military step—he'd been at West Point, you know—in a tailcoat and beaver hat, his linen blindingly white, though if you looked close you noticed it was mended, the brass buttons of his waistcoat and the brass tassel of his usually empty purse gleaming in the morning sun—"

"What a vivid description, Mr. Heath," I said. "You're making me nostalgic for a time I did not even know Poe. You must be a writer yourself—"

"Well, yes, I have committed a book or two. I published *Edge-Hill* just about that time, a novel about plantation life, then about ten years ago, my comedy, *Wigs and Democrats,* ran successfully in Philadelphia. Poe was quite good in his comic writings, too—few people know about them."

He was affable enough, somewhat on the effusive and boastful side, but what interested me most about him was his presence on the literary scene fifteen years ago. Finally I asked him, "During your editorship of the *Messenger,* Mr. Heath, did you ever come across a book called *Reflections?*"

"*Reflections,*" he repeated. "*Reflections.* I think we may have reviewed that book. What is it about? No, don't tell me, let me see if I remember." He looked up at the oil lamp overhead, fingering his goatee. "George Washington? Was it about George Washington?"

"Partly, yes. Also about great paintings and cathedrals—"

"Yes, yes. It was a kind of miscellany. We did review it. Not very favorably, as I recall. Poe may have written the review. He could be unsparing—use writers up, as we liked to say."

"Oh, yes," I said, seeing an added grievance for Reynolds. Poe "using him up" before stealing from him. "Would you happen to know the author of that book, Mr. Heath?" I noticed a tremor in my voice.

"No, I can't say that I do. It was published anonymously, as I recall."

"Is the name Reynolds familiar to you?"

"Reynolds? There is of course Jeremiah Reynolds, the explorer—"

"I mean H. Reynolds."

"H. Reynolds. H. Reynolds—" As he sat back to think better, he gave vent to a yawn. He pulled out his watch. "I fear it's time for me to retire, Mr. Dupin. But we'll talk again tomorrow."

I thought long into the night with a julep—later tossing and turning in my berth—trying to decide whether to show *Reflections* to Mr. Heath in an attempt to refresh his memory. Once again, as in New York, I wanted to shield Edgar. One's natural tendency on reading especially the "Tales from Bedlam" section was to cry plagiarism. It was thanks to the total obscurity into which *Reflections* had fallen that there were no such audible cries. Except of course by Reynolds himself—or whoever pretended to be Reynolds. In the morning I woke convinced that I must take my chance, and I appeared in the dining saloon with the book under my arm.

My new acquaintance and I sat face-to-face over hominy, eggs, biscuits, and coffee. Reinforcing myself with a second cup, I handed him the book.

He fingered the old purple linen binding, then studied the title page. "Ah, yes, this is it—*Reflections*. It does come back." He turned to one of the middle sections, getting a little lost in it, which was fine with me. He turned to the beginning, which made me nervous. Some of these items had appeared word for word under Edgar's name in the *Southern Literary Messenger* of all places; I tried to take comfort from the fact that by then Mr. Heath had long ceased to have any connection with the magazine. He turned to the end, and I prayed that he had been truthful in saying that he didn't know Edgar's tales too well.

"Listen to this," he said, startling me. "Once upon a time, a lunatic who had brutalized and killed his cat believed, when a second cat followed him home, that it was the reincarnation of his first cat returning to bring retribution upon him." Mr. Heath, the comic author, laughed. Thank God for that! For his never having read "The Black Cat."

He closed the book and returned it. "I think Mr. White knew the author."

I listened eagerly.

"He never revealed his name, but he said something about him as I recall—" Heath fell into reverie.

"Where is Mr. White now?" I asked. "Still in Richmond?" I was prepared to get off at the next stop and take a boat back to Richmond.

"Mr. White died a few years back."

My heart fell.

"Let's see. The fellow who wrote this was not really a literary man. He was in some other field—brilliant but eccentric—trying to channel that field into some form of writing—"

"Because he must write?"

"Apparently, although he was not very gifted as a writer—"

I recalled my jailer's voice outside the iron door: "No one must know I write. But I must write. Under my mask of unassailable professional dignity, behold the artist—brooding, tormented, vulnerable." They were inflated, desperate words, betraying secret doubt—words echoing in my mind now as more genuine than counterfeit. It was Reynolds's voice I had heard, I was newly certain.

"Can you remember his field? Law? Medicine? The ministry? Teaching? Business?" My list of suspects drifted across my mind.

Heath thought. "One of those perhaps—I just can't remember which."

"Do you know anything else about him? His age—or what he looked like—or where he was from?"

Heath shook his head. "May I ask why you arc so intent on discovering the author of a book that's—well, not very good?"

"For that very reason." Now that it was safely back in my hand, I could afford to say, "Its faults interest me—psychologically. The author has a brilliant mind. But it is perverted. Take the item you read aloud. I daresay the author thinks he is telling a story—"

Heath laughed. "A story? I daresay he does—poor fellow. A story in two sentences!"

"Do you see a connection between this kind of so-called story telling and being eccentric in his field—trying to channel it into some form of writing, as you said? Take, let's say, a lawyer who refuses to practice law; instead, he spends his days and nights editing law books."

"Yes, yes. Not daring to practice. Not making the commitment. Not daring to bring either his literary idea or his legal knowledge to life. That's the secret of both. Life. I see why you're so interested in this author, Mr. Dupin. You're quite correct. He is a fascinating case. Just from glancing at his book again, I see him as a kind of recluse—turning his back on everyone, on the world, on life, unable to love; feeding on himself, magnifying his own ego to monstrous proportions—oh, to the point of madness. I see him as mad." He pulled out his thick gold watch. "Oh, dear, we'll soon be in Annapolis."

It was his destination. I stood up with him and accompanied him to the stairs. I told him I would always remember our conversation. "By the way, sir, is the name Harold Tyler familiar to you?"

"Harold Tyler." He thought. "The only Tyler that comes to mind is our former president, John Tyler." He looked at his watch again. "It's been a pleasure, Mr. Dupin. If you're ever in Richmond again, be sure to look me up." We shook hands and he went below.

But Harold Tyler—his name, his face, his talk, his move-ments—burned in my mind. I went on deck and stood with my coat pulled about me, holding the rim of my hat in the wind, gazing down at the choppy blue-green waters of the bay, then suddenly swung around—feeling him behind me. So it was Tyler! Everything fitted. Tyler. Good God!

I could not explain my certainty; my evidence was largely cir-cumstantial. But Mr. Heath's one small piece of information, the psychological portrait we had drawn, my memory of that ventrilo-quized voice, my meetings with Tyler all jelled like a spectacular chemical reaction. I felt as if muses and angels had lit candles in my brain. Here was analysis, as Edgar and I had defined it during our crime detection, the poetic faculty's imaginative grasp. As Tyler loomed in my mind, all other suspects faded. I felt excited, filled by an overwhelming optimism. I was set on bold, risky action that crystallized with every clang of the lookout bell, every belch of black smoke, every mile of the churning water the side paddles pushed behind us.

As soon as we docked in Baltimore, I hurried down the gang-plank with my valise, crossed the railroad tracks and made my way to the depot. The cars for Philadelphia were leaving within the hour.

*   *   *

I ARRIVED in the Quaker city in the evening, when it appeared especially contained and sedate. As the cradle of American inde-pendence, it had held its sway for a long time, but by now it was outshone by New York. I checked into the American Hotel, near Independence Hall. The place was large enough to make me feel as inconspicuous as possible. Now for the first time I saw clearly the benefits of my sojourn in Richmond—aside from the pleasure part—in making Reynolds-Tyler, as I now thought of him, feel safe and undetected.

The city directory showed his office to be at Front and Walnut streets, and his home on Pine near Fourth, about half a mile away. On his way to work he would proceed east and north. My map showed a church on Pine near Sixth, which seemed a suitable spot for me. Early Monday morning I set out toward the river. I found an abandoned warehouse which I adopted for my dressing room. Wearing my beggar's rags, I shuffled back toward the residential streets. Standing before the church, I had a distant but adequate view of the row of small, red-brick Federal houses, one of which was Tyler's. The paucity of vehicles and passersby was a disadvantage; on the other hand, my view remained relatively unblocked. Promptly at eight forty-five a man stepped out of the house with the black shutters and I recognized Tyler. He looked up at the sky, drew his cloak about him, and started to walk east—in the same imperious, strutting way I had seen him walk in Baltimore. At every few steps he struck the pavement with his gold-headed cane. At Fourth Street he turned north. I did not need to follow him, for I knew where he was going. I continued watching his house.

At nine-thirty a woman came out, apparently through the back door. She was dressed plainly, had white hair, and was carrying a basket. She, too, was heading east but made no turn. Eventually she disappeared from view, in the direction of the markets near the wharves. At five after eleven she returned, her basket full.

As I watched through the next several cold, fatiguing hours, sometimes sitting down on the church steps, sometimes shuffling back and forth, often rubbing my hands, my feet, my body under my ragged cloak, I constructed a working hypothesis about Tyler and his household. To all previous appearances, he was a bachelor, living alone. I did not see him living with a sick mother, for example. If he did have a sick mother, she probably lived in her own house with her own servants. I estimated Tyler's servants to be two in number, the cook I had seen and a man. He did not come home for lunch, which did not surprise me. I saw him immersed in his legal editing—probably ordering up food at noontime to have at his desk. I imagined he would put his pen down at a certain hour, say five—which in fact he did, for he appeared at the corner of Pine and Fourth precisely at five-fourteen. I expected him to adhere to such a schedule undeviatingly. I knew enough about him—the abyss within him—to expect him to hold himself together by a series of rigidities: his work schedule, the way he walked, the way he dressed. Puncture one and the whole creature might deflate. I expected him to demand that his household be run the same way; I expected his cook to shop between nine-thirty and eleven every day.

But I had to test my hypothesis before I ventured to enter his house, and I repeated my vigil the next day. A cold rain was coming down and I stood flattened against a side portal of the church as much as I could. Precisely at eight forty-five Tyler appeared on his front step. Before he reached Fourth Street, a hack came, he hailed it, and got in. At nine-thirty his cook came out with her basket, now wrapped in a large gray shawl. At eleven-ten she returned with her basket full. By five the rain had let up, and at five-fourteen Tyler appeared at the corner of Pine and Fourth, on foot.

I had meanwhile been trying to decide on the best method of gaining entry into that house. For enter it I must—in order to establish the final proof that Reynolds and Tyler were one and the same. I expected to find something—perhaps some of my belongings the thugs had taken from me, or the missing miniature—if he had ever removed it from Edgar's pocket—or the pistol from which the bullet in my possession had been fired. I did not care what kind of evidence I found, as long as it was evidence.

But how to get in? I had been pondering this question for two days. As I was about to leave my vigil, a sudden gust of east wind darkened the smoke coming from the chimney of one of the houses, then the smoke turned light again. It gave me an idea.

After changing back into my normal clothes, I took my way to the Chestnut Street Theater and combed the surrounding streets until I found a shop that rented theatrical costumes. I told the man behind the counter I was interested in a fireman's outfit—projecting a bit of an actor's flamboyance. He brought out a helmet, a slicker, and heavy boots. The slicker fitted over my own clothes, buckling up to the throat. I would have to carry only my hat and shoes in my canvas bag.

The next morning, after Tyler's cook left the house with her basket, I walked up to the front entrance, weighed down by my costume, and rang.

The servant who answered was lean and surly, his pale eyes peering out from caverns on either side of his long nose unpleasantly. "Anything wrong?" he asked.

"I hope not," I said cheerfully. Elaborate explanations were not needed; the authority of my assumed vocation should suffice. "Your master may need his chimney swept—there's black smoke coming from it. I can't tell until I check your fireplaces. May I come in?"

He declined to say yes; I stepped in anyway, a nervous thrill going through me. Was there anyone else in the house? I entered the drawing room, taking it in in one glance as formal and uncomfortable; the Queen Anne sofa and chairs with their minimal cushioning and spindly legs invited stiffness. There were fewer pieces of furniture or rugs or paintings than I had seen in other drawing rooms. Restraint to the point of lifelessness. The fireplace was cold; I grabbed a poker, squatted down and probed the flue.

"Any fire going anywhere in the house?"

"No, there ain't."

I tapped the wall over the mantel, then stepped into the adjacent library, taking a careful look around. Books and little else—a writing table with a high-backed, hard-looking chair. I tapped the wall, then went out to the hall and tapped some more, muttering, "Here's where they branch out. Let's see what's upstairs." I trudged up, the man behind me. Thank God no one else was in the house. Master bedroom. A smaller one. Both were like cells in a monastery, with their narrow beds and carved wooden headboards coming to a Gothic point. In the larger room, particularly, the sparseness of furnishing was oppressive. It would not have surprised me to see a scourge. I thought it logical that the occupant of this room would lock his enemy in a dark, rat-infested dungeon.

Would he keep anything I was looking for up here? The library was still my best bet. I examined the fireplaces.

"I want you to build a small fire in the master bedroom and I'll see what effect it has downstairs. Got kindling and paper and matches up here?"

"I have 'em."

"Then I want you to build a small fire in the other room." I thought he needed a little more convincing. "We're examining all the suspicious chimneys in the area since the fire."

"What fire?"

"Don't you know about the fire last week on Spruce Street? There're a lot of fine old houses in this section, and a fire in one can burn down a whole row." Without waiting for his reaction, I wended my heavy way downstairs.

I stepped into the library, making a quick survey of drawers and cabinets. The writing table had a wide, shallow drawer in the middle and a deeper one at each side. All were locked. I pulled out my skeleton keys; a small one fitted. Stationery, writing materials, letters. In the drawer on the right side, a leather case containing one pistol. Its pair must be with him. I studied it: .32 caliber, silverplated, made by Collier; I estimated the year 1790. I looked for bullets. Not in the case. In the depth of the drawer, a box of them. I took one.

The letters might contain evidence, but there was no time to go through them. The drawers yielded nothing else. My possessions were probably in a safe in Tyler's office; the miniature of Edgar's mother also. Or it might be in some obscure nook somewhere, or lost, or discarded. Why should Tyler have kept it, once he'd made Edgar's last days the more miserable by taking it from him?

I looked around baffled, not failing to note that among the books behind glass there were no law books. He apparently kept them in his office. Here he probably wrote his unsigned pieces. There were rows of leather-bound magazines on the shelves—and the expected Greek, Latin, and more modern classics. Among them, Edgar's *Tales of the Grotesque and Arabesque* in two volumes! He did not know Poe? With what hatred and malice he must have perused them! But I still had no hard evidence. The bullet, even if it matched mine, was not decisive. And now there came footsteps on the stairs. I went out to stop the man.

"The smoke comes down a little, but it's not bad. Now light a fire in the other bedroom."

He went up again and I dashed back to the library on the brink of despair. I tried my skeleton keys feverishly on the cabinets under the books. Finally I got them open one by one. Old law books crumbling with age, law journals, books with their covers off, magazines, newspapers. The last cabinet contained a stack of books. I pulled out the top one with a rush of excitement as I recognized the purple linen cover. I pulled out the next one, and the next— almost crying "Eureka!" They were a dozen or more brand-new, uncut author's copies of *Reflections*.

I had the proof I needed. I took a copy for evidence and dropped it in my canvas bag. I locked the cabinet and stood up—just as I heard the front door open and shut. I stepped out, and found myself face-to-face with the stiff, gray-clad, stony figure of Tyler. A policeman with a drooping moustache stood beside him, towering over him.

My heart leapt to my throat as it flashed through my mind that the villain must have recognized me on the street, perhaps the very first time I stood vigil, and not seeing me this morning knew this was the day.

"Do my eyes deceive me?" He tried to be sardonic but his voice jumped. "Has the great Dupin joined our Fire Brigade?" He tried to maintain his superior smirk, but it collapsed and his pinched face looked pale. I realized how worried he was. "Constable, arrest this man!" he commanded in a trembling voice. "For trespassing—and possibly worse."

I shot back: "Arrest this man for murder, kidnapping, and attempted murder!"

Tyler's laugh was forced, nervous, hysterical. "Perhaps instead of prison you should take him to the insane asylum." He marched into the library.

The moustachioed policeman was his ally, not mine. He came at me with handcuffs.

"No need for those. I'll come along peacefully."

"I want him in irons!" Tyler shouted from the door of the library, his face twitching. The policeman obliged.

If I had managed to keep my composure thus far, my stomach was now churning. No one had ever put handcuffs on me, although I had helped to put them on many. I looked at my crossed wrists with their brutal bracelets in dismay. The policeman patted me down, took my gun, my skeleton keys, but missed the bullet nestling in my vest pocket. I gave a secret sigh of relief. He snatched open my canvas bag and pulled out my silk hat and patent-leather shoes.

"They're my own," I said.

He pulled out *Reflections*.

Tyler, emerging from the library, pounced on it. "My property!" He still couldn't charge me with burglary, for my disguise made it clear I had not broken in. Also, it was a long way from nightfall. But he could charge me with larceny, which he did—a more serious crime than trespassing.

The servant who had been hovering on the stairs saw me in handcuffs and came down courageously. "Thank God you're home, master. He might've murdered me."

"There's only one murderer among us, my man," I retorted.

It was lost on him. "He made me light fires upstairs—said he wanted to see how the flues worked—said there been a fire on Spruce Street—" He gave vent to an involuntary grin and the policeman met his eyes with half-concealed amusement. Perhaps they thought I'd been clever.

Only Tyler remained glum and nervous and pale. For he had to know that our war, now in the open, was by no means over.

*   *   *

AT THE POLICE STATION I was booked and locked in a cell, with my humiliating handcuffs removed. It was a better place than Tyler's dungeon. I was given permission to take off my slicker, put on my own shoes, and place my recently purchased silk hat next to me on the bench. Being seen as a gentleman, I was immediately better treated. A piece of meatloaf between two slices of bread and a cup of coffee were brought in, and even a cheap cigar. A police clerk asked me whether I had a lawyer.

An hour or so later, my cell door was unlocked, letting in a young man with an intense face and piercing eyes who introduced himself as Roger Baird, assigned to defend me. My name sounded familiar to him. He had read Poe and thus knew about me. He was enthusiastic to be of service to me. He considered it an honor. He knew that my present mishap was an occupational hazard in my pursuit of a serious investigation.

I explained briefly that I had evidence that Poe had been poisoned.

"I do recall the poet's strange death," he said. "Now this Harold Tyler, whose name I read on the complaint—he surely isn't the legal scholar?"

"The very same. I believe he killed Poe. He has made several attempts to kill me."

"Good God! I find the idea hard to digest."

"I entered his house for the sole purpose of getting evidence."

"I wish you had used some other disguise. One count of the complaint states that you impersonated a municipal employee, which is illegal. This count is not charged by Tyler but by the State. Do they have your costume out there?"

"I believe so."

He left the cell, then returned, his compressed lips drawn in what looked like a smile. "Our firemen's helmet carries an emblem saying 'Philadelphia Fire Brigade.' The one you wore has none. It gives me grounds to argue against the charge of impersonation. By the way, did you get your evidence?"

"Yes—although I had to surrender part of it." I gave a brief account of *Reflections* and its importance.

"The case will have to be initiated in Baltimore, where the crime was committed."

"I know the district attorney there."

"You know Mr. Lee? Personally?"

"Yes. He was a friend of Poe. He attended his funeral."

"Then there should be no difficulty—once this unpleasant business is over."

"You don't mean a prison term?" My stomach began to churn again.

"No, I mean your arraignment. We will plead *nolo contendere*. If you plead not guilty, the magistrate has to order a trial. He may still do so, but in that case he'll probably set bail, which can be arranged. But I shall move for a dismissal. If Tyler appears to press charges I intend to question him closely about the authorship of the said book; why, for example, he has a dozen brand-new author's copies in his cabinet."

But Tyler never showed—obviously afraid of such questioning. We waited in the antechamber of the magistrate's courtroom, the clerk assuring us that the plaintiff had been informed that the hearing was scheduled for four P.M. It was now four-fifteen, and the magistrate demanded that we appear before him.

He was a round, venerable man in a black robe, his bald pink head fringed with white. He read the complaint aloud and asked me directly how I pleaded.

"*Nolo contendere*, Your Honor."

Baird moved that the count of impersonation be struck and offered the helmet as Exhibit One.

"Motion granted."

He seemed like a kind old man and I breathed more freely.

Baird explained my purpose in taking the book. He said I was a famous detective from Paris and offered one of Superintendent Gaston's letters of introduction as Exhibit Two.

"I know of Poe," the magistrate interjected. "Proceed."

Baird made a point of Tyler's failure to attend the hearing—undoubtedly wary of incriminating himself.

"That is conjecture, Counsel. He may have broken a leg. Proceed."

O God, he'll order a trial weeks from now and detain me. He won't even set bail.

Baird made a motion for dismissal.

"Denied."

I wiped my forehead, my handkerchief trembling in my hand.

"The purpose for which you took another's property is immaterial," the magistrate said, looking at me over his spectacles. "Its monetary value is also immaterial. The charge of larceny stands." He removed his spectacles and slipped into human language. "You can't worm your way into people's houses and take things—of whatever value, for whatever purpose." He reverted to legalese: "However, insofar as there are mitigating circumstances, namely the purpose for which the plaintiff's property was removed, as well as its material value; and further, insofar as I am authorized to set a fine at this time, I so do, for the sum of fifty dollars, payable within three days of the present hearing. Case dismissed."

I could have kissed his pink head.

21

GRISWOLD LIVED ON SPRUCE STREET, a few blocks from Tyler, in the same affluent residential district. I wanted to see him before going to Baltimore, although I expected him to be guarded about his friend. I doubted that he had any idea that Tyler had killed Poe, but I thought it highly likely that he knew Tyler to be the author of *Reflections*. This link in my case was the weakest. The two identical bullets in my possession could be taken as an indication, but not proof, that they were both from, or for, Tyler's pistols. And the dozen copies of *Reflections* were probably no longer in his cabinet; nor my possessions in his office safe or wherever he kept them; nor the miniature, if he had it, within reach. A police search would yield nothing; and I doubted that my testimony alone that I had seen those books would be enough to convince the court and the jury. I needed a witness.

The morning was cold, raw, and gloomy, with heavy snow clouds hanging in the sky; there were few people on the street, which made me doubly cautious, with my hand on my pistol in my pocket as I walked down streets that constituted Tyler territory.

Griswold's house was another example of red-brick Federal, like Tyler's, but once I stepped inside the similarity ceased. The small sitting room where I waited while the maid took up my card offered a view of the lavishly ornate drawing room with its heavily carved furniture, tiers of paintings in thick gold frames, Oriental rugs, heavy, fringed coverlets, porcelain bric-a-brac.

Mrs. Griswold came down and I rose. She was dressed in a gold-toned gown—a striking woman with white hair, coal-black eyes, and fleshy lips. Her pale face was creased; she seemed to be in her fifties, at least ten or twelve years older than her husband.

She said rather solemnly, "My husband is not here, Mr. Dupin."

"When do you expect him back?"

"I don't."

I sympathized with her, married to such a flitter.

"He is staying at the Cadwallader House. It's a few blocks west on Locust, before you come to Rittenhouse Square."

I thanked her and left.

The place was a residential hotel. I gave the clerk my card to be sent up, but he said Mr. Griswold was having breakfast in the dining room, and I sat down in the parlor with its comfortable chairs, mirrors, hangings, and gaslights behind yellow shades.

Soon he came out, his step light, his handsome face with its pointed beard and nose drawn in an agreeable expression. But when he saw me, surprise arrested him.

"Mr. Dupin!"

We shook hands. "I just arrived from Baltimore. Where can we talk?"

"I suggest my suite." He led the way to the carpeted stairway. "How did you learn of my whereabouts?"

"I called at your Spruce Street address and spoke to your wife."

"I'm surprised she gave you the time of day. Man to man—" He lowered his voice. "That woman is the bane of my life. I was tricked into marrying her by her two aunts—two miserable witches. Everything between us has been most unsatisfactory. She has an anatomical malformation that prevents her from being a wife—and I'm of course suing for divorce. When I think of my darling Caroline—God rest her soul—"

Whom he had run from, then tried to resurrect in the most insane fashion. I didn't know what he meant by anatomical malformation. I did not trust him. I had not forgiven him for his obituary of Edgar, but it was best not to whip myself into resentment. I needed to proceed calmly and diplomatically.

His suite consisted of a study and a small bedchamber. The study was so cluttered with books and papers that he had to clear two chairs before we could sit down. We lit cigars.

"I have not forgotten my promise to send you material about Poe," I began, "but the purpose of my present visit is somewhat different. I'd like to talk to you about Harold Tyler."

"About Harold Tyler?"

"I know a great deal about him, as you do. I know he writes— that in fact he is compelled to write but keeps his writing a deep secret. I know he is the author of *Reflections,* which came out in

1836. I know the contents of that book. You recall I asked you about it in New York and you pretended only the vaguest memory of it—understandably you were trying to protect your friend's secret. But now that I know Tyler to be the author, you need not pretend any longer. We both know of Tyler's delusion that Poe stole his tales from him, that Poe stole his fame, that Poe fed on his literary corpse. We both know how consummately he hated Poe. But what you don't know, Griswold, and I'm here to tell you, is that Poe did not die a natural death, but was murdered, and his murderer is none other than Harold Tyler."

The next moment I wished I had been more circumspect, for Griswold gave a half-choked cry, his body grew stiff and he began to jerk convulsively, his head turning down to one shoulder. His face grew pale, then livid, his dilated eyes rolled, his mouth opened, foaming at the corners.

I had no time to be horrified. I leaped up and stuffed my handkerchief into his mouth to prevent his teeth from lacerating his tongue, loosened his collar, and unbuttoned his shirt and his trousers at the waist. I had seen epileptic fits before and knew there was little else one could do. Fortunately Griswold had been sitting so that his sudden loss of consciousness didn't make him fall, which accounts for most injuries during seizures, as the loss of bowel and bladder control accounts for most of the unpleasantness.

In less than three minutes consciousness returned. His body loosened up, and as I took the handkerchief from his mouth he looked about him with a bewildered expression. He tried to form words; in a little while he was able to ask, "What happened?"

"You had a seizure. Is there anything I can do for you?"

"I—want—to clean—" His eyes closed and he fell into a deep sleep.

It was best not to move him. I put a stool under his feet and a pillow under his head, and covered him with a blanket. His face was regaining its normal color. His bearded lips were slightly open, a snore breaking from them, as his chest moved up and down. The Reverend Rufus W. Griswold. I had little love for the man, but his sin against Edgar paled in comparison to Tyler's.

I went to open the window a crack, then sat down. After such an attack patients usually sleep for two or three hours, and I thought I'd sit with him for a while, then maybe go out and come back. But the exhaustion of the last few days made my own eyes close.

I woke to a commotion. Griswold was marching up and down, skirting pieces of furniture, bumping into others, emitting a pleasant fragrance of cologne, which told me he had cleaned himself. Hyperactivity is also a frequent consequence of an epileptic fit—after a period of restorative sleep.

"I must know everything, Dupin. I know I had a seizure—it wasn't the first time. Thank you for your help, you've been most kind." His nervous pacing was slowing; finally he threw himself down in a chair. There was a bottle of brandy on a table within reach and he poured two glasses with a steady enough hand. He shook his head. "Did I dream all this horror?"

"I fear not."

"He is mad, I tell you. There have been indications of his madness all along. Like his extreme secretiveness . . ." He dropped his voice. "Even though you know about his writing, I find it hard to talk about it without feeling I'm betraying him. I sometimes arrange publications for him in the magazines. 'The authorship must be kept a profound secret,' he keeps warning me. Once an editor recognized some phrases from one of his law books and Tyler flew into a passion—at me, although I had nothing to do with it. Later he apologized, begging me to invent another author who had apparently copied some phrases from his legal comments." Griswold dropped his voice and stared ahead of him. "As a writer he can be brilliant—intellectually—but he cannot move the heart. He cannot evoke any feeling, whether sympathy or horror or fear. I tried to suggest to him that his pieces in 'Tales from Bedlam' were skeletal, mere ideas, even if he prefaced each by 'Once upon a time'; that Poe had made them into real tales, giving them an enduring quality. Are you surprised, Dupin? Do you think I would've undertaken to edit Poe's works if I didn't believe in his genius? Tyler is a genius in his own way. His legal editions are known to all lawyers and he has studied everything. All the arts and sciences—chemistry, medicine—"

"Chemistry doesn't surprise me."

"He wanted to become a chemist at one time."

"It explains his expert use of arsenic."

"Arsenic? Was that it?"

I told him about our disinterment.

He poured more brandy. "I thought after my seizure I should be able to cope better with what you told me, but I can't."

It had begun to snow and the room grew dark enough to light a taper, which with the fire in the grate and the clutter of books and papers reminded me of those nights in Paris that Edgar and I would spend together talking or working or just sitting lost in dreams. Our outrage and bewilderment over Edgar's murder had brought Griswold and me closer than I would have thought possible.

"Oh, that hate." He shook his head with dismay. "It infused everything—Poe's origins, his poverty, his outcast state, his drinking, his loves. He could never find one kind or even fair word for 'that cheap, thieving scribbler,' as he called him. He told me once he had seen Poe close enough to notice the mending in his trousers. 'The scoundrel posing like a gentleman' was his scornful comment."

"He appropriately dressed him in rags before killing him."

"Yes. And yet when I heard about that, or Poe's uttering the name Reynolds on his deathbed, I couldn't, perhaps I just didn't dare, make the connection. I need not keep it from you any longer that my obituary of Poe, which caused such a furor, was written partly by Tyler—the parts that offended people the most. I still accept responsibility for the whole. I had my quarrels with Poe, and when Tyler handed me that draft I deleted only the worst parts—as I added some biographical matter. Also, I did see certain advantages in making Poe into a dark legend. But good God, when I think of that day! I still lived with Charlotte and I was in my study buried under a dozen tasks when Tyler walked in and told me Poe was dead. There was a triumphant smile on his face. I said that as his literary executor I had to write a sizable obituary, and how was I going to do it with all these deadlines hanging over me? He said he'd write one. He sat down with Bulwer's *Caxtons* and in half an hour handed me a draft, saying, 'Do what you want with it.' To think that I received the news of Poe's death—and a draft of an obituary—from his— I can't utter the word, Dupin. Is Tyler really guilty of a crime that cries to heaven?"

I told him about Tyler's attempts on my life, his hiring thugs to imprison me. "By the way, the night I met you and Tyler at Colonel Craig's home, you said you had just arrived in Baltimore that day. That wasn't true, was it?"

"I did arrive that day. But Tyler had come three days before. He insisted no one must know, he even changed hotels. He said an editor had him followed to learn his identity."

"Those were the nights he shot at me."

"I'm shocked and appalled. I'm a sinner—my life is full of error and madness—but I'm a man of God still, and such evil frightens and horrifies me. That someone I'd been close to for fifteen years—no, he is mad, mad, mad. I find no other explanation—"

I rose.

"Before you go—" Griswold handed me a letter consisting of five or six folded sheets. "Read it, but I want it back."

*   *   *

THE LETTER WAS FROM TYLER, written to Griswold three weeks before Edgar's death. My train was not leaving until four, and I sat in my room near the window, with snow drifting down outside, reading it with total absorption.

15th Sept. 1849

Dear Griswold:

Here are further thoughts on the subject we were discussing recently. Genius is highly visible to its possessor. It has been highly visible to me from early youth on. I have but to look into myself to see it shining in the depths like the sun.

There have been two profound influences on my development. First, my mother, who has always scorned sentiment. In my childhood she spoke to me of Napoleon, Shakespeare, and Plato, as glories in the desert we call mankind: "I hope someday you will be like them, not a mere grain in the desert." Secondly, an unhappy love affair when I was eighteen. In my wretched state I wanted to kill the girl, my rival, and myself, then only myself. But as I stood on the bank of the Wissahickon I lowered my pistol. "I will defy these pangs," I told myself, gnashing my teeth with rage. "I will combat my calamity and strangle the life of suffering within me." From that moment I banished feeling, banished the heart. I embraced the mind with a firmer grasp.

Reflections is the fruit of my early experience. It has been painful to see it sink into obscurity, while so much dross wins approbation. The world is clearly not ready for my book. It is the work of the head, not the heart, hence centuries ahead of its time.

The heart is in the ascendance now. Someday literature and all the arts will be expressible in a formula. Hence my "Tales from Bedlam." There is precedent for it. Jesus spoke in parables. Even earlier, stories in the Old Testament are told in a verse or two. The future will return to the Golden Age, for the world is cyclical.

Poe stole gems from me and crushed them into powder and mixed them with ninety-nine percent sand from the desert whereof he is.

His bare-faced, scandalous thieving did not stop there. Just two years ago he stole from me with total shamelessness. In an issue of the *Southern Literary Messenger*—one I missed at the time and came across only recently—an installment of his "Marginalia" is mostly copied from "Jottings" in my *Reflections*. Word for word, Griswold! When I read those items one after the other—mine, mine, and yet again mine!—I nearly fell down in a swoon. Will I ever have peace from that devil? I wake up in the night and feel him in the room, hear his footsteps, his whispering. He enters my dreams and I wake up with a cry.

He has aggravated a nervous malady that has been affecting me for some time—a restlessness that makes me unable to sit still, that makes me roam the streets wildly, alternating with an oppression of spirit that confines me in a state of rigid immobility for hours. If I reach the limit in either state—suffer brain fever or quietly expire, my blood will be on his hands.

I am deeply disappointed in you for agreeing to act as his literary executor. Rufus! Rufus! You live too much for the world. Such a shabby enterprise to involve yourself in. Do you hope to ride with him into glory? You might find yourself riding with him into hell.

Does he taunt me knowing who I am? Impossible. No one knows who I am. No one must know, until the world is ready for me.

One attribute of the devil is as tempter. Do you know how Poe steals into my dreams, my consciousness, to tempt me? He kindles self-doubt. Am I wrong to put such a high value on my own work? Is it worthless? Have I failed? Am I fulfilling the gray destiny the gods intended for me by editing dull law books? Is my idea of the sun burning in me, destining me for higher achievement, but an empty dream? Maybe somewhere during my development I took the wrong road. Maybe my insatiable thirst for knowledge is that wrong road. Napoleon was a doer, Shakespeare a maker, Plato a formulator of wisdom. Knowledge was secondary to them, a means to their loftier ends. Was there heart in their work? Heart? I despise the heart. It is but Poe the tempter whispering, urging me to despair.

I refuse to despair. My legal editing is a necessary discipline; between it and my other writing there is a mysterious connection I myself cannot fathom. But they are working together to herald forth some monumental work that will surpass even *Reflections.* Then I will be free to enter society again, from which, with your single exception, I have isolated myself. Then I will need to hide my name no longer.

Oh to shine like the sun! To hear the world hail my name as it bows down to my genius! To see Poe grovel in the dust with my foot upon his neck! This yearning is with me day and night, beneath everything I do, or don't do, whether I work, eat, or sleep, or am driven by madness or lie in a stupor, a wonder and a torment.

If Elijah came down from the heavens in a fiery chariot and told me I had taken the wrong road irrevocably, that my genius was a false coin, that there was no hope on earth for me, I would cut my throat the way I once cut a colt's that had crossed me one too many times.

You may receive this letter, my dear friend, or I may not send it.

Yrs. truly,
Harold Tyler

All that I had perceived about Tyler was here confirmed and raised to the nth power. The superstitious dimension of his hate was staggering. Poe the tempter whispering in the night. *Mon Dieu!* And the streak of violence. Wanting to kill his beloved, his rival, himself at eighteen; sometime later brutally killing an innocent colt. Self-aggrandizement with a loss of perspective, or self-criticism, bordering on madness. An uncontrollable nervous ailment, from hyperactivity to lethargy, from the heights to the depths, indeed. Mad, as Griswold said. At best, near-mad.

* * *

I NOW HAD THE WITNESS, the proof—the best I could have hoped for, yet as I sat in the small, cramped, not too well-heated railway car, with the engine puffing ahead and the snowy, darkening scenery falling behind, I was nervous and apprehensive. I kept Zaccheus Lee's promise before me: "Bring me a good suspect and I'll prosecute." But Tyler's failure to appear at my hearing yesterday was not a good sign. What if he had taken our first open confrontation as a call to disappear? And now I was chugging along not even toward him but away from him.

I arrived in Baltimore after ten. My old room at Miller's was vacant and I took it. In the morning I went to the Law Buildings.

Mr. Lee was affable, but less the politician this time than the attorney. "Well, Mr. Dupin, what have you found?"

"I must begin by making a confession."

He listened to my account of the disinterment, his prematurely creased face making him look grave. But he wasn't about to prosecute that crime. "I had an idea the last time I spoke to you that you must have found something."

I showed him the affidavit, asking for his assurance that Dr. Moran would not get in trouble.

"Granted."

Throughout my account he was interested solely in evidence and witnesses; at times I felt I was being cross-examined. "Does the shopkeeper have a record of his sales? Can you find the coachman again?"

He agreed that the series of attacks against me pointed to Edgar's murderer. He thought the seizure and imprisonment of my person was the most heinous among them. "Still, although you have witnesses to these attacks, the perpetrator remains shadowy."

"I have a pair of matching bullets, I'll come to them presently." I showed him *Reflections,* pointing to the relevant passages.

He studied them. "I see Edgar found some of his plots here. Still, is this a viable motive for murder?"

"Before this book was published," I said, "a portion of it appeared in the *Gentleman's Magazine* under the name, H. Reynolds. Edgar, as you perhaps know, uttered the name Reynolds on his deathbed. There are several witnesses."

Lee's drooping eyes opened with interest. "Go on."

"The identity of Reynolds will surprise you. He is Harold Tyler, lawyer and legal scholar, of Philadelphia."

"What?" he exclaimed. "You must be joking. Look." He stepped to his shelves of law books and handed me one: *Smith's Leading Cases Adopted for American Use,* Edited by Harold Tyler. He showed me another, edited by Harold Tyler and Horace B. Wallace. "Are you sure you mean this Harold Tyler?"

"Beyond the shadow of a doubt. Who is Horace B. Wallace?"

"A young legal scholar. Also of Philadelphia, I believe."

I made a note of the name, then showed Lee the two bullets. He examined them under a magnifying lens. "I'm no expert, but they seem close. Are they a touch heavier than most thirty-twos?"

"Yes. They're both from a pair of Collier pistols of about 1790." When I told him how I obtained the unspent one, he gave a laugh.

"You're the old Dupin, who entered the Minister D—'s house with a copy of the purloined letter and stole back the original!"

"Unfortunately it went less smoothly this time." I told him about my arrest.

"What did you find besides the bullet?"

"A dozen or so brand-new, uncut author's copies of *Reflections*. I took one but had to surrender it. By the way, would my testimony be admissible under the circumstances?"

"Yes. The Fourth Amendment concerning unwarranted entry does not apply to private persons. But Tyler could claim no such books were in his cabinet; or that they were the work of a friend who died and left them to him."

"And his lawyer could claim the spent bullet came from another early Collier pistol of the same model."

"Exactly."

"Fortunately I have a witness. Rufus Wilmot Griswold."

"Griswold?"

"He and Tyler are friends. Tyler has confided in Griswold about his authorship of this book—probably the only person he has ever confided in, except me, anonymously, outside my prison door, believing I'd carry his secret to the grave. I think Griswold would be willing to testify. But we may not need his testimony." I handed over Tyler's letter.

Lee settled down to read it and I waited, sometimes rolling the tip of my cigar in the ashtray and stealing a glance at his face, which showed variations of fascination and dismay.

He looked up. "Lots of autobiography. But what a monstrous ego!" He read on. "Ah! He admits authorship of *Reflections*. This is the crux. We'll need Griswold to testify as to the authenticity of this letter. The motive is here: the insane hate leading to the mocking character of the murder. The defense will argue that Poe meant another Reynolds on his deathbed. No matter. With what you can show with witnesses we have a case." His face shone with animation. When he finished the last page, he got up and paced to and fro, stopping before his law books. "Mr. Dupin, if you were a lawyer you would be able to have a fuller appreciation of the absolute brilliance of the comments in these books." His hand swept over four or five volumes. "They are learned, clear, illuminating, supremely rational. To think that the man who wrote them has a soul as diseased as is revealed here—it boggles the mind." He folded the sheets and put them on his desk.

"I promised Griswold I'd return the letter to him."

"Oh, it will be returned. Meanwhile, I'll have the scrivener make a copy—one for you, too, if you wish. Within an hour there will be a warrant issued for Tyler's arrest—and communicated to Philadelphia, together with a request for extradition from the governor's office. That you see is a legislative, not judicial matter. It would help to have a likeness. Did you see any portraits of Tyler in his house?"

"I recall a couple of ancestral ones, that's all."

"Do you know where we might find a likeness?"

"I doubt that any exists. Tyler is not prepossessive; with his ego he'd probably rather not display his features. In addition, he is secretive and antisocial."

"Under your direction, a skillful portraitist should be able to make an acceptable sketch—then make as many copies as we need."

"My greatest fear is he may have disappeared. God knows where. I believe he dreads exposure more than death. He may be sailing to Europe under another name, for all I know."

"We can extradite him from Europe, too." As I rose to leave, he added, "You see, Edgar was my friend. I mourned his death, and what I've learned from you shocks and horrifies me. I want to bring his murderer to justice as much as you do."

*   *   *

AT POLICE HEADQUARTERS, my physical description of Tyler was carefully recorded. Did he have any distinguishing marks such as moles or a facial tic or a scar? I could not recall any. I could only speak of his short stature, for which he tended to compensate by a ramrod-straight walk resulting in a strut, and of his elegant clothes and red hair—covered sometimes to make congruous his favorite disguise of a black beard. Then I met the artist, a tiny lady with gray hair and merry, glancing eyes, by the name of Josephine Bennett. While I spoke of Tyler's squarish face, pinched features, with the red-brown eyes close together, Mrs. Bennett sketched. She showed me a face. I thought the upper lip should be longer. Like this? More like it, yes. Something was amiss—perhaps the chin. I did not recall the chin. After several attempts I recognized it—the lower lip curling over a weak chin. The eyes were perhaps narrower, the cheeks hollower, the forehead slanting more. After an hour Tyler's face emerged from the lady's sketch remarkably well. "Bravo, Mrs. Bennett!" I exclaimed.

I returned to my room at Miller's—with its dimity curtains, oleographs of mountain scenes, blazing Franklin stove, and beautiful memories. My one fervent desire was that Tyler might be quickly apprehended. Then, until called to testify before the grand jury, I would be free to sail to Richmond and be with Elmira for longer than Christmas.

22

But Tyler could not be found. My repeated visits to Mr. Lee's office netted only that disturbing piece of information. I went to make inquiries about transatlantic crossings. No ships had sailed from Philadelphia, Baltimore, or Norfolk for the past week and none would sail for the next two weeks. One had sailed from Boston a week ago, two from New York within the past week. In the forthcoming week, one would sail from New York and one from Boston.

The police search was extended to New York, and, armed with a copy of the warrant and a copy of the police sketch, I took the two-o'clock train to Philadelphia. This time I was at least traveling presumably toward my quarry, not away from him, however slowly. Six hours and twenty-two unendurable stops later we pulled in at the Walnut Street Wharf.

I thought since Tyler's servant and I were no strangers to each other I might be able to get some information from him the police couldn't. A short walk brought me to the house with the black shutters and I gave the bell a few hard turns.

When the man first saw me he gasped, his bony hand going up to his long-nosed face. But he stood his ground on the threshold. "My master ain't home." He tried to shut the door, but I blocked it with my foot.

"Where can I find him?"

"I don't know." His voice was getting surlier.

"The police are looking for him."

"They was here. Ran all over the house."

I was glad to hear that. "Your master is wanted for a crime. Did you know that?"

"I don't want to be mixed up in anything."

"You won't be if you tell the truth. I'm working with the police."

I took out my copy of the warrant and handed it to him. He read it slowly, his thin lips moving. The word "murder" made him suck his breath back with a hiss.

"Your master didn't know when he brought that policeman here and got me arrested that I was in this house on police business. You'd better let me in and tell me all you know."

He pulled open the door hesitantly and I stepped in, closing it behind me. We stood in the hall.

"When did you last see your master?"

"Few days back."

"The day I was arrested?"

"I think so."

"Did he say where he was going?"

"No." He added, "Sir."

"Or when he would be back?"

"No—sir."

"Did he mention going to New York?"

He shook his head.

"Did he carry a valise?"

"I didn't see. I was in the back. He said he was leaving for a while and we should run the house and not worry. He said he left some money with Cook."

"Did you see him pack, or come down those stairs, or go through this door?"

"No—sir."

He was probably telling the truth. Why should Tyler have told him anything the police might get out of him?

"Does your master have any relatives?"

"His mother lives in Burlington, and he has a married sister in town."

"What's her husband's name?"

"Mr. Charles Ryder."

"Do you know his address?"

He shook his head. "It's in the book."

"What book?"

"Where my master keeps addresses. The police took it."

That was intelligent of them, I thought. When I left it was not yet nine; I was in time for another brief visit, to Horace B. Wallace, Tyler's collaborator. He too lived on Pine, a few streets further west. I hailed a cab to save time.

A servant let me into the house; I heard a murmur of voices from an inner room, punctuated by laughter and the clinking of china and glasses. A dinner party was apparently in progress. I sent in my apologies, along with my card, for disturbing Mr. Wallace.

"Which Mr. Wallace, sir? They're two brothers. Mr. John Wallace is the elder and Mr. Horace Wallace the younger."

"Mr. Horace Wallace."

I was shown into the library—the richest private collection of books I had seen in America. I was so absorbed scanning titles among the handsome, leather-bound volumes that I did not hear Wallace come in.

"Mr. Dupin?"

I turned—and started, thinking I stood face-to-face with Tyler. The man was below medium height, with carrot-red hair, a squarish, short-nosed, pinched face, and a strong, athletic body under his well-cut evening clothes. But younger—thirtyish, his expression open, friendly, his eyes sky-blue.

I apologized again for calling on him at an inconvenient time.

"It's perfectly all right, sir. Our guests are intimates, and my brother is tending to them. Won't you have a seat? To what do I owe the honor of your visit?"

When I told him he gasped, stared at me speechless, then repeated slowly, "Tyler—wanted by the police—accused of—killing Poe?" He shook his head. "Yet I am far more distressed than surprised."

"Why is that?"

"When we don't know a person, how can we be surprised by anything he does? For a year, while we worked on White and Tudor's *Leading Cases in Equity,* I saw Mr. Tyler for several hours a day at his office, but at the end of that time I knew him as little as I'd known him at our first meeting. I have never met anyone so guarded in all my life."

I wondered whether Wallace was similarly guarded, hiding not behind a wall of ice like Tyler but behind his cordiality and effusiveness. I brooded over his physical resemblance to Tyler: did it imply an inner affinity? Edgar and I had thought of ourselves as soul mates. Did he and Tyler? Even if Tyler had revealed nothing of himself? In the first place, was that true? Not that I suspected

Wallace had any part of the crime; but did he know where Tyler was, and if so, would I be able to get it from him?

"Did you know that Tyler wrote other things besides legal comments, under various pseudonyms?"

"No."

"Do you know his book, *Reflections*, published thirteen years ago?"

"This is the first I hear of it."

"How many law books did you and Tyler collaborate on, Mr. Wallace?"

"Only one. It was an intellectually rewarding experience—Tyler has a brilliant legal mind and I learned a great deal from him. But one such undertaking was enough for me. I became interested in other things—apart from my law practice. Chiefly philosophy." He switched to French, which he spoke fluently. "I'm a reader of your countryman—your namesake in fact—Auguste Comte. I was in Paris last year and met Monsieur Comte personally, and we correspond. I'm working on an essay to get his positivist doctrine better known in America."

"I share your interest in Comte. But to return to Tyler, do you have any idea of his present whereabouts?"

"I fear not, Monsieur Dupin. The last time I saw Tyler was about three years ago. I know his Philadelphia address, and I know his mother lives in Burlington, and his married sister in town. That's all I know."

I thanked him, he walked with me to the door, and I went on my way.

I thought I believed him, yet I continued to be haunted by that strong resemblance. I kept thinking crazily—sort of reliving "The Purloined Letter"—that I had just seen Tyler hiding from me right before my eyes.

I went on to the Cadwallader House. Griswold was out, so I sat down in the parlor with its soft seats and yellow lamps and waited.

He came in at eleven, in evening clothes, his step jaunty, his eyes bright. He seemed glad to see me, or perhaps merely relieved.

"I have something to show you" were his greeting words.

We went up to his cluttered suite and he handed me a thin letter. It was mailed from New York two days ago. I unfolded it.

Dear Griswold:

Poe lives and is hiding, and I know where. There I must go and bring him to justice before my enemies kill me. If I don't return, publish my best under my own name, build my fame.

Tyler

Griswold stood at my chair, waiting for my reaction. I met his narrow, greenish eyes.

"Has he utterly lost his mind?" Griswold said.

I glanced at the note again. "Shall we say he loses it when he needs to. I don't think he can face being a fugitive from the law. He has to be on a mission. Bringing me to justice would not be the same, for I am here and he must go off somewhere—I suspect to Paris. He knows Edgar lived there with me; in fact, he knows my address, since Edgar had put it in one of his tales for greater realism. Paris is the perfect locale for mixing up the two of us."

"Method in his madness."

"I wonder if he ever mixed us up before—perhaps during those tense moments whenever he tried to kill me. Once outside my prison door, he referred to Poe as my double." I scanned the note. "This confirms my belief that he has sailed, or is about to, in which case we might be able to stop him. The police have already issued a warrant for his arrest."

"Brandy?"

"Yes, thank you. By the way, Zaccheus Lee, the district attorney in Baltimore, considers his letter to you important evidence and wants to keep it for a while. I hope you understand I was obliged to show it to him."

"I didn't think you wouldn't."

"Here is a copy meanwhile." I took out the two Lee had had prepared and handed him one. Then I copied Tyler's present note into my notebook. I studied my list of sailings. "He can't be on a ship that sailed before he mailed you this note. I suspect he is either on the *Britannia,* which sailed from New York two days ago; or on the *Cambria,* which sailed from Boston today; or will be on the *Arcadia* when it sails from New York the day after tomorrow. In that case, he is still in New York. What are the pseudonyms he writes under?"

"Reynolds is his favorite."

"I know Reynolds. Any others?"

"There is also T. Meredith, which he used most recently. Also T. Lydgate and H. Perley. I can't think of any others."

I was writing them down. "Most of them have a *y* and three other letters of his own name, and of course one of his initials. He favors trochees. 'Meredith' is an exception."

"He once said he must retain some elements of his real name for his own satisfaction, but a perfect anagram would be too revealing. Maybe with 'Meredith' he was trying to run from himself."

"Interesting idea, Griswold. Can you think of any others?"

He shook his head. "If I do I'll let you know."

*   *   *

EARLY NEXT MORNING I took the cars to New York—an eight-hour trip including the ferry crossing from Perth Amboy. I went to Police Headquarters first, supplying them with other alias possibilities. I was told that a search was already on at likely hotels with Tyler's picture and physical description. I went on to lower Broadway, to the Cunard Lines, and asked if I might examine lists of passengers who had sailed on the *Britannia* three days ago and on the *Cambria* yesterday. Ship's lists were not private; my own arrival in Baltimore had been known—to Tyler, in fact. But when I failed to recognize any name, I took out my copy of the warrant and Tyler's picture. The clerk shook his head. There were of course various clerks on duty at various times; if I came back tomorrow they might be able to help me.

It was almost six, and I hurried on to the U.S. Mail Service, on Wall Street. Their ship, the *Arcadia*, would sail tomorrow. I got in just before they closed, but met with no better luck.

I studied my copy of Tyler's note. It said nothing specific about sailing to Europe, but it newly convinced me of the validity of my analysis.

At Police Headquarters, a report had just come in. Some fifteen hotels had been canvassed: over the past week no one had registered by the name of Tyler or Reynolds; most of the investigators had not had a chance of course to try the additional aliases I had supplied. In any case, no clerk had recognized the picture or remembered anyone matching the given description. Yet Tyler had checked in somewhere, three or four or five days ago. There were some twenty-five more hotels in New York, in addition to a number of boardinghouses, and I undertook to go to some of them myself.

When late that night I checked back at Police Headquarters, a sergeant told me that the clerk at the Bond Street House seemed to recognize the sketch and the description as those of one H. Wither, who had registered five days ago and stayed two nights.

H. Wither—T. Meredith. Five letters the same, initial right, back to the trochee. I tried to remember whether I had seen the name on any of the ship's lists.

I rode back to my own hotel, the City, in a state of total exhaustion, my hands and feet and ears frozen. Yet I was too excited to sleep more than an hour or two intermittently. In the morning I rushed back to Cunard. I took the list of the *Britannia* passengers from the clerk with a trembling hand. Yes, among the *W*'s at the end: H. Wither! The clerk was not the same one I had seen last evening. I asked him whether he recalled anything about Mr. Wither.

"I think he was one of the last passengers we sold a ticket to. About four or five days ago. Yes, I remember now."

"Can you describe him?"

"He was short—rather haughty and elegant—seemed to be in a hurry, yet spoke with a kind of precision. I think he had red hair."

I pulled out the sketch.

"Yes, that's him."

I thanked him and rushed over to U.S. Mail Service on Wall. "Is there any chance for a berth on the *Arcadia*, which sails this afternoon?" I asked the clerk.

"Let me see, sir." He studied the ship's list, together with the floor plan of the cabins. Most of the berths had been assigned. "I think we might have one more available in the first class." He made a further check. Yes, a berth was available.

"Wonderful!" I wrote out a check for a hundred twenty dollars drawn on my New York bank—easy to certify by messenger.

I spent the morning making final arrangements. I wrote to Miller's in Baltimore, asking the management to hold my trunk until further notice. Next I wrote to Zaccheus Lee, telling him I was on my way to Paris in pursuit of Tyler who seemed to have fled there under the name, H. Wither. "If we only had that promised transatlantic cable in operation—how easy it would be to capture him on arrival! Would it be possible, in the meanwhile, to start the extradition process?"

Finally I wrote to Elmira. "I am heartbroken to have to tell you that our beautiful plans for Christmas need to be postponed." I gave details. "To think that man had entered your sister's home and enjoyed your hospitality! . . . Once he is in custody I will return—and proceed to Richmond. May God grant that I can do this soon . . ."

23

I STOOD ON DECK, watching New York diminish in the distance once again—the ships, the wharves, the buildings, the bit of greenery that was Battery Park. But this time I was parting from a whole continent. So strange this moving back and forth between the old world and the new, like traversing centuries. There was always anticipation but also regret. In my mind there was a pair of scales slowly swinging up and down, laden on the one side by all the promises, on the other, the disappointments of America. I thought of Crévecoeur's words: "Here society is not composed, as in Europe, of great lords who possess everything, and of a herd of people who have nothing." Had the dream become an ugly reality in just a few decades, judging from the terrible conditions I had seen people living in? Or was it only in the great eastern cities that Crévecoeur's prophesy had proved false? Had I traveled westward, would I have seen his fair cities, substantial villages, where newcomers lived in decent houses? I had traveled to the South and seen slavery there, though by no means the worst aspects of it. And I recalled Mr. Dickens writing about standing on deck on his homeward journey—as I was doing now—and looking down below at some embittered immigrants who had sold their very clothes to raise passage money for their return home.

But these were few in number in comparison to the thousands who remained, who beyond their misery saw hope. This was perhaps America—the promise, the possibility, the hope. As I looked westward, one scale in my mind was distinctly outweighing the other. I had grown fonder of that vanishing land on the horizon than I had expected. There was something unabashed, innocent, wild yet mesmerizing about the new world in the eyes of old Europe. Perhaps because we all thrive on hope. It was fitting that a good part of my heart should be left there with a lovely widow of Richmond.

Soon New York vanished beyond the horizon and we were surrounded by the vastness of the sea. Somewhere eastward the *Britannia* was plowing the waves, with Tyler aboard. She had a four-day gain on us, but the time it took a ship to cross the ocean was somewhat unpredictable. I was curious about the speed of the *Arcadia* compared to the *Britannia* and sought out one of the mates, a young man with a bushy blond beard and round blue eyes. He was eager to give me nautical information.

"I think ours is a faster ship. It's a couple of years newer. We might well beat the *Britannia* to port, but you never know. You might run into dirty weather and that slows you down badly. That can happen to any ship. The average crossing these days is eighteen days. We made it once in thirteen, but then once it took us twenty-two."

I hoped the *Britannia* would run into dirty weather, as he put it, and we would have smooth sailing. I preferred being as close to my quarry as possible. The weather was good thus far, though it was cold; the rolling and pitching had little effect on me, except I found it impossible to stay long on deck, though wrapped in my overcoat and a blanket. I spent much of my time watching the sea, whether from the open or closed deck, sometimes so intensely as to believe I actually saw the *Britannia* beyond the horizon—a dot to which we were getting closer and closer.

On the fifth day a storm from the west overtook us, making the ship roll menacingly. It laid low most of the passengers and even the crew. Wild waves rose around us in all their reptile greenness and icy whiteness while a heavy slanting rain battered the decks from an almost black sky. Buckets and mops were everywhere. I lay in my berth—not such a good sailor now. But then the storm passed us eastward: it would hit the *Britannia* next.

Christmas came, with a tree set up in the lounge, carols sung in English, French, and German, and champagne served by courtesy of the captain. But I was more sad than merry, missing Elmira. Then Christmas passed quickly, as all things do on a voyage, merging with the great sameness of water and sky.

On December 28th we docked in Le Havre. We had gained two days on the *Britannia*, which had come into port on the 26th. I settled in the train for a seven-hour trip to Paris.

* * *

MY SILENT APARTMENT welcomed me in its worn, dusty embrace. I had slept in many beds and berths over the past eight weeks, but as I stood contemplating my own familiar high bed amidst the somber curtains and carpets that begged to be taken down for a good beating, there was only one in recent memory that I would have happily exchanged it for—that four-poster one in the bright, charming, cornflower-strewn guest room in Elmira's house. A sudden wild longing for her took hold of me as I roamed from one room to the other and back again, lighting tapers against the evening. I contemplated my books reaching up into the shadows, gazed at old, dusky family portraits, picked up objects like old friends in a futile effort to alleviate my loneliness—a book, an ashtray, an inkwell. They didn't make up for her absence.

My thoughts were with Edgar, too. My preoccupation with him over the past eight weeks had brought him tremendously to life again, brought him in a new way back to this very room where we two had sat so often, making day into sable night so that we could the better talk and work and dream—on this old sofa, or at the writing table, which was as cluttered as I had left it, as it had been then.

Oh, Edgar, my dear friend, whose earthly remains I dissected to become certain of the terrible crime committed against you, whose spirit has been my constant companion since—I don't want to fail you.

I heard a shuffling sound outside—either a tenant on his way to the floor above or someone coming to my door. Tyler? I listened, with my hand on my pistol. When I heard a knock I pulled it out, cocked it, and tiptoed out to the hall. I withdrew the bolt, pushed down on the brass handle and opened the door a crack, with held breath.

"*Mon Dieu!*" I heard at the identical moment that I recognized my concierge.

"*Je m'excuse, madame!*" I put my gun away and opened the door wide. "I was certain I heard a burglar."

Madame Roland came in on slow feet, a bulky, fiftyish woman with a gold front tooth and small, fat-embedded eyes, which sometimes proved sharper than one would expect.

"Did you have a good trip, monsieur?"

"Splendid, madame."

"An American gentleman was looking for you—except he called you by another name first. I can't remember it exactly—a short name—"

I was growing tense. "Poe?"

"That must be it."

"Don't you remember Monsieur Poe staying with me about ten years ago? You said we could be brothers, we looked so much alike."

"Oh, yes, I do remember. Anyway, when I told him no such person lived in this house, he gave your name. But his manner was strange—kind of not all there—"

"When was this?"

"The evening before last, about this time."

He had come here immediately on getting off the train. Why? Did he really think he could find Edgar here? Or that I had in some way preceded him to Paris? Or some combination of the two? How crazy was he? Possibly he knew that I was in Paris now—he might have even been following me. What would be his next move?

"I take it he left no card."

"No. I asked for one, at which he grew abstracted. 'Card?' he said, and laughed. 'I have no card.' Suddenly I was afraid of him, with his black beard and gold-headed cane. I was glad when he went away."

I thanked Madame Roland for her faithful report.

In the morning I went to see Gaston at the Commissariat on Rue Bonaparte. He made me wait in the bleak anteroom, with the wanted criminals' likenesses on the wall, as a matter of principle; for when I was admitted he gave the impression of having been occupied with nothing more taxing than the contemplation of the bust of Julius Caesar in a niche. Having met Tyler, I could not avoid noting certain similarities of bearing between the two men. Both short, both egotists; both strutted. In more important respects they were different, of course. Gaston was of average intelligence, average ambition, contented with his station, and he respected the law. Tyler with his superior mind, overweening ambition and pride, was a criminal.

"Ah, Dupin, you're back." Gaston offered half a pudgy hand

across his ornate desk. "You look worn. There are circles under your eyes."

"I had a wearing trip. But most profitable. I discovered that Poe had been murdered, and I know his killer's identity—"

"Very good, Dupin."

"But in his final capture I need your help."

"How on earth can I help you capture a killer in America?"

"He is in Paris."

"Are you sure?"

"I am sure. He is mentally disturbed. Before my arrival he came to my address looking for Poe, as if he hadn't already killed him."

"How odd. Do you have a warrant for his arrest?"

"I have an official copy." I took it out and presented it to him.

"Ah, copy!" He studied it as if he knew English, which he didn't, and shook his head. "I command the Sixth Arrondissement. My superior, the prefect, will not mobilize the Paris police except on an official request from the United States Government."

"An official request is forthcoming, I assure you. Furthermore, you don't need the prefect. I ask you to send a couple of men to the other arrondissements to check whether anyone by the name of H. Wither has registered in any hotel within the last three days. His real name is Harold Tyler. These are his other possible aliases." I handed over a list. "This is his likeness." I handed over a copy of the police sketch.

"I don't know, Dupin—"

"We worked together on many cases, Monsieur Superintendent. We trust and respect each other, that is why I appeal to you. But we must move quickly. We capture this killer and you'll be greatly honored both in France and in the United States—"

"Dupin, you have a way of— Very well, I'll send a couple of men around."

My sojourn in America had taught me to be impatient with the excesses of French officialdom, especially under the presidency of Louis Napoleon. But the exacting registration of transients and the efficiency with which arrondissements kept records so that within two days two policemen were able to compile a list of recent regis-trants at all hotels and lodgings through the city evoked my admi-ration.

Tyler was not staying at a hotel. He had taken a room at the Bains de Tivoli, a hydrotherapeutic sanatorium on Rue St. Lazare, under the name of H. Wither. I wondered how much of his mental breakdown he was admitting to himself. In his letter to Griswold he spoke of his "nervous malady" as "a restlessness that makes me unable to sit still, that makes me roam the streets wildly, alternating with an oppression of spirit that confines me to a state of rigid immobility for hours." It was more serious than that.

Gaston and I, with two of his men, drove to the Bains in the late morning of a cold, gloomy, overcast day. We were near the Gare St. Lazare, and the carriages, drays, and horsemen were in great profusion, while pedestrians thronged the sidewalks lined by stalls and cafés. We turned into a remarkably quiet courtyard, with a domed building in the center. Gaston and I went up to the entrance, the two policemen behind us. The large foyer was dim, with few comfortable seats, the marble floor and walls exuding coldness. Two huge frescoes faced each other, one showing classical ruins, the other a Roman bath.

Gaston pulled himself up to his full five feet five and flashed his identification at the receptionist clerk. "I wish to see one of your guests—a recently arrived American by the name of H. Wither."

"The guests are taking the baths, monsieur." The clerk consulted his watch. "The cold baths seem to be over now, so Mr. Wither should be in the steam bath."

"How long will that take?"

"In the morning it is one hour, monsieur."

"We do not have an hour. Take us to him."

I did not relish capturing Tyler naked, but it gave us more assurance he would not slip away.

The clerk tapped a bell and an attendant appeared. He led us through a corridor, then into a tiled, skylit room with stone benches along the walls. At the far end a bath attendant sat next to a stack of towels, guarding several small buckled canvas bags that seemed to contain the valuables of those in the adjacent steam bath. Our guide told him to call Monsieur Wither, then left the room.

The bath attendant went into the steam room with a towel and I caught a glimpse of vague figures in a gray fog, as a gust of heat and a whiff of sweat seeped out. We waited tensely.

The door opened, but it was the attendant again. He went to get one of the canvas bags.

"Attendez!" I leaped to him, snatched the bag from him and felt it. No gun. I let him take it into the steam room.

"Quick thinking, Dupin," Gaston said.

Tyler stepped out, the large white towel wrapped around him in the manner of a toga, his hand hidden in its fold over his chest, one moist shoulder and his legs below the knees bare. His face with its close-set eyes and short nose was red from the heat, his redder, curly hair tousled. His half-naked state was a coming out of hiding; I was unaccustomed to it, in some way disturbed by it—the red glistening curls on his chest, the small but compact torso, the muscular arms, sturdy legs, freckles.

When he saw me—or Edgar, or some mixture of us—he began to tremble and sweat broke out all over him, giving his face and body an infernal sheen.

"I don't believe in ghosts. Why do you haunt me?" He spoke in broken, plaintive tones—an eerie contrast to the icy ventriloquized voice I'd heard outside my prison door. "Do you think you're Elijah come down in a fiery chariot to tell me I took the wrong road and my genius is a false coin? I will not bow down to the heart. I despise the heart." A choking assault of hoarseness. "I recognize you as my tempter entering my dreams—whispering to me to despair. Am I dreaming you? Tell me, am I dreaming you?"

Gaston, who understood not a word, grew impatient. "You're under arrest, monsieur," he said in French, his hand similarly hidden under the flap of his coat in his favorite Napoleonic gesture.

Tyler laughed maniacally.

The moment he pulled out his hand from under his towel the two policemen had him covered with their guns. For an object flashed in his grip which I, too, for a wild moment took for a pistol, believing his cunning had defied my vigilance. I had been too preoccupied with pistols—his elegance demanded nothing less. But he was no longer elegant, he was desperate. The flashing object was the long, slim blade of a razor. Had I foolishly let it pass unexamined in the canvas bag? My fingers didn't recall the feel of such a shape. More likely he'd had it hidden in the steam room, waiting for the right moment to use it (as his letter to Griswold hinted that he might) there in the wet heat that opened pores.

We rushed upon him shouting, *"Non!* Wait! *Non!"* But we lost. An unearthly cry and the gleaming blade passed across his throat and blood gushed out. He stood dazed, then he tottered and fell.

Attendants rushed in. But the blood came in torrents and his grotesquely twisted head with eyes bulging and a hideous grin frothing blood was nearly severed. There was no helping him. A rattle and a spasm, and he was dead.

Seeing him a corpse in a widening pool of blood, I wondered about the feeling of oppression that came over me. Was it regret that he had escaped the gallows? Or just pity?

We left the body to the officials of the 9th Arrondissement. With a death certificate signed by the medical examiner, it would be shipped back to the United States, to Tyler's mother who had taught him to despise the heart.

*   *   *

I WENT TO SEE BAUDELAIRE ON RUE DE BABYLONE. When Jeanne Duval opened the door, her lovely tan face seemed more rested than the last time, which suggested that Charles was in better health and they quarreled less. She remembered my name and ushered me into an empty room with a couple of chairs in it—someday perhaps a salon—with a gracious smile.

"Auguste!" A door flew open and Charles burst in, his cat slipping in with him. "Did you get the villain?"

"Yes."

"You must tell me all about it."

"I will. How are you feeling?"

"Better, thank you. My malady is in a quiescent stage and I'm working—both on my translations and on my own poems." He looked better. His face was fuller, his complexion clearer, and he seemed to have more hair—it was perhaps his frisure.

He bundled up and we went down to a nearby café which he said he found quiet and we took a cozy table past some chess players, near the well-stoked stove. We ordered mulled Beaujolais, then sandwiches, then more mulled Beaujolais, as we talked deep into the night. My account of Tyler's doings horrified Charles.

"The evil I write about blossoms in the dream, as Poe would say. This man practiced evil."

He wanted to know about everyone I met, all I learned about Poe. When I talked myself hoarse he read me his latest *Mal* poem, holding me spellbound. Then he read from his recent translation of "The Masque of the Red Death." It was brilliant, conveying all the nuances of style, as if Edgar had written the tale in French.

"You will make Poe as great in France as he is in America."

"That's what I hope to do," Charles said.

*   *   *

THERE WAS NO SHIP sailing for Norfolk until the middle of January. One was sailing for Baltimore on the 12th, but the *Britannia* sailing for New York on the 5th would get me to Richmond sooner. I did not know which ship would carry Tyler's coffin and did not inquire. There was space on the *Britannia* and I booked passage on her.

Instead of copying out anything from Edgar's letters, I packed the whole batch to show Griswold and let him use what he needed from them.

I wrote to Elmira that I was coming, although I was sure I would hold her in my arms before she got my letter.